Hallmark
PUBLISHING

sunrise cabin

STACEY DONOVAN

Sunrise Cabin
Copyright @ 2018 Crown Media Family Networks

All rights reserved. Except for use in any review, the reproduction
or utilization of this work in whole or in part in any form by
any electronic, mechanical or other means, now known or
hereinafter invented, including xerography, photocopying and
recording, or in any information storage or retrieval system, is
forbidden without the written permission of the publisher.

This is a work of fiction. Names, characters, places and incidents
are either the product of the author's imagination or are used
fictitiously, and any resemblance to actual persons, living or dead,
business establishments, events or locales is entirely coincidental.

Print: 978-1-947892-91-0
Ebook: 978-1-947892-26-2

Hallmark
PUBLISHING

www.hallmarkpublishing.com

To my parents,
Merrill and Marilyn Johnson,
for all their encouragement and love.

chapter one

Of all the things Paige loved about the little cabin, the view of the sunrise was her favorite. She stepped outside the back door onto the small stone patio to watch, like she did every morning. The autumn chill seeped through her blue flannel pajamas, and she wrapped her arms around herself. The sun wasn't quite up yet, but almost, and the pond reflected the gold of the horizon. Above the dark silhouettes of the trees, still hanging onto their leaves for now, small pink and purple clouds flocked the brightening blue sky.

The cabin, at the end of a dead-end street far to the west of Denver, had mountain views to both the east and the west. It was a forty-minute drive, sometimes more, to the downtown elementary school where Paige taught, but in the morning quiet, she felt like she was a million miles away.

She took in a deep breath, let it out, and began her usual morning ritual.

"I'm thankful for this day," she said aloud and closed her eyes. "I'm thankful for my mom and dad." They were usually right at the top of her list. "I'm thankful for my job, and for the kids." She gave a wry smile. A couple of the children in her first-grade class gave her some trouble, but she'd been teaching long enough now to expect that. "And for my health. And for this beautiful world, and this beautiful season." She'd always loved fall.

"I'm thankful my car is fixed." Her yellow VW bug had several years and a lot of miles on it, and she'd just gotten it back from the shop. She hadn't planned on that expense, but at least it was running fine again. "I'm thankful for my creative inspiration. And I'm thankful for this wonderful home."

Sometimes, she also expressed gratitude for good things that hadn't happened yet, but she thought—or at least hoped—would come into her life. She'd read in a book once that having faith like that would actually lead to good things happening. So she added, "I'm thankful someone is about to publish my children's stories."

She tried to believe this. After eleven rejections, it wasn't easy. But staying positive had worked for her before. A couple of years ago, she'd been living in an awful apartment, and she'd envisioned having a cute little house of her own. At the time, she'd expected that such

a thing could only happen far in the future...
and then almost immediately, she'd found
this two-bedroom cabin for rent, at a price
she could actually afford. Her parents had
believed it was an answered prayer.

She didn't even care about the scuffed
brown linoleum floor in the kitchen, the rust
stains in the bathroom sink, the few missing
tiles above the bathtub, or even the draftiness
in winter. She couldn't have afforded it otherwise.

"I'm thankful for this day," she concluded.
Yes, she'd already said it once, but it was
worth repeating. It was Monday, her favorite.

She looked at her watch. The cupcakes in
the oven needed to bake fifteen more minutes,
so she might as well at least make a start on
her gardening project. Her brand-new spade,
a big bag of garden soil, and a sack of tulip
bulbs waited on the patio. It was the perfect
spot to plant them, where they'd get morning
sunshine. Until recently, a big pine tree had
shaded this part of the yard, but it had fallen
over in a winter ice storm. She'd been sorry to
lose it, but it had left a perfect, sunny spot for
flowers. She'd plant pink, purple, orange, and
yellow ones, all mixed together. They'd reflect
the colors of the sunrise.

She smiled as she thrust the spade into
the earth, right alongside the patio. The scent
of the dirt reached her nose as she dug a shal-
low trench.

"Good morning!"

She looked up to see her landlord and next-door neighbor walking across his backyard toward her. He was warmly dressed in a fleece pullover and jeans, and he moved with a surprising amount of energy for a man in his late seventies.

"Hi, Harry!" she said. "Did you get a haircut?"

He passed a hand over his gray hair. "No, I got them all cut." He laughed, as he always did at his own corny jokes, and she laughed, too. As he reached her, he gestured toward the ground. "Whatcha doing here?"

"Oh! I was planting some bulbs." Harry's brows drew together, and belatedly, she realized she hadn't actually asked his permission. He couldn't object, could he? They'd be an improvement to the property, coming back year after year. "I hope you don't mind."

"I was just surprised, since you're only renting."

She smiled and placed another bulb in the ground. "Well, this place feels like home."

Instead of looking happy for her, Harry grimaced. "I can never look at this place without thinking about Judy. She had big plans for it."

Her heart ached at his mention of his late wife. Soon after moving in, Paige had learned that Harry's wife had died the year before after a brief bout with pancreatic cancer. She and Harry had bought the cabin then, renting it out and planning to remodel it someday.

"I wish I could've met her," Paige said.

4

"I miss having breakfast with her," he said. "And I didn't always think about how nice that was, at the time."

Oh, her heart. "I'm so sorry."

"There's nothing like being with someone you love. If you get the chance..." He trailed off.

She didn't care to discuss her single status. "Maybe someday," she said, her tone light.

Harry nodded. "How are things with your agent?" he asked in a more upbeat voice. "Did she find a publisher?"

Inwardly, Paige cringed. No doubt Harry had been trying to change the subject to something more comfortable to her, but this was anything but.

When she'd first gotten her agent, Alexis Boyd at Glimmer Literary Agency, Paige had told everyone. She'd been sure a publishing deal for her children's books was right around the corner—that it would take a couple of months, perhaps.

How could she have been so naïve? That had been eight months ago. Since then, she'd received several emails from Alexis, telling her about publishers who'd passed on her work. Alexis had gotten her to revise the stories based on some of the feedback, but that hadn't made a difference.

It had been quite a while since Alexis had even emailed. Pasting a smile on her face, Paige gave the same answer as before. "Maybe someday."

Harry cleared his throat. "Well, I...I actually came over here to talk to you about something." He looked down at his shoes. "You know your lease is up next month."

"Right." Paige had signed two one-year leases with him, both for the same monthly rent. Maybe he wanted to raise it. It would pinch a little, but she couldn't complain.

"The truth is, I'm going to be selling the cabin."

"What?" Paige's whole body went cold, as though the life had drained out of it. *My cabin.* Her sweet little haven. She'd even started writing a story about it.

Harry managed to look Paige in the eye. "I'm required to give you thirty days' notice to move out, but once it's sold, I'll give you forty-five days."

That was more than fair, she knew, but she felt betrayed.

"My daughter thinks I should move down to Albuquerque and be closer to them," he said. "I've been dragging my feet. I've got a lot of memories around here. But a friend of mine asked about buying my house, and I decided it was time. I'm working with an agent to sell the cabin, too. I'd love to see more of those grandkids."

Paige softened, forgetting about her own predicament. "And I'm sure they'd *love* having you around." Harry was probably about the nicest grandpa on earth. She was glad he'd be close to his family.

He belonged there. And while she wished he would keep the cabin and rent it to her from afar, it was probably easier for him to sell. "Of course you have to go." There was no sense making him feel guiltier about it. A hopeful thought occurred to her. "Do you think you might sell it to someone else who wants to keep renting it to me?"

"I asked the agent that. Anything's possible, but he doesn't think it's likely. We'll see." Harry looked thoughtful. "I just hope it goes to someone who appreciates the place."

A screeching noise from inside the cabin gave her a jolt. The smoke alarm. *The cupcakes!* "Oh, my gosh!"

She turned and sprinted into the house. The scent of burning cake filled her nostrils. She snatched a potholder, yanked the oven door open, and winced at the smoke pouring out of it. The cupcakes in the baking tin she pulled out looked like smoldering chunks of charcoal. As the smoke alarm continued to blare, she flung open the kitchen window— and met Harry's appalled gaze.

This was bad. She'd ruined the birthday treats, and she was probably going to make him worry that she'd burn the little cabin down through sheer absent-mindedness. She shut off the oven and jogged back outside.

"At least we know the alarm works, huh?" she asked. It could shut up any time now. "I'm sorry. It won't happen again."

Harry gave her a sympathetic smile. "Well, you were distracted." The alarm stopped blaring at last.

Paige glanced down at the incomplete planting project. "I'll have to finish this later." Or would she? She wouldn't be able to see them bloom. The realization gave her a fresh stab of sorrow. "I need to buy treats for one of my students." After such a shock, she could use a treat herself.

She could get cupcakes at the café and bakery a couple of blocks away from Jefferson Elementary. If she got there early enough, she'd have time to get a pumpkin spice latte.

It had been forever since she'd stopped in at that place, and one needed to take advantage of pumpkin spice latte season when it came around.

And she'd do a little more writing on her story about the princess and the cabin. Why not? In at least one way, the place would be hers forever. She tried to take comfort in the thought.

After she said goodbye to Harry and went back inside, she took a moment to look around her. Although the bathroom and the two bedrooms had white walls, here in the kitchen and in the living room, the original log walls surrounded her, uneven, filled in with stripes of white mortar. The plank floors, although rough in places, nonetheless glowed. They were the exact color of Darjeeling tea sweetened with a bit of the red clover honey

Paige had bought from the Union Station farmer's market, though the jar was almost empty now, just a few sweet drops remaining.

The small rooms had always given Paige the feeling that she was safely tucked away with her dreams. Gradually over the course of the past two years, she'd added her own handmade touches, along with thrift shop treasures: a chartreuse lamp, a cuckoo clock, several vintage tea cups and saucers and a rack on the wall to display them. Looking around, Paige noticed for the first time that the ceiling above the fireplace was smudgy from the smoke. The chimney didn't draw perfectly. Would this deter prospective buyers? Probably not.

She had to get going. In the bedroom, she changed out of the yoga pants and sweatshirt she'd slept in and into her work clothes. Since she'd learned to sew, she'd created some dresses and skirts in bright, whimsical prints that amused her students: cats, snowflakes, dinosaurs, stars. She chose the one she'd just finished.

After putting on a little makeup and grabbing her jacket and purse, she checked the time. She wouldn't have a ton of time to linger at the café, but if she didn't hit any bad traffic, she could at least stay for fifteen minutes or so.

I am not going to let this ruin my day, she promised herself. Who knew? Maybe the sale of the cabin would be a blessing in disguise. She was a huge believer in those.

Although, it would be one heck of a disguise. After she'd moved in, she'd felt so happy, and she'd started writing more. She loved the place with her heart and soul...

Wait a minute. Was it possible *she* could buy the place?

She hadn't even thought about buying a house for quite a while. On her salary, she struggled to save money. Expenses always popped up, and she spent a not-inconsiderable amount on extra supplies for her classroom. Once she'd moved into the cabin, she'd more or less planned to rent it forever, or at least, as long as she could.

But she suddenly recalled one of the teachers at school talking about buying a home. According to him, a first-time buyer didn't need to put much down. Maybe she could actually afford to make it hers. Who knew? Maybe it was meant to be.

It was impossible.

But what if it wasn't?

chapter two

Dylan lumbered to the kitchen, still groggy, and grabbed the steel coffee canister. When he lifted the lid, two beans rattled around at the bottom. He sighed.

He wasn't in the habit of eating breakfast. A banana, sometimes, if he'd been to the store recently, and most often, he hadn't. The kitchen in the loft-style apartment was actually gorgeous: new cabinets, marble countertops, always clean. The two things he used were the refrigerator, which frequently held leftover pizza or kung pao chicken, and the coffeemaker, which couldn't help him now. He'd have to get dressed and get to a café. Usually, he fueled up with caffeine right after getting out of bed, and the variation in his routine unsettled him.

In the living room, he paused to gaze out the huge sixth-story window. Clouds hung over his downtown neighborhood. When he'd first moved in, big trees had stood in front of the newest construction. He'd admired them for surviving in a small plot of soil and breaking through the pavement; he could appreciate that type of raw determination. But then, out of idle curiosity, he'd poked around online to figure out what species they were. Their name, "tree of heaven," was ironic; they were known for not only destroying sidewalks but also putting out a chemical that killed nearby plants. Dylan had been glad when workers had removed them and planted a row of sugar maple saplings in their place. Their top leaves were starting to turn cheddary orange.

As he picked up his phone, a glum feeling settled over him. New texts. *Please don't be Mark.*

But of course, it *was* his boss. Two messages from him detailed extra changes he wanted to the presentation due that morning, and a third one explained a new assignment. Dylan briefly considered going straight to the office and drinking the coffee there, but he'd been at the office for a few hours on Saturday and wasn't ready to face it again quite yet.

In the bathroom, he scrubbed his face but skipped shaving. Even at his investment banking firm, a day's worth of stubble was acceptable. He dressed quickly, grabbed his laptop bag, and was out the door.

Soon afterward, he parked outside Dolce Café and Bakery and strode to the door. He caught another guy, with a girlfriend or wife, glancing from Dylan's new luxury car to Dylan in his perfectly tailored gray suit, in an almost automatic moment of admiration and envy.

Dylan didn't mind getting noticed like that, once in a while. He'd earned it. As a kid, he'd sometimes attracted attention for the opposite reason. When he'd shown up for school two days in a row in the same outfit, or wore pants with permanent stains on the knees, other kids had given him plenty of grief. These days, nobody could look down on him, and nobody could get under his skin.

A long line of people stood waiting to order. *Great.* He should've gotten an earlier start to the day. He tried to tamp down his impatience by looking at stocks and scanning business headlines on his phone. When he finally reached the counter, he made his usual order—black coffee, the largest size, the darkest roast—left a dollar in the tip jar, and sat down at the counter. After taking the first blessed sip, he opened his laptop and pulled up the PowerPoint presentation. He never should've taken the whole Sunday off. It always made Mondays worse.

If he finished the deck in the next hour and drove into work, he'd be able to print it out and check it before putting it on his boss's desk at nine a.m. He'd learned the hard way that errors were much harder to catch on-screen. He'd started the job four years ago, and after the first presentation he'd worked on hadn't gone over well with the client, his supervisor at the time had called him into her office to point out the misplaced comma on the one-hundred-twenty-sixth slide of a one-hundred-forty-three-slide deck. Dylan was pretty sure punctuation hadn't been the deal breaker, but he always checked carefully now.

A woman with wavy, shoulder-length blonde hair draped her red jacket over the back of the chair right next to him and sat down. Odd. There were other empty seats. She didn't seem to notice him, though, as she set a whipped-cream-topped beverage in front of her. A pumpkin spice latte, no doubt, given that it was the first day of October. In fact, little orange pumpkins dotted her purple dress, so she probably loved fall. Where did a grown woman even buy a dress like that? He could imagine one of the women in his office showing up for a meeting in it instead of their usual tailored clothing in gray or black. Honestly, it would be hilarious.

This woman looked to be maybe a few years younger than his own age of thirty-four, though the purple pumpkin dress no doubt contributed to that impression. So did the slight smile on her face and the bright pink lipstick that contrasted with her pale complexion. She dug through a huge, shiny yellow purse and pulled out a turquoise book. He was practically sitting next to a rainbow.

She looked up at him. *Busted.* He hadn't meant to stare at her. "Hi, how are you?" she asked in a tone of polite good cheer.

He didn't really have time for a conversation, even if she was cute. And okay, she was, in a quirky way.

"Eh, it's Monday," he said.

Why had *that* come out of his mouth? One of the assistants at his office always said it on Monday when people asked how she was doing. Sometimes he'd think to himself in a surly way, *Thanks, I know what day it is.*

"Best day of the week," the woman quipped and opened her book, apparently finished with the conversation.

Wait, *what?*

Nobody believed that. Maybe she wore all those bright colors because she was, in fact, a crazy person. An adorable crazy person, but still.

He focused on his laptop screen and tried to check the five-year projections in the appendix. They'd revised it four times, so it would be easy to have a mistake here...

No. This was bugging him too much. He turned back to the woman and demanded, "How is Monday the best day of the week?"

She glanced up again from the book—or the journal, apparently; she had a pen in her hand. Her blue eyes were wide, guileless. "I call it Clean Slate Monday."

"Clean Slate Monday," he repeated, as if that explained anything.

She nodded. "You know, like if your last week—or actually your last month, or your last year, or whatever—if you had disappointments, or you messed up, you can forget

15

about all that. Because it's a brand-new week. A fresh start." As Dylan stared at her, she took a sip of her latte, then wiped off a bit of foam that clung to her upper lip. She shrugged. "Anything could happen."

Dylan had no words for the feeling that thrummed through his veins. Something told him she was different from anyone he'd ever met before, and he needed to know her better.

But his cynicism rose to the surface to protect him from the unfamiliar. "Do you work on Mondays?" Maybe she was a waitress in a restaurant that was closed today. Anyone could enjoy their day off. Maybe she didn't work at all.

"I do, actually." Her tone was wry. "I'm a teacher. I have weekends off. Well, more or less."

Okay. He wasn't sitting next to a rainbow. He was sitting next to a unicorn. A person who worked Mondays through Fridays, and called Monday the best day of the week, didn't even seem real.

She went back to writing in her journal and he caught a glimpse of the page. A sketch of a house occupied half of it. No, not a house: a cabin. It looked a lot like his grandparents' cabin, where he and his sister had spent some of their childhood summers. Why would she be drawing something like that? He wondered what her life was like, and what was going through her mind.

But although curiosity was getting to him,

he looked away. He needed to stop staring at her like a creep, and whatever she was writing or drawing, it was none of his business. He had plenty of business of his own and should get back to it.

Usually, he had no trouble settling down to work. He'd gotten himself through college with a combination of scholarships and jobs that had been unpleasant, exhausting, or both: loading delivery trucks, cleaning toilets, and one summer, even gutting salmon in a cannery in Alaska. He was *made* for work.

The figures in the projections balanced out. He adjusted the formatting, advanced to the next slide, and stared at it, still acutely aware of the woman next to him. Whatever she was working on, it was probably much less crucial—and probably a lot more fun.

His phone rang. Dylan looked down and saw his brother-in-law's name on the screen.

Why was Paul calling so early? Well, it could be an emergency. Dylan answered. "Hey, what's up?" As he did, the blonde woman got up and grabbed her jacket, and disappointment flickered through him.

"Hey," Paul said. "Just reminding you to pick up Dee's cake tonight."

No. He'd forgotten all about his sister Deidre's birthday. Paul had planned a surprise party for her. He'd invited her favorite people, secretly bought decorations, and conspired with Dee's best friend to get her out of the house for some spa thing and then back home again.

Dylan had questioned this whole plan from the jump. He'd asked Paul, "Are you sure she likes surprises? I don't even like it when *one* person drops by without asking."

His brother-in-law had shaken his head. "Most people are more spontaneous than you. Actually, everybody is."

"I can be spontaneous," Dylan had said. "I just need some warning."

Dylan's doubt about the party was no excuse. He'd had one job. Bring a chocolate sheet cake with the words, "Happy Birthday, Dee!" written on it in frosting.

In response to his silence, Paul said, "You didn't order it."

"It's fine, it's fine," Dylan said with fake confidence. "I'll call around. Someone can do it." Not that he had time for calling...

But he was in a bakery. The kind that made individual treats, not big cakes, but still. He glanced over at the display of baked goods. The blonde woman stood in line at the other end of the counter, bouncing on her toes, cash in her hand, and he was glad she hadn't left yet. He asked Paul, "How many people are going to be there?"

"Eh, twenty-five, maybe. Well, thirty, if you count Dee, me, the boys, and you." He sighed. "I invited more, but people are so busy."

"Thirty's a lot." If someone had been throwing a party for Dylan, he wouldn't have been able to think of thirty people to even invite. He walked closer to the bakery counter, surveyed the inventory, and told Paul, "I'll get cupcakes."

Paul hesitated. "They can't put her name on them."

Seriously? His sister was turning forty, not seven. She wasn't going to pout if her name wasn't on a cake. Dylan kept his voice light. "It's a birthday party. Everyone's going to know who the cupcakes are for. And I'll get different flavors."

"All right, sounds good," Paul said. "Thanks."

"No problem. I'll be there at seven."

"Six-thirty," Paul corrected. "Dee's coming at seven."

Right. He had to get there early and hide behind a couch or something in the dark, and then jump out and yell, "Surprise!" Did people still do this? Apparently, Paul thought so.

Well, Dylan appreciated his organizing it. He treated Dee right, and Dylan was happy to show up and do what was expected of him.

He got in line behind the blonde. As he drew closer to her, his heart seemed to wake up, beating a little faster, and he didn't really get why. She was a random girl in a café, and not his type at all.

His last girlfriend, Lauren, had been his type, and they'd probably still be together if she hadn't taken the job in New York. She'd scored an incredible opportunity, so he hadn't blamed her. Dylan couldn't see himself ever moving there, not while Dee and the boys were here in Denver. Truthfully, he also couldn't imagine leaving the mountains behind, even if he didn't spend as much time in the outdoors as he would've liked. Lauren had made a very grown-up decision to not try the long-distance thing. Maybe it was too bad that it hadn't mattered to either of them that much.

He hadn't dated since. Vaguely, he imagined that first he'd get another promotion at the firm. He couldn't focus on relationships and making VP at the same time.

The blonde woman told the lady behind the counter, "I need twenty-five cupcakes."

No, no, no. Dylan's gaze flew to the bakery counter. Five kinds of cupcakes, six of each flavor. Exactly how many he needed. Except she was going to take most of them. "You can't do that," he blurted out.

She turned her head to regard him. "Excuse me?"

Okay. He could've sounded more reasonable. "I need them for my sister's birthday party." There. She wouldn't be able to argue with that. She'd know now that he was a nice guy, too.

"Is that birthday party at eight-thirty in the morning?"

He snorted. "No, it's tonight, but—"

"Then you have time to go somewhere else, and I don't." She smiled as if that settled it.

The lady behind the counter began putting the cupcakes in a big box.

He wasn't ready to give up yet. "I don't have time. I'm very busy."

"Everyone's busy," she said lightly. "Not just you."

Everyone wasn't *as* busy as he was. "So what is it, one of your students' birthdays?" She nodded. "Aren't the kids supposed to bring those?"

"Some kids come from homes where..." She shook her head. "There's either not enough money or not enough paying attention."

That hit him right in the gut. He'd grown up in one of the latter. His memories transported him back to the first grade, when his best friend at the time loudly asked him why he hadn't brought treats for his birthday. He hadn't remembered that in years. After his mom had died, his dad had been distant, sleepwalking through life, not keeping track of even some very basic things. Dylan had been too young to process all that at the time. He'd just felt embarrassed and angry.

This woman looked out for neglected children, and that made something turn over in his heart.

"That's very kind of you," he said.

The lady behind the counter said, "That'll be eighty dollars and twenty-five cents."

Dismay flashed across her features. Clearly, it was more than she'd expected. Well, she was a teacher; she probably didn't make a big salary.

"I'll get that," he said.

She gave him a puzzled frown and the bakery lady said, "She was here first."

He said to the teacher, "No, I—I'll get them for you." Her eyes went wide, as though he'd taken leave of his senses. "For the kids, I mean," he added.

She shook her head, though a smile played at her lips. "I can't let you do that."

"I insist." Maybe he was being overbearing. He held up his hands. "I mean, unless you say no again."

That made her laugh. "Okay, since it's for the kids, I'll let you." He loved her voice, with its wry drawl. It sounded like smoked honey. Her cheeks flushed pink. *Wow.* Was she ever pretty when she blushed.

He pulled out his wallet, counted out the money, and handed it over. The teacher gave the woman behind the counter a delighted look and said, "Yay," and the woman smiled back. As Dylan took his change, the teacher picked up the box of cupcakes. "Thank you," she told him. "That's very generous."

Dylan realized the couple behind them was watching him—the same couple he'd seen in the parking lot. While he hadn't minded them noticing his nice car or his expensive suit, he now felt self-conscious. He shrugged and said to the teacher, "My good deed for the day."

"You do a good deed every day?" She sounded impressed.

"Um...no. Almost never."

"Oh." She appeared to be at a loss. "Well, I should go."

"Yeah. Nice meeting you.—I'm actually heading out too."

She nodded and they both moved toward the exit. *Ughgh.* There was nothing more horrible than essentially saying goodbye to someone and then continuing to walk alongside them. To diffuse the weirdness, he said, "I'm Dylan, by the way."

"Paige."

Get her number.

He pushed the idea out of his head. He wasn't the kind of guy who tried to get women's phone numbers right away. And if he asked, she'd think he'd paid for the cupcakes to make her owe him, which wasn't true at all.

Still, he'd like to run into her again. As friends, or friendly acquaintances. As he held the door open for her, he said, "I don't think I've ever seen you here before." She would've been pretty hard to miss.

"It's been a while since I've been here. But it's right by the school."

He nodded. "I come here a lot to work." In fact, it had been a long time since he'd last stopped in, too.

"What do you do?"

"I'm in investment banking." He waited for one of the usual comments: how he must make a lot of money, or how he must be very smart.

She laughed. "I don't really know what that is, but it sounds awful."

It is awful.

As he brushed away the unexpected thought, she said, "Thanks again," and turned and walked down the sidewalk. He'd parked in the opposite direction, and he headed that way, but couldn't resist a backward glance. She was bending over to put the cupcakes in a bright yellow VW bug—of course, that was what she'd drive. She straightened and looked back at him. He gave what he hoped was a casual wave and turned away again.

As he got into his own car, he regretted not telling her that his job wasn't awful. Nobody loved their work. Possibly *she* did, but that wasn't the norm. That was why they called it Work and not Super Fun Time. He'd been paying his dues at the firm, and he'd see more and more rewards in the next few years. His mind went to the presentation he still hadn't double-checked. He'd give it a quick look at the office, and maybe it'd be fine.

Paige. He said her name to himself again so he wouldn't forget it. But he doubted he would, anyway, and he also doubted he'd need to remember it. He probably wouldn't even run into her again.

chapter three

As Paige stepped through the front doors of Jefferson Elementary, its faint but distinctive smell surrounded her—a mingling of cleaning products and freshly sharpened pencils. Not everyone would've found it pleasant, but Paige had worked there long enough to find it welcoming.

One of the teachers, Brittany, stood chatting with the principal outside his office. Paige waved at them both as she passed, wondering if Brittany was talking to him about the details of her maternity leave. Paige still had a couple of weeks to figure out what to bring to her baby shower.

A voice called out. "Morning, Paige! You sell those kids' books yet?"

Paige looked up to see Linda Goff, who taught second grade. Linda had been at the school forever, and often had teaching advice for Paige—whether she wanted it or not.

"Not yet," Paige chirped and strode down

the hallway, the bakery box in her hands, before Linda could ask more questions.

She'd almost reached her classroom when her best friend Jessica intercepted her. "Hey!"

"Hey. How was your weekend? Is your mom still in town?"

Jessica shook her head. "She went back home yesterday morning." Her mother and stepfather lived in San Antonio, where Jessica had grown up. "On Saturday we went wedding dress shopping."

"Ooh. Come tell me more." Jessica followed Paige into her classroom. Paige set the box down on her desk. "So did you find The Dress?"

"*No.* I've tried on so many pretty dresses, but there's always one little thing I don't like." This didn't surprise Paige. Jessica paid a lot of attention to details. "And let me tell you, those dresses are not made for short, curvy ladies." She was smiling, but Paige could hear the insecurity in her voice.

"You'll find the right one. You're going to be a stunning bride." She meant it, too. Jessica, with her curly dark hair, big brown eyes, and flawless amber skin, would look beautiful if she went down the aisle in a flannel nightgown.

Jessica's mouth turned down. "My mom keeps telling me about how much weight my cousin lost for her wedding."

Paige had heard a lot of stories about Jessica's big but close-knit family. "You don't mean the cousin who got divorced three months later?"

Jessica nodded. "She did look great on her wedding day, though."

"Well, I guess that's all that matters," Paige quipped, and they both laughed.

Jessica sat down on top of Paige's desk. "And guess what? Yesterday I volunteered at Furever Friends. I took three dogs on walks."

Paige looked at her askance. "I thought you were going to get through your wedding first, and *then* help rescue cats and dogs."

"I know...but it's good exercise. And you know how I want to adopt a dog with Steve as soon as I move in." Jessica had talked about this so many times that Paige had teased her about marrying Steve for his big fenced backyard. Jessica lived in a dog-friendly apartment building, but she'd be moving into Steve's very nice three-bedroom house.

Paige asked, "Did you meet any you wanted to adopt?"

Jessica laughed. "Pretty much all of them. But especially the senior dogs. Some of them are so *sweet*." She scrunched up her shoulders.

"I can't wait to meet your future furry friend," Paige said.

She wanted to tell Jessica about the cabin, but class would start soon, and she'd need at least an hour to go over all her hopes and fears.

Jessica pointed at the box. "So what's in there?"

"Cupcakes. It's Sam's birthday."

Jessica lifted the lid. "Oh, man. These are like, gourmet." She gave Paige a quizzical look. "They're way too good for six-year-olds."

"Yeah, that occurred to me after I got them." She should've gone to the grocery store.

"Next time you won't break the bank." Jessica closed the box again.

"Actually..." Paige didn't know why she was hesitating to tell her best friend this. "I didn't buy them."

Jessica raised her eyebrows. "I don't see how you could've stolen twenty-five cupcakes. Which, by the way, would be wrong. Impressive, but wrong."

"The guy behind me in line paid for them."

Jessica's mouth dropped open. "Just totally out of the blue?"

"Yeah." Well, that wasn't exactly true. "But before that, I was sitting next to him and we were talking."

Her friend's eyes narrowed. "How old was this guy?"

"A few years older than me, I guess?"

"Was he cute?"

Extremely. Or *handsome* might be the better word. The truth was, Paige had sat down right next to Dylan on purpose with a vague idea of striking up a conversation. Then she'd almost chickened out, but when he'd seemed to be looking at her, she'd said hello.

Jessica added, "He must've been very interested in you."

"It wasn't like that!" She'd already told herself about three dozen times that it hadn't meant anything. "He was just being friendly. And generous."

"Sure. People buy stuff for strangers all the time. You won't even tell me what he looked like?"

"White guy, tall, brown hair, brown eyes, wearing a nice suit." After Jessica spread her hands wide in impatience, Paige added, "*Yes*, he was good-looking." She felt that flutter in her nerves again, the same one she'd felt earlier with Dylan. Some kind of unspoken connection had flared between them.

But that was nonsense. She'd just met him.

Jessica asked, "What did you talk about?"

Still trying to act casual, Paige shrugged. "I told him about Clean Slate Mondays."

Jessica's eyes widened. "What did he think of that?" Paige knew that sometimes her best friend found her optimism a little over the top.

"He wasn't convinced." And he wasn't the kind of guy to ever be taken in by fanciful notions, she was sure. "Listen, he wasn't dating material. He's a banker or something. And he was working on a spreadsheet." She shuddered.

"Um, excuse me. Steve works on spread-sheets."

Paige winced. Jessica's fiancé was an in-ventory controller. The truth was, Paige had never found him to be very easy to talk to. But he and Jessica loved one another, and that was the important thing.

Dylan's corporate vibe wasn't the only reason she had mixed feelings, though. "He asked me if I worked on Mondays. I work *very hard.*" Of course, things weren't as difficult as her first year on the job, when she'd still been trying to figure everything out at once, and the sheer mental effort had left her exhausted at the end of the day. But it still took a lot of organization, energy, and prep work at home.

Jessica gave a dubious shrug. "He was making conversation."

"He also said he was busy. Like I wasn't." Well, maybe he did work long hours, given the fact that he'd been poring over columns of numbers before seven a.m. But still.

"He paid for your order. What else does he have to do, write 'I'm interested in you' on a big sign?"

Paige smiled. The truth was, when he'd said *That's very kind of you,* and had looked at her like he could see straight through to her soul and appreciated it, Paige had melted. And that had been before he'd paid for the kids' treats.

Jessica said, "I don't suppose you got his

name and number." She was already shaking her head at the lost opportunity.

"Just his first name. Dylan."

"Well, that's something," Jessica said. "Does he go to that café a lot?"

"It sounded like it."

"Great! All you have to do is hang out there in the mornings until you see him again."

"Because that wouldn't be pathetic at all," Paige said...as if she hadn't considered doing that exact thing. Her ears burned with sudden embarrassment.

Jessica looked up at the clock. "I better go."

For reading circle time, Paige had picked out a book about a lost dog. "This book has our sight word of the day in it." She pointed to the word she'd written on the board. "Kind. K-I-N-D. Does anyone know what this word means?"

"It's like, what kind of cupcake do you want," Sam burst out. Paige had told him privately about his birthday cupcakes at the beginning of the day, explaining that they'd have them after lunch and he'd be able to choose his favorite flavor first. Sam's eyes had lit up, and clearly, he hadn't thought about much else.

"Yes, exactly," Paige said. "*Kind* can mean

a *type* of thing. For instance, there are lots of kinds of animals: dogs, cats, and so on."

"And birds," someone added.

"Dragons."

"Dragons aren't real!"

"But they're still animals!"

Paige said, "Kind also means something else. It means nice. If we yell at each other, that's not being kind. But if we share with each other or say nice things to each other, that's being kind."

"I shared crayons with Ava yesterday," Katy said.

"That's a good example of being kind," Paige said. One time, when Linda had stopped into her classroom, she'd told Paige she shouldn't ever let the kids talk unless they raised their hands and Paige called on them. But during circle time, Paige relaxed things a little. "Okay, I'm going to read today's story."

Clara, a little girl with light brown bobbed hair, raised her hand. Secretly, the girl was Paige's favorite, although she tried to encourage all of them. Paige asked, "Yes, Clara?"

"Could you read one of your stories instead?"

Several voices assented to this plan. Paige lit up inside. At least somebody liked her writing. The most important somebodies, in fact.

"Miss Reynolds?" Jaden had his hand raised.

"What is it, Jaden?"

"Um, why are stickers sticky?"

Well, he's got me there. It wasn't the first time the child had stumped her with a question. He was easily her brightest student, and not particularly good at following directions or staying on topic.

"I'll get back to you on that," she told him. She was going to have to do more with science in this class.

Clara raised her hand again. "Yes, Clara," Paige said.

"Do you have a new story?"

"I've started writing a new one," she admitted. "It's about a princess who finds a magical cabin in the woods."

"I wanna hear!" Sam said, bouncing up and down where he sat.

"Stop it!" a girl said. Paige looked over to see Tommy tickling the top of her head.

"Tommy Bradley," Paige said in her nononsense voice. "You know you're supposed to keep your hands to yourself. You come over here and sit down right next to me."

"Okay." He shuffled over to her and sat. Paige dug her journal out of her purse and flipped to the right page. "Here's a picture I drew of the princess and the cabin," she told them, holding it up so they could see.

"Why is the house magic?" one of them said.

"You're a good draw-er," said another.

Clara raised her hand. Paige asked, "What is it, Clara?"

The little girl's eyes were wide. "My mom... is a real artist! She had a galley show!"

Paige smiled at her pride. "Get out of town!" She didn't bother to correct her pronunciation. Hey, a galley show wasn't such a bad idea. Paintings or photographs hung inside a ship? It might be fun.

Clara's face crumpled.

Immediately, Paige asked, "Sweetie, what's wrong?"

"You told me to *leave town.*"

Oh, no! Paige might've laughed if the poor child hadn't been so distressed. "No, no! I would *never* want you to leave town! 'Get out of town' is just an expression. It means... 'That's amazing!' It's great that your mom is an artist and had a show."

"Clara, Miss Reynolds likes you," the boy next to her said, rolling his eyes.

"That's right," Paige said firmly. "Clara, I didn't mean to hurt your feelings, and I'm sorry. Do you forgive me?" Children needed to learn forgiveness. She'd even done a weekly unit on it, earlier in the year.

Clara nodded, looking much sunnier.

"Thank you," Paige said. "How about I read the story now?" Clara nodded again. "'Once upon a time, there lived a princess who was far away from home. She traveled through a deep, dark wood. Wolves howled. The cold wind blew.'"

"She's going to meet a witch," a little boy said.

"A wolf's going to eat her."

"Shhh, let's stay quiet for the story," Paige said. "'And then she came to a meadow full of tulips, and in the middle of the tulips stood a cabin...'"

chapter four

In his office, Dylan finished booking his next upcoming trip to a conference in New York. Out on a Monday, back on a Thursday morning. He wasn't looking forward to it. Hours of meetings. Awkward conversations with strangers. And delivering a presentation about how Hammersmith Capital was basically the most incredible firm on the planet. At least it was only a two-day conference, though after that he'd be meeting with a prospective client.

He closed the laptop and shoved it into his bag. It was five-forty-five, and he had to slink out without looking like he was slinking. That was the only way he could make it to Dee's party on time after buying her cupcakes at the grocery store.

They'd probably be a lot cheaper than the cupcakes he'd bought for Paige. He'd surprised himself by doing that. He wasn't in the habit of making random generous gestures.

It had been for a good cause, he told himself. And seeing her blush had been a reward.

Where did she live? Where had she gotten that sunny attitude of hers? What *was* she writing in that journal?

It had been a random encounter at a coffee shop. That was all. He needed to get out more.

And he needed to get out now. The first half of his route held no danger: the kitchen was on his way, and anyone might believe he was on his way for yet another cup of coffee.

Brian Walker, whose cubicle was right by Dylan's office, looked up. He was the new hire—or newer hire. He'd been hired a few months ago, and on his first day, he'd filled his cubicle with pictures of his family and friends. That had struck Dylan as soft and sentimental, but he'd dismissed it with a mental shrug. To each his own.

Dylan hadn't as much as said hello to the guy in three days, so he said, "Hey Brian, how's it going?"

Brian sighed. "Not great. I think this girl I went out with is avoiding me."

Seriously? In what world was *How's it going?* an invitation to tell someone, a coworker no less, how it was really going? Someone needed to explain this to him. But Dylan didn't have time to go into the finer points of what passed for social interaction at Hammersmith Capital. "Sorry to hear that," he said lightly. "Hope she comes around." He started to move on.

"I don't know," Brian said, completely missing his cue to stop talking. "I should call her and ask what's up, right? Are we a thing or not a thing?"

Dylan could think of no reasonable way to get out of the conversation. "I wouldn't do that." It sounded needy. In any relationship, business or otherwise, the person who cared more had less of the power. "You don't want to be too nice. I'd wait for her to call."

"Yeah, maybe." Brian looked unconvinced.

"Well, good luck." Dylan continued toward the exit before the guy could say anything else. He passed his coworker Josh's office, where Kyle stood talking to Josh. "Did you see the look on his face? I thought he was going to *cry*." Both men laughed. Kyle caught Dylan's eye and Dylan automatically smiled, as if he'd be in on the joke if he had the time.

"Hey Cain," Kyle said, coming over to the office door. "Got your email about Wakefield Properties. Why do you think that tax break is going away?"

"It's for green companies, and they're not green." It irritated Dylan. The tax break had been intended for undeveloped forestland, not commercially run golf courses.

Kyle's broad, freckled face lit up with amusement. "It's crazy, right? It's a ton of money, too. But we already checked it out. It's totally legal."

"Yeah, all right."

"You worry too much," Kyle said good-naturedly as he retreated back into Josh's office. Finally, Dylan was alone to make his escape.

He was almost to the exit when the door to the men's room opened and his boss emerged.

"Hey, Mark," Dylan said.

Mark squinted at him. From behind the glint of his glasses, his small blue eyes, almost colorless, were barely visible. "You getting takeout? I might want something. Unless you're going to Jade Palace. That place is trash." Dylan loved Jade Palace.

Restaurant runs were common around this time of day. The company paid for them: a thoughtful perk to encourage them to work through the dinner hour and beyond.

"I've actually got to head out. It's a family thing." Dylan hoped the tone of his voice suggested some kind of emergency rather than a grown sibling's birthday party.

Mark blinked and licked his lips, his tongue flicking out quickly like a lizard's. Dylan braced himself. Mark did that every time he had a last-minute job for someone. "I need you to take another look at the modeling for Hartley. We've got some new inputs."

"Another look" meant a couple of hours at least. "I'll be in tomorrow morning at five."

Dylan could almost hear his future self cursing as he climbed out of bed.

His boss pursed his chapped lips. "Did you hear Jeffries is no longer with us?"

Kevin Jeffries? He'd been hired less than a

year ago. Had he left, or had he been fired? "Is that right?" Dylan asked.

Mark nodded. "We're not making a big announcement."

Fired, then. They never announced that. Everyone pretended the person had never existed. Dylan got a heavy feeling in his chest. Kevin and his wife had just had a baby girl.

It wasn't a job for a new dad. Maybe Kevin would be better off in the long run.

Elaine approached them, her purse over her shoulder. "I'm going to Jade Palace," she said. "Dylan, you want your usual?"

Elaine, a heavyset brunette who was always perfectly put together, was a few years older than Dylan. That made her the oldest person there who hadn't made VP yet.

"Thanks, but I've got to go," Dylan said. "Family emergency." Elaine made a noncommittal *mmm* noise that might've meant she didn't believe him. Dylan half-raised a hand in an awkward farewell and headed for the exit.

An hour later, two packages of grocery store cupcakes in hand, he knocked on the front door of Dee and Paul's one-story house in the suburbs.

Dee opened the door and beamed at him. "Hey, come on in!" The laughter and conversation of guests buzzed in the house behind her.

Judging from her casual sweater and jeans, she truly hadn't expected a party.

"Happy birthday, sis." After shifting the cupcakes to one hand, he leaned down to hug her. "I guess I'm late."

"Not really. I just got here."

Dylan spotted his father across the room: a man of about seventy, with thinning, graying hair and glasses. He'd dressed up for the occasion, in a button-down shirt and khakis. As soon as they made eye contact, his dad came over. He looked slightly hunched, and Dylan recalled Dee saying that his back had been giving him trouble.

"Hello, there," his dad greeted him. "How's work?"

"Brutal," Dylan said. "With all that's going on with the markets, it's making things hard." His dad had always been his own height, about six feet even, but now it seemed like Dylan was looking down a little to talk to him. It unsettled Dylan, almost making him feel sorry for his father, when he preferred not to have any strong feelings about him at all.

"You should take a break sometime. Why don't you come over and watch the game with me next week?"

They never watched the game together. In fact75, Dylan never visited him at the townhouse he'd bought after he'd retired a few years ago. "Yeah, maybe. Monday nights are always bad, though."

One of Dee's children, Connor, ran up to them. "Grandpa, guess what?"

Dylan's dad leaned down, giving the boy his full attention. "What?"

"Mom says I can get a pet lizard. If I get all A's and B's."

"Well, that shouldn't be too hard. You did it last time."

Dylan raised his eyebrows at the reply. When he'd been a kid, his dad hadn't even looked at his good grades before signing his report card—or if he had, he hadn't commented on them.

His father now asked Connor, "What got you interested in lizards?"

The boy basked in the older man's attention. "My friend Quentin has one. Do you want to play my new videogame with me?"

Dylan's father looked sincerely regretful. "Oh, you know those aren't my thing."

So he'd at least tried before. As a grandpa, he was doing a good job. *Better late than never.*

Dylan went to the kitchen and set the cupcakes down on the counter. Dee leaned closer to him and said, "That's Allison in the gray sweater." She inclined her head ever so slightly in the direction of the women he'd just passed.

Dylan glanced over and saw the tall brunette looking right back at him. She smiled and then returned her attention to her friend.

"Am I supposed to know who that is?" he asked his sister under his breath.

"I told you about her," she whispered back. "Connor is friends with her son? She lives down the street? Come on. It's been forever since you dated."

Dylan opened his mouth again to explain that the timing wasn't right for a new relationship of any kind when Dee straightened and said, "Hi, Allison!" Dylan turned around as the brunette walked over to them.

"Hi! Do you need any help?"

"Oh, no, I think Paul took care of everything. I don't think you've met my brother. This is Dylan. Dylan, this is my friend Allison."

"Nice to meet you," Dylan said.

"You too. Dee's told me a lot about you. You're in investment banking, isn't that right?" When he nodded, she added with a smile, "So you must be pretty smart."

"Oh, I don't know about that," he answered easily. "What do you do?" He listened as Allison talked about pharmaceuticals, asking at an appropriate moment, "How long have you been working there?"

How long had Paige been a teacher? Her students probably adored her.

She hadn't worn a wedding ring, but for all he knew, she had a boyfriend. Maybe a fellow teacher, someone with whom she could happily discuss crayons or phonics or whatever teachers talked about for hours on end. Or maybe he was a guy with a beard who brewed his own craft beer and played in a band. Thinking about the possibilities set Dylan's teeth on edge.

"Dee told me you run marathons," Allison said, shifting the conversation back to him. She had good social skills. He had to give her that.

"Yeah, I've run a few of them."

He'd almost always been a runner. In middle school, he'd joined the cross country team, and at every meet, he'd gone as hard as he could.

He'd never won, though he'd usually come close. He hadn't been born with natural athletic gifts. In place of them, he'd developed a high threshold of exhaustion and pain. At a sports banquet, he'd gotten an award for athletic and academic performance combined. Grueling effort resulted in approval. He'd learned that equation before he'd gotten to high school.

"Everyone come sing happy birthday," Paul called out. The interruption relieved Dylan. Paul stuck birthday candles into four of the cupcakes. "One for each decade," he said.

"I don't know what you're talking about," Dee joked. "I'm turning twenty-nine." Someone flipped off the lights and the candles cast a golden glow on her face.

She looked good for forty. More important, she looked *happy*. She seemed to like her part-time receptionist job, and she truly loved being married to Paul and being the mom to a couple of energetic sons. Despite her joking, she didn't seem to mind the milestone birthday. So why did it give Dylan a vague sense of panic, as though time were suddenly moving all too quickly?

They all sang "Happy Birthday" and then Connor called out with gusto, "Make a wish and make it good!" Everyone laughed, but it startled Dylan. Their grandfather had always said that.

Dee scrunched up her face. "Hmm, let's see," she said, making a show of deciding what to wish for. Then she blew out all four of the candles, and people cheered.

A few hours later, the last guests left, including Dylan's dad, who hugged the boys goodbye. Paul was already loading the dishwasher, and Dylan gathered up empty wine glasses.

"I've got something to show you," Dee told Dylan, getting her phone out. "You will *never* believe this." Some weird story about someone they went to school with, Dylan guessed.

She showed him a picture.

"Oh, wow," he said. Grandma and Grandpa Cain's cabin had a real estate sign in the front yard: *Coming Soon.*

"I drive by there every once in a while," she said. "I already showed Dad. I think part of him wanted to buy it, but he says he's getting too old to move again."

"I want to see," Connor said. "What is it?"

Dee showed him. "This was your great-grandma and grandpa's house." She beckoned to her younger son. "Come here, Noah, look. Your Grandma Cain's mom and dad lived here."

Connor's eyes got bigger. "It looks like Abraham Lincoln's house."

Dylan laughed. "Yeah, exactly, it's a log cabin."

"We used to stay with your great-grandma and grandpa on some weekends," she told the boys. "And some summers."

"And your mom and I would come over on Christmas morning and open presents," Dylan added. "They always had a real Christmas tree."

Their dad hadn't put up a tree after their mom had died. Dylan's memories of his mom were hazy—no more than fleeting images—but Dee remembered those early, happy times well. For Dylan, the best times had been at the cabin.

Connor frowned. "Why were you there so much?"

Dee gave Dylan a quick glance. "Just for fun," she answered her son, her voice light. Dylan wouldn't have expected her to explain that their dad hadn't been the best father.

Dylan gestured for the phone again and took another look at the photo. He wished he could see a glimpse of the inside through the windows. His grandparents had often left them open on warm nights to let in the breeze and the chirping of crickets.

"I wonder if there's any of Grandma and Grandpa's stuff in there," Dee mused.

"I don't think so. Aunt Maureen cleaned out the place when Gandma went into assisted living."

She frowned. "I wish Dad had gotten the cedar chest for me." Her voice carried a hint of bitterness.

"What cedar chest?" Then he remembered. "The thing she kept sweaters in?"

"Yes! She had things from her wedding in there. Like her bridal veil. She'd let me put it on and pretend I was getting married. And there was, um—a sixpence, I think. Brides back then would put one in their shoe for good luck." Dee shook her head at the loss.

"You should buy the cabin," Dylan blurted out. Connor and Noah could grow up there. It would be amazing.

She laughed. "Seriously?"

The boys probably wouldn't like not having their own rooms, though. And Paul and Dee might not want to share a bathroom with them. "It's small, but you could build an addition."

She shook her head. "We just bought this house last spring. And the cabin isn't even in the same school district." She tilted her head and admitted, "Not that I didn't think about it."

Dylan's memories of being there were sun-lit, easy, so unlike the drabness of the rest of his existence then...and his existence now. He'd never been one to dwell on the past. Just the opposite, really. But now he thought, *I want it. I want it all back.*

He couldn't get it all back, of course. He was a grown man. His grandparents were gone, in a better place. But the experience of being in the house, and all the good feelings he'd had there...he could have them again.

"I'm going to buy it," he said.

Her eyes widened. "Really?"

"I've been thinking about buying instead of renting. It's a good investment."

"That's why you want to buy this house?" she teased. "For financial reasons?"

Dylan nodded. "Sure." The whole idea of buying it made him feel light inside, the way buying a new car hadn't—the way no other purchase could have. It felt like life and pos-sibility opening up again. "And the boys would love it there."

Dee's eyes sparkled. "Wouldn't that be wonderful?"

"I like it," Noah declared.

She leaned over and gave him a quick hug from behind. "It's not a sure thing. Your uncle isn't going to be the only one who wants it."

Dylan said, "Nobody's going to want it as much as I do."

"You know what, if you tell them we used to stay there as kids, I bet it'd help."

"That's the *last* thing I'm going to do."

She blinked. "Why not?"

"Because *then* the seller would ask for the moon. 'Actually, we want *twenty million dollars* for this place.'" Connor and Noah giggled. This was good. The boys were learning sound bargaining practices.

"You've got a point," she admitted. "Well, I'll let you tell Dad."

"Sure." Dylan didn't expect to tell him any time soon, though. Why would he, until it was a done deal?

Dee wanted him to talk to their dad more. He knew that. But she'd always been bossy, the way big sisters could be, even if these days she expressed her bossiness in more tactful ways. She had all kinds of ideas about how Dylan's life ought to go, but Dylan was pretty sure he knew better than anyone else what was right for him. Maybe he and Dad weren't close, but they got along okay, and that was more than a lot of people could say.

Dee looked down at the photo on her phone again. "I still miss them, you know? Especially on birthdays."

That had probably been why she'd driven by the place this week. "They knew how to do birthdays right," Dylan said.

"And Sunday mornings," Dee reminded him. "Remember how Grandma would always make muffins?"

The memory came back to Dylan so vividly that he could almost smell them. Fresh-baked, flavored with maple syrup, studded with pecans. "They were so good."

Connor said, "Uncle Dylan, I have a question."

"Yeah, buddy, what is it?"

"Will you take me to Happy Harvest?"

Dylan frowned at the sudden change of topic. "What's that?"

Dee said, "Happy Harvest Farms. You can go there and pick apples and choose your own pumpkin from the patch. We were going to go, but we've got the church yard sale."

Connor gave his mother a wide-eyed, resentful look. "Brandon said this is the last weekend for the apples. And you get to climb the trees and it's awesome."

Poor kid. That did sound like more fun than hanging out at a yard sale while his parents volunteered. But Dylan couldn't make plans for Saturday. Who knew what would be going on at work?

"Your uncle's very busy," Dee said.

Paige came to his mind yet again. *Everyone's busy*, she'd said. *Not just you.* And again he had the sensation of time moving too quickly, summer to fall to winter, grandparents gone, a beloved cabin gone, he and Dee not exactly *young* anymore...

He could do it. The idea of visiting an orchard actually did appeal to him, and spending a few extra hours with his nephews was a good idea. "I'll take them."

Connor punched a fist in the air. "Yes!"

Dee's eyebrows raised. "You're sure? You'll have to keep an eye on them."

Really? He was a grown, responsible man. "I've taken them places before."

"Well, it's been a while. They've gotten faster and sneakier."

"We'll be good," Connor said. "I'm going to go tell Noah!"

chapter five

On Thursday night, Jessica and Paige sat at Paige's kitchen table. Paige cut orange construction paper pumpkins for an art project, and Jessica graded her students' math tests. She put stickers on every paper, with encouraging messages ranging from *Brilliant!* to *Good Effort!*

Sometimes they made monotonous work more fun by meeting to do it together. Of course, they talked so much that it probably took about five times as long to get it done.

"Are you going to do a Halloween art project?" Paige asked as she traced a pumpkin.

"Oh, yeah. It's ready to go. I've got all my art projects ready through Christmas."

Paige stared at her. "How are you always so far ahead of me? Especially when you're about to get married?"

Jessica gave a modest smile and shrugged. "I like to plan ahead. And I want to have plenty of time with Steve to relax after the wedding."

"I wish I were more organized," Paige admitted. "If I do have to move, it's going to be a huge job. That spare bedroom is stuffed full of fabric, and holiday decorations..." She shook her head.

"It would be so great if you could buy this place," Jessica said, not for the first time that week. "You *love* it."

"I have to get approved for a loan first."

"I'm sure you can. Maybe you could even make some improvements."

"Like what?" Paige asked, although she could think of several possibilities. She grabbed a new sheet of construction paper and set her cardboard pumpkin template on top of it.

"Like insulating it. Didn't you say it got pretty drafty last winter?"

Paige traced around the pumpkin with a pencil. "It's not that bad. I wear big sweaters and use the fireplace. I kind of like doing that anyway, you know?"

Jessica shuddered. "Not me. From October to May I'm a miserable icicle."

"Texas girl," Paige teased. "At least you have Steve to keep you warm."

Jessica's mouth tightened into a grim line. "Things were *very* cold between us last night."

Uh-oh. Paige paused, scissors in hand. "What happened?"

Jessica shook her head. "Oh, it wasn't serious." Her expression and her tone of voice told a different story. "It was a stupid argument that, I don't know, blew up into this big thing."

"I'm sorry." Paige's instinct for looking at the bright side kicked in. "I think even happy couples have bad fights sometimes. You guys are both probably stressed out about the wedding details."

Jessica perked up a little at this. "It's true. Did I tell you my mom and my aunt had a fight about the seating chart?" She looked back down at the paper she was grading. "Shoot, I'm out of stickers. Do you have any?"

"Hang on." Paige got up and opened the kitchen drawer that held plastic sandwich bags, aluminum foil, and her sticker stash. She flipped through them. Rainbows, stars... didn't she have any with words on them? She dug further. Something was caught in the back corner of the drawer. She tugged it free and pulled out a folded piece of ivory paper. What was that?

She unfolded it to see delicate but steady handwriting. A piece of stationery, but not a letter. The top of the page read: *Sunday Muffins.*

Wow. The recipe must have been left behind a long time ago, though she hadn't come across it before. She smiled and brought it over to Jessica. "Look."

"Sweetie, that's not stickers," her friend said.

"Ha ha. Look at it! Someone left their recipe here."

"That is pretty cool." Jessica scanned it. "And it's old."

"Why do you say that?"

"They don't make that brand anymore." She pointed. "See? She crossed it out and wrote 'shortening' instead."

"Oh, wow. She must've used this recipe for a while."

Paige took it back and put it on the fridge with a rainbow magnet. "I wonder why it says *Sunday* Muffins."

"So she wouldn't get them mixed up with her Saturday Muffins?"

Paige laughed. "Well, I'm going to make them soon."

"Do you think that's a good idea? I mean, no offense." Paige had told her about the cupcake-baking debacle. And she probably hadn't forgotten about the time Paige had invited her over for dinner.

"If at first you don't succeed," Paige said. She told her kids that all the time. Jessica still looked skeptical. "What? I'll concentrate this time!"

Jessica got a sly look on her face. "Speaking of delicious things...have you been back to that café?"

How in the world did her best friend know her so well? Part of the job description, Paige supposed. Still, she played innocent. "What café?"

"The one where you got the cupcakes? No,

wait, the one where a rich, handsome busi-
nessman *bought* you cupcakes?"

Paige could feel her face flush. "I have, actually. But only to get pumpkin spice lattes."
There was no point in admitting the truth.
If he'd wanted to see her again, he would've
stopped in too, right? "Maybe you don't love
the fall, but I do."

"*Sure,*" Jessica said. "You're not hoping to
run into him. It's just that nobody else makes
pumpkin spice lattes. Oh wait, they do."

"It's right by work!"

Someone knocked on the front door, and
Paige's heart dropped. "It's my landlord. He's
going to show the real estate agent around."
Jessica's mouth twisted in sympathy.

She opened the door to find Harry and a
man who looked to be not much older than
she was. He was powerfully built, his light
brown hair cropped very short, and he wore
a bright blue button-down shirt and dress
pants.

"Hi, Paige," Harry said. "Sorry to bother
you."

"Come on in."

The real estate agent closed the door behind both of them and stuck a hand out to
Paige. "Trent Jackson, Paragon Realty."

"Hi, I'm Paige." She pasted on a smile.
"This is my friend Jessica. We're just working
on teacher stuff."

"I'm sure you won't be in the way," Trent said. *Um.* Shouldn't he be concerned about being in *her* way? He looked around him and said to Harry in a wry tone, "Well, it's definitely got that vintage charm."

Paige bristled. Harry said, "That's what they say about me, too." She laughed, but Trent barely paid attention. He walked over to inspect the mantel.

"For the showings, we'll need to do a lot of depersonalizing." He picked up a framed photo of Paige's parents. "Family photos, those have to go."

How dare he? Paige resisted the urge to walk over and snatch it out of his hands.

He set it down, moved to the sofa, and picked up one of the brightly colored throw pillows Paige had sewn herself. "And we want to get rid of home décor like this, keep everything neutral."

Heat flooded her cheeks.

"Excuse me," Jessica said pointedly to Trent. "My friend still *lives* here."

"This is just for staging," Trent said, unbothered. "It's not personal."

"Right," Jessica said. "It's *de*-personal."

Trent smiled. "Exactly. And de-cluttered. We put away all the knickknacks like this." He reached for the brass apple on the side table, a gift from one of Paige's students—and knocked the table lamp to the floor with a crash. Paige gave a little scream.

"Oh geez, sorry," he said, looking down at the ceramic shards on the floor. At least he sounded sincere now. "I'll pay you for that."

The chartreuse lamp had only cost her eight dollars at a thrift shop. She'd loved it, though.

"Where's a broom?" Trent asked. After he'd swept up the pieces, Harry, looking more contrite than ever, steered him into one of the bedrooms.

"Oh, honey." Jessica patted her arm. "I love the way you decorate. And you made that twill shower curtain."

"Toile," Paige corrected her unthinkingly.

Jessica lowered her voice. "Go tell your landlord you want to buy the place. Do it now, while he feels bad for you."

Paige got up and walked over to Harry, who now stood with the real estate agent in the doorway to her bedroom. Hopefully, she hadn't left any embarrassing personal items in plain sight. The agent was saying, "It would be great if we could de-clutter here a little, too, but it's not as crucial as in the main area."

Paige decided to ignore him. "Harry, how much are you going to charge for this place?"

Harry's eyebrows raised. "How much am I listing it for?" He exchanged a look with Trent.

"We were going to discuss that next. Why? Did you know somebody who's interested?"

"Yes," she said. "Me."

His face brightened. "Is that right?"

"We'll see." Although Paige tried to feel doubtful, a spark of hope shone inside her.

The following afternoon, Paige glanced up at the schoolroom clock. Her art project had gone more quickly than she'd expected. She'd already spread out the painted construction paper pumpkins on the long windowsill to dry, and the children had all washed their hands.

"We've got a few minutes until the bell. What song would you like to sing?"

"Greasy grimy gopher guts!" a boy yelled.

"Hmm, I don't know that one," Paige lied. It had been a favorite at her childhood summer camp, and even then, she'd found it disgusting. How did a kid today still know about it?

Clara's hand went up. "Yes, Clara," Paige said.

"Do you have more of your cabin story?"

The simple question made Paige's stomach knot. Maybe reading more of the story would somehow jinx her chances at getting the cabin. "You know, I don't think that story is ever going to be a real book." The way things were going, none of her stories were going to be real books, but still. "I think it's just for me."

"Can it be for us, too?" Deion asked.

He was a shy boy and rarely spoke up. Paige couldn't bear to say no to both Clara *and* him. "Okay."

She dug her journal out of her purse, opened it to the last section, and read.

"'One day, the princess looked out the window and saw a gigantic scary bull. He stomped down the hill and tromped right into her cabin.'"

"What's a bull?" someone called out.

"It's a cow who's a boy," Paige explained. "And he has horns."

Another child piped up. "My dad says that when he's mad. *That's bull!*"

"When my dad's mad—"

"Well, we don't say that in this class," Paige cut in loudly. Clara raised her hand. "Yes, Clara."

"Did you draw the bull?"

"I did, actually." She flipped to the next page and turned the journal around, holding it up so they could see.

A few of the children gasped. "He's scary," a boy said.

"He is," she admitted, turning the book back around. Maybe she shouldn't have given him red eyes. "But don't worry. All my stories have happy endings, remember?" How she hoped that could be true in her real life.

A girl asked, "What did the princess do? Did she fight the bull?"

Good question. Maybe she should've written it that way. But no, she didn't want to promote violence.

"She could fight him with a sword," a boy said.

"Or a rock."

"He's too big to hurt with a rock."

"If it was a *big* rock."

Jaden waved his hand in the air. "Miss Reynolds!"

"Yes, Jaden?"

"Um. If you burn a log, where does the log go? Does it turn into air?"

A great question, and for once, Paige could actually understand how his thoughts had gotten there. It was a story about a log cabin, after all. "I don't know, but I'll find out."

Jaden gave her a sweet smile. "Will you get back to me on it?"

He couldn't have been any cuter. "Yes. I will.—Okay, I'm going to read now. 'His big tail swished and he knocked a lamp to the floor. *That was my favorite lamp!* the princess said. And the bull said, *Ha, ha, ha! I don't care!*'"

"Uh-oh," Clara breathed, and then the school bell rang.

chapter six

Dylan yawned as he pulled into the last parking spot at Dolce Café and Bakery, his nephews Connor and Noah in the back seat. The place was apparently even more popular on Saturdays. Since the time he'd run into Paige there, he'd been back four times.

He wasn't looking for her, exactly. No. It turned out the café was a good place to caffeinate and catch up on emails before he went into the office.

Anyway, he should probably give up on the idea of seeing her again. It had been, what, two weeks now?

"Why are we going here first?" Connor asked.

"Because your uncle is in desperate need of coffee."

That was true, anyway. He'd stayed till around one a.m. at the office the night before, updating a presentation, immediately scrapping the update after getting new information from Elaine, and then making a new set of changes.

When he'd gotten home, he'd taken a while to unwind, the way he sometimes did when he worked late. He'd watched a couple of episodes of a TV show before going to bed, which he regretted now. The show hadn't even been that good. Depressing, too. He always teased Dee for watching Hallmark movies, but maybe she was on to something.

Despite the late night, Dylan had picked up his nephews at the appointed time, and he gave himself a lot of credit for that.

"You always need coffee," Noah declared as they got out of the car.

"That's right, buddy."

They went inside and he quickly scanned the café. His gaze stopped briefly on a blonde woman at the counter, hunched over her phone. *Not Paige.* He felt a foolish jab of disappointment as he got in line.

Connor asked, "Can I get a cupcake?"

Dylan raised an eyebrow. "I thought you said you wanted cider donuts at the orchard."

"I could get both."

"Ha. Your mother would kill me."

Connor straightened. "Miss Reynolds!" Dylan looked up, startled, as Connor trotted over toward someone. A blonde woman in a bright blue sweater...

Holy smokes. It was Paige. And Connor

knew her? She met Dylan's gaze and her mouth fell open.

Connor reached her side, and she beamed down at him. "Hi there! How are you?" Dylan got out of line and walked up to her with Noah.

Paige's brow furrowed slightly in confusion. The sweater brought out the blue in her eyes, bright as an October sky.

"You're not Connor's dad."

"Uh, no. Uncle." He found himself short of breath. "I'm his mom's sister—her brother." He didn't usually trip over his tongue like this. A dozen times a week, he made calls to important clients. Even when they asked him questions that he didn't, strictly speaking, know the answers to, he didn't stumble.

"Connor was in my class last year." She looked to Noah. "And you're his little brother, right?" Noah nodded.

"She was my favorite teacher," Connor told Dylan.

"I'll bet." He said it without thinking, a little more emphatically than necessary, and her eyes widened.

Connor asked, "How do you know her?"

"We met here a little while back," Dylan replied, without quite being able to take his eyes off Paige. Again he imagined a boyfriend. Any moment, a man would probably come up and put a proprietary arm around her waist.

She said, "I'm kind of addicted to the pumpkin spice lattes here."

"We're going to pick our own pumpkins," Noah told her. He was gazing up at her, clearly smitten.

"Wow. That sounds like so much fun!"

"It's a place called Happy Harvest Farms," Connor explained. "You can pick your own apples off the trees, and they have cider donuts."

She nodded. "I've been meaning to go there! I tried to get someone to go with me, but they said no."

"You should dump him," Dylan said lightly.

Her cheeks flushed pink. "Oh, it wasn't—it was my best friend. There's no him."

No boyfriend. She was single. This simple bit of information buzzed through him. She'd let him know that on purpose, too.

She turned to Connor again. "You know Miss Garza?"

Connor nodded. "I wanted to be in her class. But I got Mrs. Goff." He made a face.

"Mrs. Goff is a good teacher, too," Paige said in what sounded like an obligatory tone.

Connor shrugged, clearly unconvinced. "Why didn't Miss Garza go with you?"

"I tried to talk her into going, but she's very busy lately. She's planning a wedding, and it's very complicated."

Connor screwed up his face. "Why?"

"Right now, they're having some disagreements about flowers." She cast an amused glance at Dylan.

65

He shook his head. "What a hassle. Everyone should just go to the courthouse."

Her expression softened. "Oh, I don't think that. I mean it doesn't need to be big or expensive. At all. But it should be someplace special. Because finding someone you love enough to spend the rest of your life with, that's amazing."

"I—see what you're saying." He'd been talking to this girl for two minutes, and they were discussing true love. How did that happen?

She said with a laugh, "I didn't mean to make a speech."

Noah grabbed his wrist and tugged. "Let's get apples!" Dylan didn't blame him for being antsy. They'd been standing there in the middle of a coffee shop for a little while now.

"Have you ever had apples you picked yourself before?" she asked Noah. He shook his head. "They taste so much better than apples from the store."

"You could go with us," Connor said.

Awesome idea. Maybe having the boys around wasn't so bad. He doubted she'd take them up on such a spontaneous suggestion, though, so he gave her a graceful out. "Miss Reynolds probably has other things she wants to do today. Though she's definitely invited," he added, as if that weren't one-hundred-percent obvious.

"I'd love to," she said, surprising him.

It took him a moment to remember it was his turn to talk again.

"Great! Uh, why don't we give you a ride? We can drop you off back here later. That way we won't get separated." And that way, they'd have a lot more time to get to know one another.

"It's better for the environment, too."

"Yes, exactly." That hadn't been on his mind, but the fact that she thought of it pleased him. "Let's go."

"Did you want to get a coffee first?"

Right. He'd come here for coffee. In fact, until he'd seen her, he'd been pretty sure he couldn't stay alert behind the wheel without it. He felt wide awake now, though, and his heart seemed to be beating at a brisk pace without the aid of caffeine. "Oh yeah, definitely. And I'll get your PSE."

"My what?"

"PSL," he corrected himself. Pumpkin spice latte. He'd let a work term slip in there. She wanted coffee and whipped cream and spices, not a public sector enterprise. "Sit down, I'll get in line."

Smooth, he thought as he walked away. *Get it together, Cain.*

In the car, Paige chatted with the boys, and he and Paige talked, too. "A couple of months ago I ran a half marathon that went up this hill," he commented at one point. "This was the last mile." Was he trying to impress her? Of course he was.

She scrunched up her shoulders. "That's

thirteen miles, right? That hurts to even think about."

Farther out in the country, they came upon a hand-painted wooden sign that read "Welcome to Happy Harvest Farms!" Apples and pumpkins with smiling faces surrounded the words.

Dylan found a place to park in the grassy fields that served as parking lots. From the backseat, Connor said, "Awww! There aren't any apples on the trees." As Dylan shut off the car, he looked in the direction of the boy's gaze. Sure enough, the nearby line of trees held no fruit, although small piles of half-rotten apples lay in the grass beneath them.

Paige said, "I bet when we walk a little farther, we'll find trees with lots of apples."

He appreciated her optimism. He didn't even care about the apple picking, but both Paige and his nephews apparently did, and he hoped he hadn't devoted part of his day to something that would disappoint them. Okay, he was more concerned about Paige. If his nephews had been disappointed, he would've chalked it up to a lesson about how you didn't always get what you want and then taken them bowling or something.

They walked up the hill toward a wooden building with a sign out on the front that read "Country Store." On tables out in front, piles of apples, gourds, and vegetables gleamed in the sun. The smell of cider doughnuts filled the air. Inside the store, Dylan approached the woman behind the counter.

"Hi!" she said. "How can I help you?"

"How does this work? Picking apples."

"You grab a basket there." She pointed to where they were stacked in the corner. "We sell them by the peck, the half peck, or the quarter peck. You fill it up and bring it back here to pay."

"What's a peck?" Connor asked.

"Oh, it's usually around thirty, thirty-five apples," the woman said. "Here's a map of our different varieties. The Red Delicious are pretty much gone." She shrugged. "Though honestly, they're my least favorite. We've still got everything else."

Dylan thanked her and then studied the photocopied hand-drawn map. "What kind of apples do you want?" he asked Paige and the boys. "They've got Golden Delicious, Jonathan, McIntosh, Honeycrisp, Cortland, and Granny Smith."

"What's the difference?" Connor asked.

"I have no idea," Dylan said. "Except I'm pretty sure Golden Delicious are yellow."

"I like red," Noah said.

"Tell you what," Paige said. "Let's get a few of all of them."

Connor grabbed one of the big baskets. "No," Dylan said. "You each get a small one."

"Do you mind waiting a minute?" Paige asked. "I'm going to get a couple of things."

"Yeah, no problem. What are you getting?" He moved closer to see the jars in her hands.

"Red clover honey." She showed him. "I bought this from their stand at the farmer's market a few months ago. It's really good. And jalapeño jelly."

"I never heard of that. Is it really hot?"

"Only a little spicy. I love it," she said. After she paid for the jars and tucked them into her big purse, they grabbed baskets and headed out toward the closest grove. The autumn air was cool enough that he was glad he'd worn a sweater, and the trees and the wide-open spaces made him feel a little freer.

"Sometimes I forget how much I like to be outside," he said. He was glad Connor and Noah had wanted to come here, that they weren't the kind of kids who only wanted to stare at screens. He'd *loved* being outdoors when he was their age. There had been a pond not far from his grandparents' cabin, and he'd walk around it sometimes looking for frogs. There hadn't been many, but once in a while, he'd see one before it hopped into the water with a splash.

"Isn't it great? Especially on a day like to-day." She waved an arm at the trees behind her. "The sign says these are Jonathans. All I know is, they're mostly red."

As they approached the closest tree, the smell of the ripe apples, both on the tree and lying on the ground, made Dylan want to grab one and eat it right there. He'd never thought

70

about apples being tempting before, but he'd only had them from the grocery store, uniform in size, chilled, and waxed. Walking in a sunny orchard was a very different experience. Apparently, he wasn't the only person who'd had the urge to eat one on the spot, because a few browning cores lay in the grass along with the fallen apples.

Noah gave a little shriek. "A bee!"

"There are lots of them out here," Paige said pleasantly. "They pollinate the trees in the spring. We wouldn't have apples without them." She was such a teacher. Noah looked uncertain, and Paige added, "If you leave them alone they'll leave you alone. They'd rather eat apples than sting you." She darted a friendly glance toward Dylan.

Well, he was tempted, definitely, and by more than fruit. *I'm going to ask this girl out.* It surprised him. This wasn't at all part of his plans, and changes in plans unsettled him, but he knew he was going to do it.

"I can't reach any of them," Connor said, stretching up his hand to demonstrate. "I have to climb the tree."

"You don't have any other choice," Dylan agreed.

"I'm going to climb too!" Noah ran over.

Dylan told Paige, "This is the real reason they wanted to come. To climb trees."

"Be careful," she called over to them. Then,

to him, she said, "I don't want him to break an arm like last year."

"Right," Dylan said. Connor hadn't been happy when the injury had kept him from playing soccer, though he'd enjoyed showing off all the signatures on his cast. "He broke it on the playground swings, right?"

Paige nodded. "I heard he swung as high as he could and then jumped out. I think he was showing off."

"*My* nephew?" he asked in mock disbelief. "No way."

Paige walked up closer to them. "I kind of want to climb one myself."

"Yeah?" he asked, amused. "Well, you're dressed for it today." Her worn jeans fit her curves perfectly. He kind of wanted to *watch* her climb a tree. "The last time I saw you, you were wearing a dress with pumpkins on it."

She grinned. "I learned how to sew a couple of years ago. I make some dresses with patterns like that because the kids like them."

"That's dedication."

She shrugged. "Or...maybe teaching gives me a good excuse to wear dresses with dinosaurs on them."

"Do you need an excuse?" he asked. She laughed. "Well, you're still colorful. Look at those shoes." She wore bright yellow canvas sneakers. "It's like you're walking on sunshine."

"I am," she said, and then looked away.

They decided their next stop would be the

Golden Delicious grove—Paige's favorite, she said—and they headed down the dirt road past families with small children. To anyone else, *they* probably looked like a married couple with kids. It probably should've disturbed him more than it did. Paige was easy to talk to, and the morning felt magical, a temporary escape into another world where he didn't have to work so hard or worry so much.

"You like being a teacher?" he asked.

"I do. Although the first couple of years were rough."

He hadn't expected that. "How come?"

"Oh, I had a lot to learn. About how to set up the classroom and plan the lessons. And I wasn't good at dealing with kids who misbehaved. I hadn't learned my no-nonsense voice yet."

That didn't surprise him at all. She seemed naturally sweet. "Do it," he said.

"What?"

"Let me hear your no-nonsense voice."

"Nooo." She waved him off.

"Oh, come on."

"Dylan, I told you *no*."

He stopped short. He'd been joking around, but somehow, he'd offended her.

"That was my no-nonsense voice," she said quickly.

He laughed. "That was pretty good."

Her smile faded. "So what about you?"

"I definitely have a no-nonsense voice."

"No, I meant do you like being a...was it an

investment banker?" While he considered how to answer this, she said, "You know, I'm sorry about what I said before."

"What do you mean?"

She winced. "About your job sounding awful."

"I wasn't offended."

"Hey, stop!" Connor said. "We're passing the Golden Delicious." He walked from one tree to another. "The only ones left are way up there." He scrambled up into the branches.

"These really are my favorites," Paige said. "I'm going to climb. Are you?"

"Uh. No." She was serious about this?

"Why not?"

Because I'd look ridiculous. "I've never climbed a tree in my life." She was clearly unsure whether to believe him, and the way she scrunched up her face was adorable. "Besides, those branches aren't that thick. I'd probably break one."

"No, you wouldn't," she said, but he caught her giving him a quick look up and down. Then she said, "Watch my purse," and dropped it at his feet. She sauntered over to the next tree and swung herself up to the lowest branch. When she climbed to the next one, her foot slipped on a branch, and she squeaked. Dylan rushed closer. She regained her footing and laughed, looking down at him.

"You're making me nervous up there," he said lightly.

"You're making *me* nervous."

What did she mean by that? She tossed one apple to him, and then another.

When everyone's baskets were full, they headed toward the pumpkin patch, but then took a detour to explore the corn maze. The boys trotted ahead of them. "Connor, don't get too far away," Dylan called after him. "And don't lose your brother!"

"I won't!"

Paige said, "It's nice of you to take them places."

"I should do it more often." The last thing he'd expected that day was to be walking with Paige among cornstalks that towered over his head. He smiled. "I'm glad I did today."

"Me too," she said.

If he was going to ask, now was the time. "So, you want to go out with me?"

Her eyes sparkled. That was a good sign. He liked his chances, or he wouldn't have asked, but one never knew.

"Go out with you where? And when?"

"Uh, I hadn't gotten that far yet." They both laughed. "Dinner, next Saturday night? I'll pick you up."

She bit her lip. "You know..." Was she backing out of it, after all? "I don't really know you. I don't even know your last name."

"Oh. Cain. It's Dylan Cain." He didn't blame her for being hesitant. There were a lot of creeps out there, and while he hoped he didn't seem like one, there was no way for her to know for sure. Maybe his suggesting to pick

75

her up had set off an alarm in her head. "We could meet for lunch." If she drove herself, in broad daylight, she might feel better about it.

Her shoulders relaxed. "I'd like that. Sorry to be weird."

"You weren't. It's fine."

"Well, here," she said, holding out her hand. "I'll put my number in your phone."

Yes. She trusted him that much, at least. He pulled up his contact list and then handed the phone to her. As she typed in her name, he asked, "Is next Saturday good?"

She smiled. "It's perfect. I don't have much of a lunch break during the week."

"What do you like for lunch?"

"Um, places with breakfast food? But I mean, anything's fine."

"Breakfast for lunch is great. I think some people call that brunch." She rewarded him with a laugh.

"Uncle Dylan!" Connor peeked around the corner. "We went that way, but it was a dead end. Are you coming?"

"Where's your brother?" Dylan asked. He hadn't been paying attention to them at all, and the last thing he needed was to lose him in a maze.

"He's right *here*." Connor gestured as Noah came into view.

"Just a minute, you guys," Dylan told them.

Paige gave the phone back to him along with her own. "Give me yours, too."

With a great sense of satisfaction, he complied. After he handed it back to her, she fiddled with the phone for a moment, then held it up and took a photo of him.

"Hey," he said in mock protest.

"I need your face next to your name." Her mouth twisted. "You don't *really* mind, do you?"

He'd already pulled up the camera on his phone. "Not as long as I get to take one of you." She shook her head, and he insisted, "Fair is fair."

"I hardly have any makeup on," she mumbled.

"Paige, come on," he said, more seriously. "You look beautiful."

Her expression softened and her mouth curved upward. He snapped the picture.

"Uncle *Dylan*, let's *gooo*," Connor said.

Okay, the kid was killing the moment. But Dylan couldn't complain. If it hadn't been for his nephews, he might never have met up with Paige again, and this had been the most fun he'd had in a long, long while.

chapter seven

On Monday afternoon, Paige read the latest installment of the story to her classroom. "The knight said, *Come with me'*—Yes, Neveah?"

"How can the night talk?"

Paige sat puzzled for a moment, and then understood. "Oh! It's not 'night' like 'night and day,' it's 'knight' with a silent 'k.'" She got up and wrote it on the board. "Does everyone know what a knight is?" Clara raised her hand. "Yes, Clara."

"It's like a prince but he has a sword."

"Yes, very good! But only for scaring away bulls and monsters," Paige added. She still didn't want to promote fighting. Clara raised her hand again. "Yes, Clara?"

"I think princes are boring."

"No they're not!" another girl shouted.

"It's funny you should say that," Paige said. "Because this prince—I mean this knight— seemed boring at first. But then, it turned out he wasn't." Clara's hand went up again. "Yes, Clara?"

"Is he a real person?"

Paige's face heated. "This is a story," she said, not exactly lying to the children, even under pressure. "I'm going to keep reading it.—The knight said, *Come with me to the magical orchard!*"

The bell rang. Paige put the journal away and helped the children gather their coats and belongings. Once they'd gone out to the busses, she stopped by Jessica's classroom.

Jessica was standing on a chair to put up a new bulletin board display. A border of colorful fall leaf cutouts surrounded a half-finished message. When she saw Paige, she smiled. "Hey! How was your weekend?" As she stepped down, she scrunched up her face and added, "I bet it was better than mine. You would not believe how complicated wedding centerpieces can be. I was going to have tropical flowers in square vases, but then the vases looked too big, so I..." She cut herself off. "Aaand that's all super boring."

"I like hearing about it," Paige protested. "And you don't think it's boring. You love planning all that stuff."

"I do."

"I think you'll miss it once the wedding is over." Jessica looked sheepish at Paige's words. "What?" Paige asked.

"I may have signed up to help organize a charity ball at the shelter."

"Seriously?" Paige gaped. "You're going to drive yourself crazy." Jessica might've been the most organized and energetic person Paige knew, but still, she was only human.

Jessica waved her hand in a placating gesture. "It's for *next* fall. The planning won't even start until after the New Year."

"Oh, well that sounds okay, then," Paige said, significantly less worried. "And the wedding's given you so much event planning experience."

"Exactly." Jessica smiled. "How was *your* weekend?"

"I had a great one, actually."

At her cagey tone of voice, Jessica lifted her eyebrows. "Oh, *really.*"

All day, Paige had been itching to spill. "You know the guy who paid for my cupcakes? I ran into him at the café."

Jessica gave her a skeptical look. "Ran into him?"

"I...might've been hoping he'd show up there again."

"And he was hoping the same thing," Jessica said.

This hadn't occurred to Paige until that moment. "Do you think?"

Jessica rolled her eyes. Paige's heart warmed. Jessica had one-hundred-percent confidence in her irresistibility. Paige would've felt the same way about Jessica if her friend were still single.

"Well, he was with his two nephews," Paige

said. "And one of them was Connor Matheson. He was in my class last year?"

"Oh wow, really? That funny kid, right?"

Paige nodded. "Dylan and I talked a little, and then Connor asked if I wanted to go to Happy Harvest Farms with them...and I said yes."

"You've been wanting to go there! Did you have fun? Did you like him?"

"I did," Paige answered to both questions.

Jessica stapled the last of the letters that spelled out LEAF THROUGH A GOOD BOOK. Paige recalled her friend had prepared this particular bulletin board display back in early July. Jessica hopped off her chair. "Tell me everything."

"He asked me out."

"What?" Jessica bounced on her toes. "This is so exciting!"

"It's not *that* big of a deal."

"Yes, it is! What are you guys going to do?"

Paige suddenly felt shy. "We're just meeting for brunch."

"That's perfect."

"Do you want to see a picture of him?" Paige dug out her phone.

"Um, *yes*." Paige pulled up the photo, and Jessica snatched the phone from her. "Oh, my gosh. He is *cute*." She looked up at Paige. "What's he like?"

"He's nice. And he's funny."

"I have to meet him," Jessica declared.

"I'm not bringing you to brunch." Paige

took the phone back, noticed the time, and gasped. "I've got to go. I'm late."

"Late for what?"

"The bank."

"The mortgage." Jessica's eyes reflected her worry. "Go, go, go."

Paige sprinted across the parking lot, then slowed to what she hoped was a dignified walk as she approached the bank's front doors. Her reflection showed in the glass. She was wearing the most conservative dress she owned, navy with polka dots, with a plain navy cardigan over it. Was it still too frivolous? No. They gave mortgages to people wearing polka dots. They gave mortgages to all kinds of people, and she was responsible and upstanding, a *teacher*.

I believe it can be my house, she thought. *It was meant for me.* She took a deep breath and went inside.

She'd talked to a woman on the phone, but she wasn't sure where to find her. A few people sat at large desks in the common area. Paige approached one of them, and the woman looked up and smiled. "Can I help you?"

"Hi! Yes, I have an appointment with Lavonne Davis."

"Paige Reynolds? I'm Lavonne. I wasn't sure you'd make it."

Her tone was light, but Paige's stomach clenched. Already she was making a bad impression. "Sorry I'm late. Busy at school today." *Yeah, busy day talking to your best friend about a cute guy.*

"You said you're an elementary school teacher, isn't that right?" Paige nodded.

"I already started to fill out a mortgage application for you. Let me pull it up." Lavonne typed into the computer, pulled up a form on the monitor, and put on a pair of reading glasses. "You're a first-time buyer...and you were thinking around this amount, is that right?" She pointed to the figure on the screen.

The number still seemed huge to Paige, but she said, "Yes."

Lavonne went over Paige's personal information: her job, her salary. "And how much were you thinking for a down payment?"

Paige named the amount in her savings account, rounded down by seventeen dollars to an even number so she wouldn't sound desperate. She added, "I heard first-time buyers didn't have to put a lot down."

"That's true, but even for an FHA loan, we need at least three-point-five percent. A lot of first-time buyers borrow from their parents. In fact, that's becoming more and more common. Is that a possibility?"

"No," she answered immediately. Her parents had paid for her college, including the student teaching, and had also gotten her into her first apartment, paying the required first and last month's rent and even buying her many of the things she needed: a dresser, a sofa, staples for the pantry. She hadn't gotten financial help from them since then, and she wasn't going to start again now.

The back of her neck burned with shame. Why hadn't she saved more? She could've cut back on things. Fabric. Pumpkin spice lattes. Art supplies for the classroom. It had all seemed reasonable, but now, so many of those expenses seemed foolish. And her rent was high on a teacher's salary. If she hadn't been renting the cabin, maybe she would've been able to buy it. The thought galled her.

Lavonne said, "Well then, you'll need to look at another way to get to that down payment."

Paige remembered what Jessica had said. "Maybe a different bank would be willing to go with less down."

Lavonne gave a slight shake of her head. "Less than three-point-five? I don't think so." She took off her glasses. "Is there maybe a car you could sell?"

"No." She was single. Why would she have two cars?

"Well, give it some thought. There may be a solution you're not thinking of yet." She gave an encouraging smile.

"Okay, thanks."

As Paige left the bank, she thought, *I'm going to need to find a new place to live.*

But she should stay positive, right? She'd

always believed in optimism. It was just hard. Even though she'd tried to sound confident with the bank lady, the truth was, the house was going on the market Saturday. Someone might make an offer on the spot—someone who wouldn't love the place like she did, but who had more cash on hand. Her chances of getting a book deal that fast were about the same as her chances of winning the lottery. And she didn't even play the lottery. She got in the car.

Maybe things weren't as bad as she thought. She hadn't talked to her agent for such a long time. There was only one way to find out. Still sitting in the parking lot, she got out her phone, and then paused.

Come on, call her, she urged herself. Were other people scared of their own agents? She pressed the number. It rang three times, and then her agent answered in a brisk voice. "This is Alexis."

"Alexis, hi. It's Paige Reynolds. I was calling you about *Muffy and Kerfuffle*?" After a moment of silence, she added, "The rabbit and squirrel stories?"

"Of course. Hello."

Another moment of silence. Paige realized she hadn't asked anything. "I was just wondering if anyone had been interested in them lately."

"Actually… You know, I don't like to discuss a deal until it's final."

Paige's heart leaped. "But there's a deal?"

"There *might* be a deal," Alexis corrected her. "An editor at Vandergast Books is interested, but she hasn't met with their editor in chief yet. But my guess is we'll get an offer in the next couple of weeks."

Joy flooded Paige's soul like sunshine. "That's amazing!"

"Yes, I'll be thrilled if it goes through." Alexis sounded more calm than thrilled, though. And why not? She did book deals all the time. "Listen, I'm going to be in your neck of the woods the weekend after next. There's a YA conference downtown at the Winslett Hotel. Hang on, let me check my schedule... I've got a break after my last panel on Saturday, November third. Why don't you meet me then at the hotel lounge? Let's say around five. Hopefully by then I'll have real news for you."

"Yes, I'd love to!" Paige scrambled for her journal and wrote down the details. "Thank you," she told her agent. "I mean, thank you for everything."

"Fingers crossed," Alexis said.

Paige pulled up to Harry's house instead of her own and rang his doorbell. When he opened the door, his eyebrows raised. "Paige. Come on in."

The interior of the house was dark, lit by

only one lamp, and she was tempted to switch on another one for him.

Harry said, "I'm sorry about that real estate agent the other day."

For being rude, or breaking her lamp? Maybe both. "No, I understand. It's just that... I wonder if you could hold off selling it until I get the money."

Harry sighed. "I'd like to sell to you, Paige. You know I would. But I can't wait too long. I already put a deposit down on a place and the first month's rent. It's a very nice senior community my daughter recommended. And like I said, I already have a seller for this house."

"Could you wait a month or so?" She felt rude pressing the issue. "My agent says she's very close to getting a book contract for me."

Happiness dawned on his features. "That's wonderful! After all your hard work, too." Paige had told him before about how she'd written a dozen other children's stories, and had tried and failed to get an agent for a few of them, before finally finding someone to represent her rabbit and squirrel books. "You'll know for sure soon?"

"She said maybe a couple of weeks. If I can get more money for the down payment, the bank says they'll approve me."

Harry nodded. "Well, the buyer for this house is closing on Friday, November ninth. I could hold off until then before selling the cabin to anyone." He frowned. "I have to warn you, though. If I get a much higher offer from someone else, I may still go with that."

Paige felt foolish for not even considering that possibility: getting enough money for the loan she'd asked for, only to be outbid. Her spirits sank. She couldn't imagine getting enough of an advance to get an even higher mortgage.

Maybe there wouldn't be a bidding war. At least she had a chance.

"I understand," she said. "Thanks, Harry."

chapter eight

On Saturday morning, Paige put a big, cozy cardigan over her pajamas before she stepped outside the back door of her cabin, mug of coffee in hand, to watch the sun rise. A stripe of pale gold shone on the horizon below the gray, cloudy sky. Not every sunrise dazzled. Even if she looked at the weather the night before, she could never tell how it would go. But they were all worth her attention.

The aspens beyond the pond had lost many of their leaves, and the remaining ones, pure gold, trembled in the slight breeze. Paige imagined the trees clinging on to their happiness as long as they could.

She took in a deep breath and let it out. Closing her eyes, she said, "I'm thankful for my parents. And for Jessica. And for my good job, and the kids. And I'm thankful for...well, for the cabin, and the fact that I'm going to be able to buy it. And for the fact that I may get a book contract." She winced. The book she'd read about positive thinking had said one shouldn't leave room for doubt. "I mean definitely, I'm sure that's going to happen, so I'm thankful for that," she continued. "And I'm thankful for this day."

As she went back inside, her phone rang from the bedroom—her mom's ringtone. Paige trotted back, dug around in the covers to find the thing, and then picked up. "Hey, Mom!"

"Hi there! Didn't know if you'd be up yet. Hang on, I'll get your dad on speaker."

As her mom told her about a fabric sale, Paige debated what to wear to brunch with Dylan. Should she go casual? The last time he'd seen her, she'd been wearing jeans. She set out a pair of jeans and a striped sweater on the bed. She wasn't feeling it, though.

"Some of those prints were a dollar a yard," her mom was saying. "I went a little nuts. I couldn't help it."

"I probably would've done the same thing," Paige confessed. She tossed the jeans and sweater in the closet on the floor. Maybe something fall-ish? She pulled out the first dress she'd ever sewn for herself, printed with fall leaves, and lay it on the bed.

"I got a few yards of a cute heart print. Do you think you might want that?"

Maybe the fall-print dress was more appropriate for teaching children than for going on a date. Hmm…

"What do you think?" her mom asked, and Paige realized she hadn't answered her.

"Hearts might be cute for a skirt."

"I'll save it to show you, then. But if you don't like it, that's fine, too. I'm making a lot of those little dresses for the bazaar at church."

"That reminds me. How do you guys like that new pastor?" Their former one had retired after twenty-odd years, and her parents had worried about who might follow him. Paige still went to church with them sometimes, but last Sunday she'd gone to Brittany's baby shower.

Her dad chimed in. "His sermon wasn't bad. A little long."

As her parents weighed the strengths and weaknesses of their new minister, Paige continued scrutinizing the dress. Her stomach tied in knots. Dating was a normal thing. She'd done it before. So why did she still feel like she didn't know how?

She deposited the dress in the bottom of the closet, pulled out a floral skirt, and lay it on the bed. This dithering was ridiculous. *Why am I acting like a teenager?*

Because you really like him, came the mental response.

But she couldn't even know that for sure, could she? She found a pink cardigan to pair with the skirt. There. That looked nice. It was fine.

"He had a cute children's sermon," her mom was saying.

"That's important," Paige said.

"Yeah, the kids liked the story. That reminds me, have you heard from your agent lately?"

When other people asked about this, they embarrassed her, but Paige knew her mom and dad believed wholeheartedly in her genius. They weren't realistic, but she wouldn't have even gotten this far without their faith in her. When she'd been growing up, they'd praised her writing and drawing, providing her with an endless supply of colored pencils, pads of paper, pens, and notebooks.

Usually, when they asked about her agent, Paige didn't have anything to say, and she was glad that today was different. "She thinks I might get a deal with a publisher called Vandergast Books?"

"Honey, that's wonderful!" her mom said.

"We'll be able to see her books in stores," her dad said.

Her mom beamed. "And in libraries."

"Nothing's for sure yet," she cautioned them. "I've got my hopes up, though. If I got a deal, I could afford the down payment on this place."

"Is that right?" her dad asked. "Wouldn't that be something?"

Soon after, Paige stepped into the Marigold

Café. Immediately, it charmed her, with its natural wood interior and cheerful paintings in brightly colored frames. Several couples and one large family waited in the sitting area at the front, and other groups stood around, waiting for their name to be called.

"Paige, hey."

She turned around to see Dylan walking in the door. He looked even more handsome than the last time she'd seen him, in a navy sweater and jeans, though at the orchard he'd had perhaps a couple of days' worth of stubble, and now he was clean-shaven. Did he usually skip shaving on weekends? Had he shaved for their date—for her? "You're early," she said.

A smile played at his lips. "So are you. You look great." The warmth in his voice and the way his gaze lingered on her made it clear he meant it. She got a fluttery feeling in her stomach. Wow. Actual butterflies. Much better than knots.

He gestured toward the hostess station. "Did you put our name in yet, or—"

"No, I just got here."

He approached the hostess and said, "Hi, party of two. Last name Cain."

She wrote it down. "It'll be about a forty-minute wait." She handed him a buzzer.

He took it reluctantly. "Forty minutes." Looking apologetic, he turned back to Paige. "They didn't take reservations. You want to go somewhere else?"

"Oh, but this place is so cute. I love it." As soon as she said that, though, *she* had reservations. Could she make conversation for forty minutes, with no distractions, before they even sat down? Would it be awkward?

"It seemed like your kind of place," he said. It warmed her heart that he'd put some thought into choosing a place that suited her—and it impressed her that he'd gotten it right. The café was even on a block of fun shops she'd like to look into...

"I've got an idea," she said. "Did you see that costume shop next door?"

He shrugged. "Yeah, I think it's a pop-up store for Halloween."

"Do you want to go costume shopping with me?"

"You're going to dress up for Halloween?" Then he nodded, looking amused. "Of course you are."

"For work! The kids love it."

"All right. Let's do it."

As they entered the store, he asked, "So what do you want to be this year?"

"I don't know yet." She found the aisle of women's costumes. Most were in plastic packages displayed on the wall, but some hung on a clothing rack. "What do you think?"

"Princess," he said immediately.

Even though she'd been jotting down a story about a princess, hearing him say it made her think of different implications. "Why?" she teased. "You think I'm spoiled?"

"You know I don't think that."

His answer pleased her. She ventured down the aisle, scanning the choices. "For all you know, I *am* spoiled. You don't know me."

"I'm starting to."

Warmth curled inside her. "So, it's been a long time since I've been on a date." Inwardly, she winced. "Is it weird that I said that?" And maybe asking that made it even weirder.

But he still looked relaxed, his hands in his pockets, regarding her with—well, she would've had to call it affection. "You say what's on your mind. I like that."

"What about you?"

"Do I say what's on my mind?"

"No, I meant—" She turned back to the costumes and attempted a casual tone. "Do you go on a lot of dates?"

"Oh, yeah. You're my second date today." She shot him a look and he laughed. "It's been a little while."

Of course, she should've known he was joking. She was glad to hear he didn't go out with women all the time. Maybe it meant this was special to him. It was feeling that way to her.

He picked up a pirate costume. "What about this? *Arrgh.*—Do lady pirates say *ar-rgh?*"

She came over to look. "That's...a little revealing for me. And definitely too revealing for work."

"Right." He hung it up and picked up another one. "So I guess you don't want to go as a sexy chicken."

"They do not have a sexy chicken costume." She looked. Oh yes, they did. "Good heavens."

"It's actually disturbing. I'm going to hang it behind the um, regular chicken costume here."

"Shouldn't you go find one for yourself?" she asked.

"Not going to happen." He appraised a nurse ensemble, then put it back.

"Oh, come on. Cowboy?"

"No way." She raised her eyebrows at the vehemence of his tone, and he added, as though it should be obvious, "I hate the Dallas Cowboys."

"Hey now, that's my Uncle John's team." She had no strong feelings about football, herself. "If you're a Broncos fan, you could dress up like a horse."

"Ha ha."

"How about a knight?" She grinned, thinking of how she'd written him into her latest story. "I could totally see you in a knight costume."

"You're not going to see me in any costume. I wouldn't even have a place to wear it." He looked through more choices on the women's rack.

"Doesn't anyone in your office dress up?"

"Absolutely not.—Oh, here we go. This is your costume."

She guessed he'd found something wildly inappropriate. He held up a full-length dress in sky-blue with a diaphanous skirt, matched with a huge pair of sheer, iridescent fabric wings. A crown of pink and blue silk flowers hung from the top of the hanger.

"Ooh."

"Have you ever been a fairy before?"

"No." She took the costume from him and checked the tag. "This might fit me."

"Go try it on and see." He gestured to the fitting rooms in the back. "And then come out so I can see it."

"I'm not showing you."

"Oh, fine." He was smiling, not really giving her a hard time.

She went to the dressing room and tried it on, her expectations low. They only made costumes in a few sizes, so they were generally either too small or too loose. To her surprise, the dress fit beautifully. She put her arms through the elastic loops of the wings to fasten them to her back, and then settled the flower crown on her head.

Okay. She adored the costume. She wasn't going to go out and show him, though.

No, she was. She slipped on her ballet flats, stepped out of the dressing room, and found him more or less where she'd left him, engrossed in his phone. "What do you think?"

He looked up and then gave a wondering laugh.

"You're laughing at me," she said automatically.

"No. I mean yeah I am—you're dressed like a fairy. But you look amazing." The tone of his voice and the admiration in his eyes were more than she'd expected, and she ducked her head, her cheeks suddenly heating. "You have to get that."

She could feel herself smiling. "I think I will."

She retreated to the dressing room. As she changed back into her regular clothes, she could see her own delighted expression in the mirror. In the past, first dates, even with guys she'd liked, had been somewhat awkward ordeals. Somehow, she and Dylan skipped a couple of steps, right to the fun part.

He stood with her in line, pretending to try to convince her to buy some of the tacky trinkets displayed close to the cash register. "You need these."

"What are those?"

"Temporary tattoos that look like wounds."

"Ew, why? So it looks like I got in a fight with another fairy?"

He laughed. "What about these?" He held up a bag of rubber balls that looked like eyeballs.

"That's disgusting." She waved them away.

"But they glow in the dark."

"Why do they make those gross things?"

He picked up a big package of glow bracelets. "Now this is a good deal."

"I don't need—" She stopped short and studied it. "Fifty for twelve dollars? That's an *amazing* deal." She took the package from him.

She paid for her items, and as they walked out of the store together, she said, "You're probably wondering what I'm going to do with fifty glow bracelets."

They lingered on the sidewalk. There was no reason to go back into the restaurant yet, and the waiting area had been crowded. "Make a memorable fashion statement?" he suggested.

"Good guess, but no. See how they're rainbow colors? I'm going to save them for my kids for April third."

After a moment, he played along. "What's April third?"

She grinned. "National Rainbow Day."

"Oh, yeah. How could I forget?"

"You should mark it on your calendar," she said.

"You buy your students a lot of things, don't you?"

"All teachers do. But maybe I do more than most."

The buzzer in his hand went off, flashing with red lights. "Oh! That's us!" she cried, rushing toward the restaurant.

"Hold up," he said behind her, laughing. "It's like you've got wheels on your feet."

chapter nine

Well, how about that, Dylan thought as he got into his car. *That was a great date.*

When they'd said goodbye outside of the restaurant, she'd hugged him. He'd only kissed her on the cheek, since she'd seemed nervous at first about dating. She'd felt so good in his arms. When he'd said, *I want to do this again soon,* she'd said, *Yay.* Did she even realize how freaking cute she was? Dylan smiled to himself. She had to have an inkling.

Amazing, how rare a great date was, though people tried hard to get them. They signed up for apps, subjected their photos and what amounted to their resumes as human beings to the scrutiny of strangers, and attended events they didn't especially enjoy, all in the hopes of meeting someone. It was always so hard. But with Paige, it had been so easy.

His mind replayed what she'd said at the

costume shop. *I could totally see you as a knight.* As a kid, a bona fide nerd before being a nerd had been anything close to cool or even acceptable, he'd been into King Arthur stories, in these old-fashioned books at the school library with black-and-white illustrations. They'd probably been published in the sixties. It embarrassed him to recall how much he'd loved them. Standing up for what was right. Being brave. Being brave even when it came to saying how you feel, because in that department, the Knights of the Round Table were not messing around. If they were into a lady, they said so.

He was into her, definitely. And now he was headed to the cabin open house. All in all, an ideal Saturday.

Once he pulled onto the interstate, he realized her yellow VW bug was one car ahead of him and one lane over. Not many of those on the road. He could see the back of her head. They were both on their way to the west side of town.

He couldn't wait to see the house again, even though he didn't know what kind of shape it would be in. For all he knew, the place was missing part of a ceiling, or filled with mold. Even major things could be fixed, though.

Not for the first time, he wondered who lived there now. Mr. and Mrs. Burke, his grandparents' next-door neighbors, had bought the place as a rental property after his grandma had died. That had been a long time ago. Chances were good that they'd sold it since, and maybe sold their house, too.

He changed to the right lane to take the next exit. Now he was right behind Paige. Odd, but not *that* much of a coincidence.

Until they made the same two turns after that. Now they were on a road with few cars. Ordinarily, he would've enjoyed this drive, past rugged boulders and scattered spruce trees and Ponderosa pines. Instead, the back of his neck prickled. She'd been understandably skittish about dating someone she'd just met, not allowing him to pick her up and drive her home. And now, if she noticed him behind her, she was going to think he was following her.

Well, she'd know better soon. The cabin was on a dead-end street. There was no chance she'd be going that way.

They made the same right turn. And then the same left turn, onto dead-end Juniper Lane. He almost felt like she was following *him*, except that was impossible, since she was in front. Had she noticed him? As far as he could tell, she wasn't staring in her rearview mirror.

Maybe she lived right by the cabin. Maybe they'd be neighbors... But no, she pulled right into the driveway of the cabin.

He laughed out loud. They were both going to the same open house. What were the odds? He'd never been a big believer in divine intervention, in romance or in anything else, but he couldn't help thinking this might be some kind of master plan.

He parked along the side of the road so he wouldn't box her in. She walked toward the front door, but when he got out, shutting the car door behind him and locking it, she stopped in her tracks. As he approached, she stared, open-mouthed. "Did you *follow* me?" she demanded, just as he'd feared.

"No! I'm here for the showing."

She gaped. "You want to buy my cabin?"

"*Your* cabin?" She lived here? "Wow. This is crazy." He laughed, but she didn't join him. Her mouth was turned down and the light had gone out of her eyes. If she were selling the place, why wasn't she happy to see a prospective buyer?

A man about Dylan's age came out the front door. He was good-looking, in a jock-ish way, and when he spotted Paige he gave her a tight, insincere smile. "Paige. I didn't think you were going to be here for the showing."

"I changed my mind. I need to work on my lesson plans." She looked back at Dylan and managed a tense smile. "I'm renting it." *Of course.* He should've figured it out sooner. "So you can't buy it. You won't, right?"

Confusion overtook Dylan. "Um..." He searched for the right words.

Her slight smile disappeared and her eyes reflected hurt. She turned and went inside without another word. Why was she so upset?

The man stepped up to Dylan. "Hey, how're you doing? Trent Jackson, Paragon Realty."

Dylan shook the proffered hand. "Dylan Cain." He reminded himself again not to divulge his past with the place, and to stay cool, even though he couldn't wait to see inside it again. The more eager he seemed, the less likely he'd get a good deal.

"Come on in, take a look around. It's good you're early. I think we're going to get a *lot* of people coming through today. A true log cabin, in commuting distance of downtown... property like this doesn't come on the market often." Trent had the easy patter of a man who enjoyed his job. As they reached the door, he said in a lower voice, "Oh, and uh, don't mind the tenant. She's not happy the owner decided to sell."

"Right." He could see that, although she didn't have any reason to blame Dylan for it.

"If I were her, I wouldn't want to move, either. The owner was way undercharging."

Having to move unexpectedly would be a real hassle for Paige, but Dylan suspected there was more to it than that. *My cabin*, she'd said. Maybe she wanted to buy it herself and lacked the means to do it. Dylan didn't know how much money first grade teachers made, but he knew it wasn't a lot. That was why he'd paid for her cupcakes, after all.

Well, he was sorry she'd have to leave a place she liked, but he couldn't honestly be sorry she wasn't in a position to buy it. She couldn't love the place like he did. She didn't have his history. Paige had just been shocked to see Dylan, which was completely understandable. In a minute or two, she'd come to her senses.

He stepped inside. The living room was smaller than he remembered, and the floors were scuffed. They'd been slick and polished when he'd been a kid, and he and Dee had loved running and sliding on them in their stocking feet. But other than that, the place looked the same, down to the way the sunlight slanted through the windows. It *sounded* the same, with the small fire in the crackling fireplace. A wave of nostalgia engulfed him.

Paige sat at the kitchen table with her laptop, refusing to look at either of them. Dylan wanted to say something to her, but the right words didn't come to his mind. Instead, he said to the agent, "Living room's small."

"Yeah, these older houses are cozy," Trent allowed, "but you get a lot of details you won't see in a new house. Like, I love this fireplace. Original stone."

It didn't seem all that cozy, with Paige freezing him out. And what right did she have to be angry with *him*? It wasn't his fault the place had gone up for sale, and he had every right to be interested in it.

They'd had a good time at the orchard and at brunch today. He'd thought there had been something real between them, and that she'd felt it, too.

And now that feeling had completely dimmed. It seemed like she didn't even care, or it didn't matter, just because of the coincidence of him being interested in the house.

Trent said, "Anyway, go ahead and look around. I'll be in here if you have any questions." He sat down on the sofa as though it belonged to him.

Dylan went into the kitchen despite Paige's stubborn presence somehow taking up more space than physically possible.

More memories flooded back to him. The smell of his grandparents' coffee in the morning. The way his grandmother had liked watching the birds at the backyard feeder from that kitchen window. One time, in the middle of winter, she'd urged him in a whisper to come and look. Along with other birds crowded around, no less than six red cardinals had been at the feeder and on the ground next to it, stunning against the white snow. Their grandfather had hardly believed it when they'd told him later. Male cardinals, he'd said, didn't get along. Ordinarily, they couldn't be around one another without fighting. Even now, as sensible and even skeptical as Dylan usually was, the sighting had made him think there was something magical about the place.

His grandfather had taught him and Dee how to play pinochle at their old kitchen table, a round wooden one, not unlike the one Paige was sitting at now. In fact... Dylan looked closer. The top was scratched, and some of the veneer had chipped off the edges. He called back to the agent. "Did this table come with the place?"

"That it did," a different voice said.

Dylan looked up to see a man in maybe his late seventies, hands stuck in the pockets of his jacket, standing in the living room. Something pricked at Dylan's awareness, and then the shock of recognition hit him. Mr. Burke, his grandparents' neighbor, the one who'd bought the cabin so many years ago. It was still his.

"That table was part of the house when I bought it," Mr. Burke said, walking over. "The couple who lived here before had this for decades."

Paige looked down at the table, then up at him, wide-eyed. "I knew you were friends with them, but I never thought about the table being theirs." Clearly, the story had made her forget to be silent and resentful.

"That's right. The cedar chest in the bedroom, that was Leona's, too." Dylan had to keep his jaw from dropping. *Dee is going to flip.*

"Hello," a female voice sang out from the other room. A middle-aged man and woman came through the door, and Trent greeted them. Dylan's competitive spirit roared to life. Whoever these two were, they were not getting his cabin.

Mr. Burke turned to Dylan. "What do you think of the place?"

"I like it." Dylan's thoughts swirled. If he told Mr. Burke who he was, there was no way he could pretend to be a disinterested buyer. And the last thing he wanted to do was disclose his past in front of strangers, and especially in front of Paige, who had apparently found it easy to decide not to like him.

His connection to the cabin felt very personal. Not because of his grandparents, but because of the reason he and Dee had spent so much time with them in the first place: the death of their mother, and their checked-out father. It was a lot to get into.

He wasn't used to talking to people about the details of his past. Even with his last girlfriend, he hadn't done that. In a strange way, although they'd been an official couple for months, nothing had ever gotten too serious or intimate. Over nice dinners at nice restaurants, they'd discussed their clients, the weather, sports, and TV shows they both watched. They'd never even once had a fight, and he was already more or less having one with Paige. Then again, he and his ex had never shared anything worth fighting about.

Mr. Burke peered at Dylan. "You know, you look so familiar." Dylan shrugged. Was it possible that he looked much like the ten-year-old boy he'd been? Even then, they hadn't seen the Burkes frequently. His grandparents had been friends with them, but not close. A couple of times, they'd come over when Grandpa had grilled burgers and hot dogs. More often, there had been conversations over the fence.

The older man shook his head. "Ah, my memory's playing tricks on me." Dylan felt a pang of guilt at that. True, he hadn't seen the guy in more than two decades. But Mr. Burke seemed awfully sharp, and he and his wife had always been nice to him and Dee.

He glanced at the man's left hand. He still wore a wedding ring, so they hadn't gotten divorced. The older man took a drink of the water. "Hey," he said. "Know why the Clydesdale gave the Shetland pony a glass of water?"

Dylan blinked. "Because the pony was thirsty?"

"Nope. Because he was a little hoarse." Mr. Burke laughed, and Dylan couldn't help but join him. He recalled Mr. Burke's love of goofy jokes. Who knew where he picked them up?

The other couple came into the kitchen. "With the new construction, we'd want to build further out," the woman was saying, making a pushing gesture at the back wall of the kitchen, as though she could knock it over with the palm of her hand.

"I see what you're saying," the man mused. "But it's a great view. Maybe we could add a big patio area there instead. If we made the new house wider"—he gestured with his arms—"we'd still have plenty of room for the open floor plan."

Trent joined them. "It is a great location, isn't it? It would be a cheap teardown, too."

Paige's head popped up again, anger sparking in her eyes. Dylan couldn't help but find that gratifying. The voices of more visitors came from the living room as the couple spoke virtuously of using some of the wood from the log cabin for a feature wall in the modern home they'd build.

Mr. Burke interrupted them. "No offense, but I think I'd prefer to sell to someone who likes log cabins."

The man and woman whirled around to stare at him. Trent turned pale. Clearly, this had thrown him for a loop.

"I'm glad to hear that," a younger woman said as she entered the kitchen with her husband, a man with shoulder-length hair and a beard.

"We're into the rustic look," he said.

Mr. Burke smiled. "See? Now you're the kind of couple I'd like to sell this house to." Dylan's hackles rose. The first, middle-aged couple exchanged an irritated look and retreated. Dylan could hardly blame them, but he enjoyed seeing them leave.

"We've already got a log home plan picked out," the bearded man continued. His wife beamed up at him. "And I think our builder will love this site."

Paige's eyes narrowed at the newcomers.

Mr. Burke said, "A plan?" His agent shot a warning look at the bearded man.

"It'll be in the spirit of the original home," he said. "We just need a bigger place. We're going to start a family, and we like to entertain."

Dylan's ire rose further. "You wouldn't have to build a whole new house," he told the bearded man. "You could add a second story." He shouldn't be giving advice to a rival, but he couldn't help himself. Didn't anyone appreciate the cabin?

"The rooms are small, though," the woman told him.

Mr. Burke studied Dylan. "Is that what you would do?"

"I like the place as it is. But if I—happened to get married someday, and had kids, then yeah." Talking about the possibility of a family in the future, while Paige was listening, unnerved him. "I wouldn't tear the place down. You've got to respect the past."

The bearded man pressed his lips together in annoyance. "It's not a historical landmark."

The agent cleared his throat. "It's easy to get emotional about a property, but Harry, I'm sure once you weigh the pros and cons—"

"I'll sell to whoever I want to." He looked to Dylan. "Keep looking around. Let me know if you have any questions."

Dylan had never appreciated an old man's stubbornness more. The younger couple looked even more exasperated than the first couple had, and they headed out. The agent rubbed the back of his neck, no doubt thinking this was one of the worst open houses he'd held in a while.

Paige's gaze had returned to her computer screen. She couldn't possibly be focused on her work.

Dylan gave a nod to Mr. Burke and the agent and moved on to the back bedroom that had been his grandparents'. This truly did look different. A handmade floral quilt covered the bed, and multiple strands of clear twinkly lights hung on the wall behind it. Little boxes and canisters of various shapes and sizes—wood, beaded fabric, porcelain—covered the top of the dresser. He'd encouraged her to try the fairy costume, and this room did look like a fairy's lair.

Even if he'd been walking through a stranger's house, he would've felt odd intruding on a private space like this. Because it was Paige's bedroom, it made him even more uneasy. But this was an open house. Walking through the rooms was literally the point.

A dress—green, printed with cats—hung on the closet door. Maybe she'd picked it out for tomorrow, or maybe she'd considered wearing it to brunch. Something in his chest ached. Then he spotted the cedar chest at the foot of the bed. Remembering Dee's words about the bridal veil and the sixpence, he lifted the lid but found only folded blankets.

"Get out of there." His head snapped up at Paige's quiet but forceful voice. Her no-nonsense voice.

He straightened. "I was just—"

"Going through my stuff?" The other couple

still stood in the kitchen, debating something about the foundation, and she wasn't speaking loudly enough to be overheard. "It's bad enough you're tromping through my house, ready to buy it out from under me."

Her words prompted a rush of guilt. But he felt like she was trespassing, too, by using furniture that had belonged to his family. "I haven't even made an offer yet."

"Are you going to?"

"Yes." She wilted at his answer. "If I don't, someone else will."

"That doesn't mean I have to like it."

Her downturned mouth and the dejected slump of her shoulders melted his heart. He decided to risk putting himself out there.

"Paige, I had a good time today. I thought you did too. I'm sorry you'll have to move out; I am. But I really want this place. Can't we still see each other?" If she agreed, he'd tell her all about the cabin.

"We can only see each other if you promise not to buy my house."

"That doesn't even make any sense!"

The other couple appeared at the doorway, but stopped when they saw Dylan and Paige. The man said, "Uh, are we interrupting something?"

"Nope," Paige said and walked out.

chapter ten

It was eight p.m. on a Tuesday night, a respectable hour to go home by anyone's standards. Dylan swung by Mark's office to say, "Hey, that call with Circa went great." He still hadn't figured out what they actually did at Circa Biologics, and as far as he could tell, no one else at Hammersmith knew, either.

"You're meeting with them after the conference, right?" Mark asked.

"Yeah, we've got a meeting and then dinner." Dylan suspected that getting them as a new client would seal the deal of his promotion to VP.

"Good, good. Maybe Elaine can help you with the prep."

"I don't know. She's got a pretty heavy workload right now." That was true, and Dylan wasn't sure he wanted to share, anyway.

Mark shrugged and said in a lower voice, "It's not like she's got a husband to go home to." Elaine was single, but so were Dylan, Josh, and Kyle, and nobody sneered at them about it. Mark was married and never mentioned his wife. While Dylan was still trying to think of how to reply, Mark continued. "Did you get the call with Wakefield set up?"

He'd forgotten. "I haven't heard back from them yet."

"Might want to give them another nudge."

"You know, they've been having some issues," Dylan said. This had been on his mind, and maybe he hadn't forgotten the call so much as put it off. "Adding extra charges? It's technically legal, all in the fine print, but—"

"It's got nothing to do with us," Mark said, which was true. Dylan didn't even know why he was bringing it up. "You heading out?"

"Yeah."

"All right. See you bright and early tomorrow."

As Dylan walked out of the office, the place was quiet, though Elaine still sat in her office, typing away. He knocked on her half-open door.

She looked up. "Yes?"

"Hey, sorry to interrupt. Do you remember the name of that admin at Wakefield? The one Rick said to follow up with?"

"Mmm, hang on." Elaine pulled out her black planner, flipped to the middle tab, and rifled through a few pages. "Yes. Rita Muller. Email is her name with no periods or caps, last name just like it sounds, M-U-L-L-E-R, at Wakefield dot com."

"Thanks." Elaine had been an optional attendee on the call where Rick had mentioned it. Wakefield wasn't even her client.

"No problem."

He felt a pang of guilt for not sticking up for her to Mark. Their boss made comments in such an offhand way that they were hard to counter in the moment, even if one wanted to, and contradicting Mark wasn't ever the smart career move.

"Are you heading out soon?" Dylan asked her. "I'll walk with you to the garage." She went to the parking garage in the dark all the time, he knew, but someone had gotten her purse snatched a few weeks ago.

She shook her head. "I'm in the middle of that massive merger for VHL. Thanks anyway."

He nodded and was about to walk on when he heard a voice behind him say, "Hey, Dylan." He turned around to see Brian slouched at his desk.

"Hey. How'd the Grange presentation go?"

His shoulders slumped even further. "Not good."

It had been the first time that Brian had actually participated in a presentation, instead of only doing the grunt work behind the scenes. Kyle had done most of it. How bad could it have been? Hiding his reluctance, Dylan backtracked his steps to hear more about it. *He's not cut out for this*, he thought, not for the first time.

But maybe it wasn't true. Maybe Brian just needed some guidance. Mark had no interest in helping his employees. Elaine was far more helpful, but even more buried in work than Dylan was. He asked Brian, "Would you like some advice?"

Brian said in a quieter tone, "From the guy who's about to make VP? Yeah, definitely."

Oh, really? From the first, Brian had been a little too eager to pick up and pass along gossip. But that wasn't always a bad thing, was it? "Who said I was about to make VP?"

"I don't know, everyone?"

Well. If that happened, then working his tail off would've been worth it, after all. "All right, I heard you talking to the Grange guys the other day. You're sounding too eager. Even a little desperate."

"I am desperate," Brian said. "You know what my student loans are like?"

"See, that's exactly what I'm talking about." The mentor role wasn't familiar to him, but Dylan warmed to it. "You've got to stop putting all of your cards on the table. Telling everybody your business."

"I should pretend things are better than they are?"

"Yes." Now he was getting it. "Make people think you've got the world on a string. Make them think they're lucky to work with you."

Brian gave a rueful smile. "You sound like my cousin giving me dating advice."

Dylan started to say that dating and business were similar, but then he stopped himself. He'd shown Paige how interested he was in her...a fact he wasn't at all comfortable with, now that she was mad at him.

Instead he said, "There you go again. Don't talk about dating problems at work. Or money problems. Don't...act like you need anything, or want anything really badly, ever."

Brian's forehead furrowed. "Okay, I mean, maybe."

"And another thing. With the Grange account..." He shouldn't be saying this. But he knew it would help. "Don't let anyone else around here know how bummed you are, because you'll be reminding them that it didn't work out. In fact, don't get bummed. Walk it off."

Brian nodded. "I see what you're saying."

Good. Dylan felt a satisfaction in knowing that he could pass on his wisdom to someone who would take it to heart. "All right, well, have a good one." He started to walk away.

"Hey, Dylan."

Dylan stopped and turned around. "Yeah?"

"Does this job get any easier?"

What a question. "No, it gets harder," he said honestly. "But you get used to it being hard."

Brian regarded him for a moment. "Okay, great, good to know."

Dylan shrugged and walked on.

As he headed out to the parking garage, he considered what to do with what was left of the evening. He could hit the gym, but he'd gone in yesterday morning, and he wasn't in the mood to run on a treadmill. Probably he'd opt for takeout and TV.

He got into his car. It still had that new-car smell, which now vaguely annoyed him. He'd learned that day that his boss Mark drove the same vehicle. There had been nothing wrong with Dylan's other car, the one he'd sold, other than the fact that it hadn't been new, and had been an economy model. At his workplace, a nice car was expected. A nice address was, too. *What do you drive, Cain? What neighborhood are you in?* These things came up.

His work/takeout/TV/sometimes-gym rut suddenly struck him as depressing, almost-VP or not. Denver was a big town. Why was his world so small?

If things hadn't gone so wrong, maybe he would've been looking forward to a date with Paige—maybe a proper dinner-and-a-movie. At a red light, Dylan picked up his phone to look at her picture again. He hadn't stared at it much. Only once or twice.

Maybe more. Whatever. A totally normal number of times.

He'd told Paige she was beautiful, and she'd blushed. It still surprised him. Not her reaction—she seemed like the blushing type, never mind that she must've heard it a bunch of times before—but him saying it in the first place. He wasn't the kind of guy who went around saying things like that to women he didn't know well.

A text from his sister on his phone screen read, *Connor left his sweatshirt in your car. Can you bring it by?*

Dylan craned his neck to look at the backseat where the boy had been sitting. Sure enough, a balled-up black sweatshirt lay on the floor, though he hadn't noticed it before against the black interior.

The driver behind him honked. Sheesh, people could be so impatient. Dylan straightened and proceeded through the green light.

"Oh, thank you," Dee said when he showed up at her door, sweatshirt in hand. Paul and the boys were in the living room behind her, watching TV. "He wears that thing all the time. I don't know why."

Connor looked up as she spoke. Dylan had noticed the Batman logo on the shirt, and he remembered Connor also had a Batman poster in his room. Dylan said, "It's because he's awesome, that's why."

His nephew grinned. "Hi, Uncle Dylan. Did you go on that date with Miss Reynolds yet?"

Dylan froze. He'd been sure the boys had been out of earshot when he'd asked Paige out. Maybe the kid wasn't really Batman, but he had the hearing of a bat.

Dee laughed at her son. "Don't be silly." Then she glanced at Dylan, who hadn't laughed, and her eyes widened. "Wait. *Did* you ask her out?"

He gave a reluctant shrug.

"Oh, my, gosh." She spaced out every word. "I knew you guys *saw* her. I didn't know you *liked* her."

"We just went to brunch. And nothing's going to come of it," he added pointedly.

Paul winced. "Bad date, huh?"

Dylan suddenly turned to Connor. "Hey, buddy. *Do not* talk about this at school." Even if Paige was angry with him, he didn't want kids—or other teachers—gossiping about her at work.

Connor's eyes widened. Dylan rarely spoke to him in such a serious tone, and apparently it had an impact. "I promise."

"Sit down for a minute," Dee urged. "Do you want a cupcake? I've got a few left over."

"No, that's okay." Noah was playing with a race car track on the rug in front of the TV, and Dylan sat down next to him. "Whoa, look at this," he said to his younger nephew, who smiled at up at him.

"Don't feel bad that it didn't work out," Dee said as she sat down on the couch. "She's not your type."

"You don't like her?" Dylan asked. "Connor said she was his favorite teacher."

"Oh, no, it's not that," Dee said quickly. "But she's so...free-spirited, and you're so focused. You two probably want different things."

He set one of the toy cars at the top of an inclined track. "No, actually, we want the same thing." He pushed the car with one finger, and it streaked down the track and smashed into another car.

"How so?" Paul asked.

"After the date, I went to the open house, and it turns out...Paige lives there. She's renting it. And she's mad at me for wanting to buy it."

Their shocked expressions gratified him. "That's crazy!" Dee said. "Talk about a coincidence."

"The first time I saw her, she had a journal, with some drawings in it." This had been on his mind since the showing the other day. "I saw she had a sketch of the cabin. Except I didn't know then it was *our* cabin."

Dee pursed her lips. "Is that why you started talking to her?"

"Not exactly." It had intrigued him right away, though. The cabin might've actually drawn them together...and now, it had driven them apart.

Paul asked, "What was it like to be in that house again?"

Dylan shook his head. "All those memories. It was like time travel, almost. And Mr.

Burke was there. He still owns the place. It was strange to see him, too."

"Oh, my gosh." Dee shook her head. "Was he freaked out to see you again?"

"I uh, didn't tell him who I was." At her quizzical look, he added, "There were a bunch of people around. It would've been too weird."

Paul nodded. "Did you make an offer?"

"I called the agent a couple of hours ago. He says Mr. Burke would like to sell to me. He wasn't too impressed with all the people who wanted to tear it down and build a new one."

Dee make an indignant noise. "Tear it down!"

"That's great he wants to sell to you," Paul said, and Dee nodded.

"He's not accepting any offers till the ninth, though," Dylan said. "He's giving Paige a chance to get the money together for a down payment."

"Well, you're just going to outbid her," Dee said. He must've looked uneasy, because she added, "Did you have a good time with her? Before the open house?"

What could he say? He'd thought he and Paige had a connection, and he'd been completely wrong. If she'd liked him, she would've been more understanding. He would've explained more about why he wanted the cabin, once they were in private, but she hadn't even given him a chance.

Whatever. "I don't know. She doesn't want to date anyone who wants to buy her cabin."

"Did you tell her it's really ours? I mean, how it's been in our family?"

"No. I didn't want to get into personal stuff with someone I just met." He didn't talk about his past with anyone, in fact. Growing up, he'd been nerdy and needy—everything he didn't want to be as an adult. If he talked about his childhood, people might see glimmers of that same terribly vulnerable boy in him now, and he wouldn't be able to stand that. Besides, Paige had gotten mad at him for no good reason. That didn't exactly inspire trust. He shrugged. "Honestly, I don't have time to date right now anyway."

Dee rolled her eyes. "I've heard that before."

"It's different now. There's a good chance I'm going to make VP."

"That sounds like a big deal," Paul said. He'd always been supportive. Dylan appreciated it.

"It doesn't mean you can't find a girlfriend," Dee pointed out.

"Hey, you know how easy it's going to be to find a girlfriend, once I make VP?" he joked. Dee didn't laugh, and darted a glance at Connor. Even Paul looked uncomfortable. Okay, that was more of a joke one made with the guys at the office.

It wasn't even his kind of joke, and he felt a flash of self-loathing. "I'm kidding. But seriously, I have a lot going on now. VP, then girlfriend. That's a rock-solid plan." His sister shook her head. "What? You think I should not buy the cabin, just so I can date Paige?"

"No," Dee said emphatically. "I think you should date, period. But she's being ridiculous. Someone's going to buy the place, anyway. Why shouldn't it be you?"

That was what Dylan kept telling himself, and naturally Dee was thinking the same, since she loved the idea of seeing her kids play in the same place she'd played when she was young. But he could still see Paige's discouraged face so clearly in his mind.

She was a happy person by nature, embracing Mondays even though she had a busy job, climbing trees when the opportunity presented itself. There was a good reason why she'd been Connor's favorite teacher. The sunshine inside her warmed everyone around her. He hadn't known her long, but he was sure she was upset about more than the considerable hassle of moving. The cabin meant something to her.

chapter eleven

"I talked to Harry again this morning," Paige told Jessica before their classes started on Wednesday morning. She'd decided to finish planting the tulips, as an act of faith, and her landlord had ambled over to chat with her. "He said if I can't buy the house, he'll probably sell it to Dylan." Harry had been nice about it, pointing out that Dylan liked the cabin just as it was.

Jessica scrunched up her face. "Why? He just met Dylan."

"He said there was 'something about him.'" It had struck Paige as irrational—and it made her feel irrationally betrayed. "I just don't get it. If Dylan wants to buy a house, there's a million options in Denver."

"Exactly," Jessica agreed. "If he really liked you, he'd buy another one!"

"That's what I'm saying!" Dylan had sauntered into her living room with the real estate agent, acting like buying someone's house from under her was a totally normal way to conclude a date.

"Men are the worst," Jessica declared.

Paige looked at Jessica askance. "But not *all* men." She was a bride-to-be, after all.

She grinned. "No, definitely not. Last night he helped me fill out that evaluation report."

"That's true love."

"Did you get yours done yet?"

"No. I swear they love coming up with useless things for us to do."

Jessica's eyebrows drew together. "Are you okay?"

Paige sighed. "I'm fine. Just grouchy."

"That's not like you."

It wasn't. What was with her? "I didn't do my morning ritual this morning."

"Where you say everything you're grateful for?"

"I know you think it's crazy."

Jessica shrugged. "It's a little out there for me, but I'm glad it works for you." She glanced up at the clock. "You've got a few minutes to do it. It's probably more fun than working on that evaluation form." She left, closing Paige's classroom door behind her.

Paige shut her eyes and took a deep breath. She'd have to do it silently, since she was at work. *What am I grateful for today?*

Dylan's face came into her mind.

No, no, no. That was completely wrong. Well yes, you were supposed to love your enemies, as much as you could. And he wasn't even an enemy, for heaven's sake...just a disappointment. But did she really have to feel grateful for disappointments? That might be a little more spiritually advanced than she could manage.

Come on, she told whatever part of her brain summoned her reasons to be grateful. But although a few of the usual ideas came to mind—her parents, her health, Jessica—she couldn't shake the image of Dylan.

This wasn't working. She couldn't concentrate here. In fact, she'd never done the gratitude thing anywhere else but the cabin. She'd gotten into the habit of it there, a natural response, maybe, to the view of the sunrise from the back door. *And he wants to take that away from me.*

She didn't need to be spiritually advanced to know that nobody needed their dream house in order to be grateful, and nobody could take one's gratitude away from them. She was being childish, and not in the good way. The thought made her grouchier than ever as her students arrived.

During circle time, Paige read aloud her latest installment in the cabin story. She knew it made no sense and had given up hopes of shaping it into an actual children's book, but the kids always requested her personal stories.

"'And then the knight said, *You're not really a princess. You're a fairy.* Then big, beautiful wings grew on her back, and wheels grew on her feet.'" A few of the children laughed, and Clara said, "I did *not* see that coming."

"Clara! You didn't raise your hand!" Paige blurted out.

The little girl looked crushed, and Paige immediately regretted saying it. She hadn't even been reprimanding the girl. "It's okay," she reassured her. "I was just surprised." She continued. "'But when the fairy and the knight came back to the cabin, the bull was inside!'"

"Uh-oh," one of the children said. "That knight's going to get that bull."

"'The knight said, *Hello, bull! I want to live in this cabin and make the fairy sleep outside in the rain. Will you help me?* And the bull said, *Sure!* Then the knight and the bull laughed together. *Ha ha ha ha ha!*'"

The children stared at Paige.

She closed the journal. Honestly, it was a terrible story, but at least it kept the kids' interest. "That's as far as I've gotten," she said. "But I'll probably have more tomorrow."

Neveah said, "I think the princess should take the knight's sword, and shake it at the knight and the bull like this"—she demonstrated—"and tell them to both get out of her house!"

The boy next to her, his imagination

piqued, joined her in brandishing an imaginary sword, emitting battle cries. "Rrrraaa! Rrrraa!"

"Miss Reynolds."

Paige whipped around to see Linda Goff standing in the doorway.

"Mrs. Goff!" What did she want? Of course she'd walk in when the children were pretending to do battle. To the kids' credit, they'd clammed up and sat up straighter at the sight of her.

"I came to borrow some chalk," she said.

"Sure." All she had was the multicolor chalk she'd bought herself, because she hadn't been able to resist. She gave Linda one of the boxes.

"Thank you."

After she left, Paige glanced at the clock. "Actually, it's time for you all to have your math test." Some of them groaned.

That evening, Paige tried to grade their tests. Ordinarily, this wouldn't have been difficult. Other than the trouble of deciphering some of the children's handwriting, first grade math tests were straightforward. She usually did them while watching TV. But the home inspector was coming over soon, and she struggled to stay focused.

Dylan had opted to pay for the inspection

now, even though he had no assurance that he'd be able to buy the house. That was what people did, Paige supposed, when they had a lot of money to throw around and were determined to take over one's house as soon as possible. If she did get a publishing offer and an advance, and she could buy the house, it would be great to have an inspection already done and paid for. She wished she could just *know* whether she'd be able to buy it, or whether she'd have to pack up, move out, and get settled someplace new. She could deal with anything better than she could deal with uncertainty.

Her mind wandered back to their brunch date. When they'd said goodbye and he'd kissed her on the cheek, he'd given her a quiet little thrill. She'd appreciated him not moving too fast, too. He was a decent guy in general, and she'd had such a wonderful time with him…right up to the moment when he'd shown up for the open house.

If she'd lived in an ordinary apartment somewhere and they'd started dating, they might've never run into a big issue like this, or at least, not for a very long time. Circumstances and timing worked against them.

She'd always seen herself as easygoing and kind. Could she keep dating Dylan even if he bought the cabin and she had to move out? Maybe, with a great deal of effort, she could be easygoing about this too. Except that "easygoing" and "great deal of effort" didn't exactly go together, and the very idea of it still stung, and she'd probably eliminated any possibility of their dating again by being so angry the last time she'd seen him.

The knock came at the door, and her muscles tensed. The home inspection guy, right on time. She went over and opened the door.

Dylan stood there. Maddeningly, he looked as attractive as he had on their date. He held himself stiffly, not exactly looking her in the eye. "Hi. I guess the guy isn't here yet?"

Paige shook her head. "Not yet."

"I'll uh, wait in the car till he gets here."

She opened the door wider. "You can wait inside. Come on in."

He did. After a moment of hesitation, he sat down on the sofa, but on the edge, as though he expected to have to jump up again at any time. Half-heartedly, she asked, "Do you want tea or coffee or something?"

His eyebrows shot up. "Uh, no. But thanks. That's nice of you."

"Well, I'm a nice person." She went into the kitchen, grabbed the copper kettle from the stove, and filled it under the faucet.

He got up again and came over to stand in the doorway of the kitchen. "I know you are." Paige retrieved a cup and saucer from one of the cabinets. "I'm trying to be a grown-up about all this. From now on," she added, because if she were completely honest with herself, she hadn't exactly managed that the other day. She wanted to give herself a pass, since her heart had felt like it had been stomped on. But of course, that was the whole point of maturity. Anyone could deal gracefully with easy things.

Dylan said, "I really am sorry."

She tore open the paper packet of the tea bag. "I might buy it myself. Harry won't close until November ninth."

"Yeah, he told me."

The back of Paige's neck prickled. Had Harry told Dylan about her children's books and her hopes for them? Too many people knew already, and to have the guy who was now her rival know about it seemed downright embarrassing. "How much did he tell you?"

"Um, what you just said?"

Paige hazarded meeting his gaze. His brown eyes were filled with sympathy, rankling her even as it melted through her defenses.

He said, "Obviously he didn't tell me about your personal finances." She should've known Harry wouldn't do that. "I still don't know that much about you."

"You really don't," she retorted, surprising herself.

And she'd said she was going to be a grown-up. She sighed. "Sorry. I'm scared that even if I can buy it, you'll outbid me because you're a fancy banker guy who gets whatever he wants."

"Nobody gets everything they want, Paige." The frustration in his voice threw her.

"What do you want?"

He huffed. "I don't know how to answer that."

"But you want this place. If I make an offer, are you going to outbid me?"

After a moment, he admitted, "Yes."

At least he's honest about it. "I don't even know why you *want* this place. You seem like someone who would live in, like, a fancy downtown apartment with concrete and glass everywhere, and white walls, and a view of the city to make you feel like a conqueror."

The corner of his mouth tugged up. "Hey, that is not fair. I have a black accent wall."

"You see my point." She waved her hand to take in the cabin. "This isn't your kind of place."

"Yes it is," he said, with a firmness that surprised her.

The kettle whistled, and Paige turned off the stove. Pondering his motives, and not completely paying attention to what she was doing, she poured the hot water into her teacup. "Ahh!" she cried out as she missed and hot water hit her hand.

Dylan launched himself to her side, grabbing her hand, though not touching the top of it where she'd been burned. "Oh ow, come here, get it under some cold water." He urged her over to the sink. Paige's heart skittered at his sudden action and his touch. He turned on the faucet, passed his fingers briefly under the stream of water, and then thrust her hand underneath it. "Keep it there for a minute."

"It's fine," she protested. He was overreacting, his concern plain on his face, embarrassing her even as it warmed her from within. She withdrew her hand, shut off the faucet, and blotted her hand on one of the vintage tea towels hanging from the handle of the oven.

He frowned. "Let me see." She held up her hand, and when he took hold of it lightly to look at the reddening skin, tingles went through her that had nothing to do with the slight burn. "It doesn't look bad," he admitted. "Does it still sting?"

She shook her head. "Really, it's nothing." She was very aware of how close he stood to her, making her feel unsteady, and he looked at her intently, as if he were about to say something else. Or do something...

Someone pounded on the front door.

"The inspector," they said in unison. Dylan straightened and released her hand. They both moved a couple of steps toward the door, and then Dylan stopped and gestured for her to go ahead and answer it, as if to say, *It's your house. At least for now.*

Once Dylan and the inspector were making their rounds, Paige took the teabag out of her cup, poured in a tiny drizzle of the honey she'd bought at the orchard, and stirred. Then she sat down at the kitchen table and opened her laptop. She browsed Pinterest, looking for inspiration for bulletin board decorations, art projects, and lesson plans. She overheard the inspector saying that the bathroom pipes should probably be replaced, and they'd have to rip out the plaster to do it.

The men came back into the kitchen and the inspector tapped the kitchen window. "This one, too. So that's five in total that need to be replaced. Otherwise they'll let in a lot of cold drafts in the winter."

"I could've told you that," Paige said from her seat at the table. They both looked over her and she shrugged. "It's freezing in here in the winter. That's how I got addicted to tea. And did you notice the electrical problem in the bathroom?"

The inspector frowned. "What problem, exactly?"

"When I plug in my blow dryer, half the time, it doesn't work. There's something wrong with that outlet." She pantomimed a thoughtful look. "I wonder if something's chewed the wires? Maybe there are rats."

"I better take another look at that," he muttered and headed back to the bathroom.

Dylan gave her a suspicious look. "Are you coming up with things to discourage me?"

"This place has a lot of problems." She shrugged and took another sip of tea.

The inspector returned. "She's right, that's faulty wiring. Can't believe I missed that." He wrote on his clipboard. "You're going to have to take out the plaster to replace it. That's going to cost you."

"Wow, that's too bad," Paige said complacently.

Dylan sighed. He told the inspector, "It's not a problem. Anything else?"

"I've still got the outside to do." The man tromped out the back door.

Dylan studied her. "If this place has so many issues, why are you so attached to it?"

"If you knew more about me, you'd understand."

"Maybe that's true."

If they'd been seeing each other for a while, and he'd known her better, maybe he would've steered clear of the idea of buying the cabin. Even a few weeks of dating might've been enough.

That gave her an idea.

She asked, "What if you gave me a few weeks to convince you I should get the cabin?"

Dylan had been leaning against the doorframe, but now he took a couple of steps into the kitchen. "What do you mean?"

"I mean..." She was making this up on the spot. "I take you to other places that mean a lot to me, and tell you about me and my life, and then you'll see why I was meant to live here."

His mouth dropped open. He hadn't been expecting that, which gave her a tiny measure of satisfaction. There was something so staid and controlled about him that gave her the urge to catch him off guard. When they'd been at the orchard, she'd climbed a tree partly to get at the best apples, but also partly to shake things up.

"If I convince you by November ninth that I deserve the cabin," she said, "then if I can make an offer, you won't make one."

He shook his head. "You know someone else still might, though, right?"

"Harry says it's either me or you." Dylan didn't blink. "You already knew that, didn't you?"

He gave a reluctant shrug. "He said something like that."

"Besides. With you, I have a chance of changing your mind."

"What makes you think that?"

Because you like me. Or at least, he had. "Because you're a nice person, too."

He raised his eyebrows, looking nonplussed and…a little pleased? "So we'll still be dating."

"Not dating," she said firmly. "I'd just be— teaching you. About myself."

"Isn't that what dating is?"

He had a point. And the mischievous look in his eyes was awfully hard to resist. But she *was* resisting. "As long as you want to buy this cabin, we're not dating." All he had to say was, *Fine, I'll buy some other house.*

"Okay, you're on," he said. "You've got until November ninth to convince me." He held up a finger. "Under one condition."

Her hackles rose. "What?"

"I get to try to convince you that *I* deserve it *more.*"

She gave a short, disbelieving laugh.

"What?" he challenged her. "It's only fair, right?"

She raised her hands. "No, it is, you're right. But there's no way you can convince me of that."

He actually got a smug look on his face, like a poker player holding a royal flush. Was there something she didn't know...?

No. He was just being arrogant.

He asked, "When do we get started?"

chapter twelve

At nine o'clock the following Saturday, Dylan pulled up to the cabin. He had no idea what he was on time for. He only knew he didn't want to be late.

How in the world did Paige intend to prove to him that she should own that place? Naturally, he needed to find out. Anyone would've been curious.

He could've told her right there in the kitchen that he'd spent a lot of his childhood there. She might've given in on the spot, for all he knew, admitting that he had a much better claim.

But that was exactly why he *hadn't* told her. If she'd immediately acknowledged defeat, she wouldn't have been arranging times to meet with him and tell him about herself, now would she? There was no way he could pass that up.

Well, he'd tell her soon. But if they got to

know each other more first, she'd feel better about him winning this particular conflict.

Maybe he could buy the cabin and still date her, after all.

That probably wasn't going to happen. He needed to put it out of his head. She'd told him point-blank that she could never see him if he bought the place—that it would be too weird. He had no reason not to believe her. It didn't mean he couldn't enjoy some time with her for a little while.

He got out of the car, went up to the front door, and knocked. About half a minute passed, and then he knocked again. After what felt like a long time, during which he wondered if he'd somehow been stood up, she opened the door.

She wore a blue dress printed with black cats. "I couldn't find my purse," she said, a bit breathless. The big yellow bag was slung across her shoulder. He'd expected to be invited in first, but she stepped outside and locked the door behind her.

"Uh, where are we going?" Dylan asked.

"You'll see," she said lightly, walking to her VW bug. "Come on, I'm driving."

He shrugged and followed her. As she reached the car and unlocked it, he asked, "Hey, isn't that dress bad luck?"

"What?"

He pointed. "Black cats."

"Ohhh." As he went around to the passenger side, she explained, "Black cats are lucky for me."

What? They both got into the car, slamming the doors almost in unison. He said, "Okay, I give up, how are black cats lucky? Did you have one once?" He could easily imagine her doting on a cat. Or a dog, for that matter.

"No." She turned the key in the ignition and started the car. "But things that are unlucky for other people are lucky for me." She pulled out of the driveway.

"What kinds of things?"

"Oh, you know. The number thirteen. Walking under a ladder. I always get good luck from those."

"How do you know?"

"I won a cheesecake in a raffle on the number thirteen, and…" She shook her head. "I don't know. I just do." It figured. She was too positive to see anything as bad luck.

Despite her cheery conversation, she seemed nervous, her shoulders tense. Was she having second thoughts about this whole thing? She'd given herself a real challenge. He asked, "Seriously, where are we going?"

"That's for me to know and you to find out."

He snorted. "You've been hanging around children too long."

"Not possible," she protested.

He doubted many teachers would say that. "You really do love your students."

She nodded. "I've always loved kids.—But you do, too. At least your nephews."

He shrugged. "I get them out of Dee's hair once in a while."

"It's really nice you're so close to your sister, too. I'm an only child, and I always wished I had a sister or brother, you know? Not that I can complain. But I bet it was fun growing up."

Talks with her tended to get personal, fast. Already, she was bringing up his past and his family. As if sensing his discomfort, she changed the subject. "I feel like this conversation should give you a hint about where we're going."

"Hmm. Children...fun...are we going to that pizza place with the ball pit?"

"No, somewhere funner than that."

"You're driving me to Disneyland," he teased.

"That's right. We'll be there around midnight tonight."

He knew she was joking, too, but a part of him loved the idea of taking off with her and getting away from it all. Going somewhere to have fun and no other reason. Walking with her on the beach...

Yeah, right. Like that would ever happen. "Can you at least tell me how far we're going?" He'd assumed the destination would be in town, but he might've assumed wrongly.

She pulled into a parking lot. "We're already there."

Dylan blinked. "The library? This isn't fun."

She gasped in genuine shock. "How can you say that?"

"I just thought we were going somewhere exciting."

She shook her head as they got out of the car and walked to the library entrance. As they went through the front doors, she said, "We're surrounded by books. In your imagination, you can go anywhere in the world. You can even go to other worlds...including ones that don't even exist. What's more fun than that?"

He followed her down the stairs. "You're assuming I *have* an imagination." Until recently, he would've said that he didn't. That had been okay with him. In his line of work, daydreaming wasn't a plus. But somehow, being around Paige made his mind wander and envision things he never would've thought of before.

"Everyone has an imagination."

"Isn't that something that first grade teachers are required to say?"

The lower level had colorful chairs, floor pillows, and a rug decorated with the alphabet. The children's section. Of course.

"Wait here," she ordered. Dylan complied, but felt foolish standing there while a couple of moms with their kids looked him over. Paige roamed the shelves, searching. After she grabbed one book, she hunted for another. Finally, she came back to him. "Here." She thrust the two books at Dylan, who took them reluctantly.

"What are these?"

"Two of my favorite books from when I was a little kid." She gestured at one of the nearby chairs. "Sit down."

"This chair only comes up to my knee."

"We'll sit on the floor then."

Dylan felt a twinge of regret about the whole venture. Story time, really? He opened his mouth to suggest that they at least find adult-sized chairs in a different section, but before he could say anything, she plunked herself down on the blue rug. She was like a duck in water here, and he was... like a grouchy cat in water, or something. Begrudgingly, he sat down on the floor facing her. Out of the corner of his eye, he caught one of the moms staring at him with a bemused expression. He asked Paige, "What are we doing?"

She pointed to the top book in his hands. "Favorite story number one. It's about a family in the eighteen-hundreds. They had to make everything for themselves. Like clothes, and they made dolls out of corncobs, and they made their own butter—"

"That sounds horrible," Dylan said flatly. "Most days I don't even want to make my own sandwich. Why did you like this?"

"Well, for one thing..." She reached over and opened the book, her hand grazing his as she did so. As she flipped through pages, he caught a hint of her perfume: crisp and sweet, like caramel apples. She stopped and pointed at an illustration. "They built their own log cabin."

It actually did look quite a bit like his grandparents' home. She said, "Even when I was little, I thought it sounded like the perfect house. I used to daydream that I lived in one."

Dylan studied her face. She wasn't lying. He wasn't positive she was capable of lying. "Kids imagine all kinds of things," he said. "Probably other days you imagined you were in a cave or something."

She wagged her finger at him. "That brings me to my second one. Look."

The large volume was titled *My Amazing Word Book*. She took it from him, paged through, and then returned it to him open. "See? It shows all different kinds of houses." There were a couple of dozen illustrations, each with a word beneath. A-frame home. Yurt. Houseboat. Castle. "When I was little, my mom would ask me which one I liked best," she said. "And I always said this one." She pointed to the log cabin.

She appeared completely sincere, but... "I don't believe you," he said, only half-joking. "This is some kind of elaborate ruse. It's not even that elaborate."

"It's true!"

"You picked it over a castle?" He pointed to the illustration. "Every kid would pick the castle."

"Not me."

He shut the book. "Okay. You've established you liked log cabins as a kid."

She looked smug. "It's a better argument than you were expecting, wasn't it?"

"Mmm..." He pretended to think about it. "No, not convincing. Is that all you've got?"

"We're going one other place today." She lifted her chin in defiance. "And that's just for starters."

She drove him into the city and toward the university neighborhood. "Are we going to the DU Library now?" he asked.

"No, we're going somewhere bad." *Oh.* What was she getting him into? He imagined a junkyard, and then worse places. She glanced at him askance. "It's not *dangerous*."

That didn't mean it wouldn't be depressing. Or weird. Probably both. "Maybe I shouldn't have gone on this mystery tour. Do normal people go along with things like this?"

"You went along with it, and you're normal."

"I don't know," he muttered. "I might've fallen off the wagon."

After taking one side street and then another, she parked along the side of the road. "Here we are."

They sat on a block of one-story houses and a couple of apartment buildings, all with neat front yards, on a tree-lined street. "Oh, yeah," he said ironically. "This is horrible. You've proved your point."

"Come on, get out of the car."

He did, continuing to tease her. "I mean, look at the cracks in these sidewalks. It's disturbing."

She rolled her eyes as she reached his side. "Here." She pointed at the apartment building right next to them, a two-story red brick. "The Washington Arms."

Dylan peered at the sign out front. "Why is it named after a founding father's arms?"

"No idea." She gestured for him to follow her and walked up to the side of the building. "This is where I lived for a year before I moved into the cabin. Right there." She pointed. "First floor, in the middle there."

Dylan stood with her in the lawn. "I don't think we should be staring right into their window."

"Okay, don't stare." She turned away and he did the same, so they were facing one another. "This was a terrible place to live."

His gaze swept the whole building. "It doesn't look bad." He'd lived in worse places, as a student, anyway. It surprised him that Paige would be so critical.

"Oh, it *looks* nice," she said. "My neighbor upstairs had loud parties all the time, even on weeknights. Everyone complained to the manager, but he never did anything. So finally, somebody called the cops."

"Did that help?"

"That made it worse. One day I came home and there was a waterfall in my bedroom. All of this water pouring from the upstairs bath-tub. He wasn't even home."

Okay, that was bad. "They started running a bath and then forgot and left the house?"

"Oh no, I could understand that." He believed her, although he wouldn't have had much sympathy for it, himself. "I found out from one of the neighbors he did it on pur-pose. He thought I was the one who called the cops."

He felt his jaw drop. "You're kidding."

"I wrote a note to him to explain, and I went to slide it under his door...which was probably stupid. When I was almost down the hallway he opened the door and yelled at me to stay away from him. So then I was really scared of him."

Anger stirred within him. How could any-one be mean to Paige? No one should get away with intimidating her like that.

"The rest of the time I was here, I avoided him. Every time I went to do the laundry or get the mail, I'd be afraid he'd be there. And then because of the water, I got mold in the bedroom. The landlord kept promising to do something about it, but he never did. The last couple months of my lease, I slept in the living room—oh no." Her eyes widened at the sight of something behind him.

Then she flung her arms around him, pressing her cheek against his chest.

Reflexively, he returned the embrace, feeling a rush of warmth inside even as confusion overtook him. *What is happening?*

She didn't let go. *This is weird, right?* He liked it. A lot. He hadn't known if he would ever get to hold her in his arms again. But it was weird. "Uh, Paige? Are you all right?"

She lifted her head and peeked around him, and then pulled away. "Oh. Never mind," she said, a little breathless.

He turned around and saw no one. "Who was it?"

"I thought I saw my ex-neighbor. But it wasn't him." She drew in a breath and then pressed her hands to her mouth. "I am so, so sorry. I didn't want him to see me, and I didn't know what to do."

"No, it's fine! Totally fine. You're sure it wasn't him? Because if it was, I could go fight him. How big is he?"

She laughed. "It wasn't him. Let's get out of here."

As they walked back to her car, Dylan realized a small part of him wished it *had* been the guy. It made no sense at all. Dylan wasn't in the habit of picking fights, because he was a rational adult. But still. This jerk of a neighbor had made her miserable. And Paige, of all people, with her cheerfulness and kindness, deserved better. He stopped and looked back at the apartment building. "Do you think he still does live there?"

"I have no idea."

"Did he ever apologize? He owes you an apology."

She looked at him as if he'd lost his mind. "He's probably gotten evicted by now. Let's go."

Once they were in the car and driving again, she said, "So you can see why I was happy to move into the cabin."

Dylan scrubbed a hand over his mouth. He'd already known how much she loved living there, and this whole excursion had been a lot more convincing than he could've ever imagined.

"I admit, that was awful. I'm sorry you had to deal with it." She darted a glance at him. "If you rented a new place, though, it might be fine." *Or it might not.* The thought troubled him.

He ought to tell her now about his grandparents and his summers at the cabin. But if he did, he might not ever get to see her again, other than a possible awkward encounter as she moved out and he moved in. She'd relinquish her claim, he felt sure, and that would be that. They weren't dating. They weren't really even friends.

After they got back to the cabin, she said, "I'd invite you in, but my parents are visiting later, and—"

"No, that's fine," he said quickly. He honestly didn't expect her to be a good hostess, under the circumstances. He asked, "You have anything else planned?"

Her mouth curved upward. "I do, actually. What are you doing on Halloween?"

"I don't do anything for Halloween, remember?"

"You do this year," she chirped. "Come over. Right around...what time does the sun set?"

"This time of year?" He considered it. "Maybe six o'clock."

"Okay, come then," she said.

He gave her his best skeptical look. "On Halloween, after dark, I should come over to the house of someone who has a grudge against me. I've seen horror movies like this."

"Very funny. My best friend Jessica will be there, too, plus her fiancé Steve."

Oh, great. Now he really was apprehensive. Paige's friends would know how much she loved living at this place. They wouldn't exactly be fans of his, under the circumstances. Honestly, he'd gone along with this whole thing to spend time with her, not with strangers.

"So you'll have accomplices," he said. "I really don't like the sound of this."

"Well, if you're too chicken..." She shrugged.

"Oh, no, I can't let that stand. I have my faults, but I am not a coward."

"Great," she said. "See you on Halloween."

chapter thirteen

As Paige cleaned up the pumpkin guts and wet newspapers on her side of the kitchen table, she told Jessica about the questions her student Jaden was always asking her. "The other day he asked me how we know that time doesn't speed up or slow down sometimes."

Jessica squinted at Paige over her pumpkin. With her painted-on nose and whiskers and the pointy ears attached to her headband, she made a cute cat. "You're kidding."

"Right? I don't even know how he comes up with these things."

"What did you tell him?" Jessica asked.

"I said we knew that time didn't go faster or slower because of clocks. But he said if time sped up, the clocks would go faster, too."

"He's got a point," Jessica said, as Paige threw the mess into the trash.

Right now, time seemed to be moving quickly, barreling toward the deadline of

November ninth when Harry would be selling his house and would wait no longer for her to make an offer on the cabin. She was no closer to being able to do it than when she'd first asked him.

Why was it so upsetting to her? Sure, it wouldn't be any fun to pack up and move again. Her VW bug, in particular, didn't hold a lot of stuff, so she'd need to either rent a U-Haul or make a whole lot of trips. Neither option appealed to her. And yes, it would be hard to lose the house...but she'd be losing something bigger than that. The cabin had seemed like proof that good things could happen if you only had faith. What if that wasn't true? Where did that leave her?

In less than a week, though, she'd meet with her agent. Wasn't it possible that Alexis already had good news, and wanted to give it to her in person? Since Paige had never gotten good news from the agent before, she couldn't be sure how Alexis would handle it.

"Done!" Jessica put the big knife down on Paige's kitchen table and stretched. "Geez. I had no idea carving pumpkins could be so exhausting."

"It is when you do three of them," Paige said. Her own fingers and arms were aching. "Especially after doing two yesterday."

Jessica took off the apron Paige had given her to protect her black velvet outfit. Paige was wearing her fairy dress, but her wings hung from a hook on the wall. She'd taken off her flower crown and hung it up there as well, because as she carved, it kept slipping down over one eye.

She came around to look at Jessica's jack-o-lantern. "Oh, I love it! It's so goofy." She gave Jessica a hug around the shoulders. "Thank you for doing this."

"Do you think it looks too much like my other one?" Jessica pointed to the one next to the sink. "They have the same number of teeth."

Only Jessica would worry about this. "No, it's fine."

"I still feel like I should've done a scary one."

"*No.* This is a pumpkin patch for smiley pumpkins only." Jessica raised her eyebrows at the firm tone, and Paige felt obliged to explain. "When I was a kid I got scared easily. At Halloween, all the gory costumes and monster decorations..." She shook her head. "They weren't for me. They still aren't."

"Mmm. I get it. I can't watch really scary movies." Jessica wiped her hands on a towel. "Steve makes fun of me."

Paige finished cleaning up the table. "I'm still sorry Steve couldn't make it. I feel like I haven't seen him in forever."

Jessica snorted. "I kind of feel the same way. There was a dog at Furever Friends that I wanted him to meet...he's the sweetest thing. I figured if Steve liked him maybe he could go ahead and adopt him now, you know? But he

155

didn't want to go with me because he had a really bad cold. And I guess he still does."

"I'm glad he stayed home to get better. It would be awful if he was still sick for the wedding. And it would be even worse if *you* were sick."

"I know, right? My dress doesn't have pockets for a handkerchief."

"I'll carry anything you need," Paige said, and then did a double take and set her knife down. "You finally got a dress?"

Jessica's eyes danced. "Yep."

"Now you tell me! Show me!"

"Okay, hang on." Jessica washed her hands and dried them off with paper towels. Then she got her phone out of her purse.

"I don't know why it took me so long to get one," she mused as she pulled it up. "You were probably thinking I'd wind up going down the aisle in my yoga pants." Jessica held the phone out to her. "Look."

In the photo, Jessica wore a gown with a closely fitted bodice topped by a froth of ruffles around the shoulders. The skirt was an enormous, diaphanous bell. "Oh, my gosh," Paige said. "It's beautiful."

"Look, it's not even too long." Jessica said. "Well, it won't be, because I'm going to be wearing really high heels." Paige couldn't help but wonder if that was a good idea. Navigating what appeared to be about twenty yards of layered satin and tulle, in high heels? If it had been her, she'd never make it to the aisle without falling on her butt.

She kept her reservations to herself. Maybe she didn't possess enough grace to pull that off, but Jessica might. Besides, she'd already purchased the dress. Once Jessica's dad had walked her up the aisle, Paige would make sure to stay close by and grab her if she was going down.

"You're going to look like you stepped out of a fairy tale," Paige said.

"Speaking of which, don't you need to go put your wings on? You're going to get trick-or-treaters any minute now."

Paige glanced up at the cuckoo clock. Ten till six. "And Dylan'll be here soon." The trash can was full, so she pulled the garbage bag out and tied it shut.

"And why is he coming over again?"

"I told you. I'm trying to convince him not to bid against me if I turn out to be able to buy the place." She set the trash out on the back patio and closed the door again. "Be nice."

"Why should I? He's betraying you."

Paige picked up her wings. "Well...maybe I'll be more convincing if I'm nice though, right?" She threaded her arms through the shoulder straps.

Jessica rolled her eyes. "Yeah, yeah. You catch more flies with honey or whatever." She frowned. "Though I don't know why anyone wants to catch flies. Unless they're a frog."

"Ha ha." Paige adjusted the wings on her

back and settled the flower crown on her head. Then she grabbed one of the pumpkins on the table. "Okay, let's take these outside."

In the front yard, Paige had already created a pumpkin patch display. Dozens of tiny plastic jack-o-lanterns on stakes surrounded the area, and larger plastic jack-o-lanterns of various shapes and sizes were already arrayed there. Jessica followed Paige, carrying one of the pumpkins she'd just carved. Paige said, "We want to mix the real ones in with the fake ones."

After a few trips, all of the jack-o-lanterns were arranged. "It's a lot easier doing this with two people," Paige said.

"I didn't even do that much." Jessica shook her head at the finished display. "This is so over the top."

"Oh, it's more than you think. Hang on." The sky had deepened to dark blue. It was time. Paige flitted back to the master switch near the front door and flipped it on.

"Whoa!" Jessica stared at the display. Strings of orange lights wrapped around the front posts of the cabin and outlined the roof and the door. All the plastic jack-o-lanterns in the patch glowed and grinned, now sitting on a bed of twinkly purple lights. Paige walked back to the pumpkin patch to take in her work, delighted by the results. Jessica stretched her hands wide for emphasis. "This is amazing!"

"It is," a male voice said. They both looked

up to see Dylan, not at all festively dressed in a black sweater and jeans, coming up the front walkway.

Paige's heart did a little skip as she saw him. *We're not dating*, she thought. Her heart needed to get with the program.

Jessica had no trouble remembering their current status. She folded her arms across her chest, scrutinizing him.

Well, that was fine. That's what best friends were for. They could hold a grudge so you didn't have to. Paige smiled and said to Dylan, "Happy Halloween."

"That's still a great costume," he said. The morning they'd spent at the costume store, and the light, sparkly feeling she'd had as they'd laughed and bantered together, all came back to her, and she felt a stab of regret. Shifting his gaze, he said politely, "You must be Jessica." Jessica nodded without saying hello.

"Come on, let's go inside," Paige said. As they went up the front walk, she prodded Dylan. "You like what I've done with the place."

"Um, yeah." Dylan looked as though he'd just remembered why she'd invited him over. He reached the door and took in the wreath of fall leaves and little pumpkins, also illuminated with tiny orange lights.

Paige opened the door. "So Dylan, what's one thing you hate about living in an apartment downtown, on Halloween?"

He blinked as they went inside. "Uh...nothing?"

"Really? Nothing?"

He shook his head, looking bemused.

"Because I'll tell you what I hated about it." She reached up to the top of the bookshelves and brought down a huge pumpkin-shaped bowl filled with candy. "I didn't get any trick-or-treaters." She set the bowl on the table near the door.

"Why did you have that up on the shelf?" he asked.

"So I wouldn't eat them all, obviously." She grabbed one and unwrapped it. They were her favorite: chocolate-covered peanut butter pumpkins.

"I didn't think kids even trick-or-treated anymore."

"Not in apartment buildings, they don't. And when I first moved in here, Harry told me that they only got a few kids at Halloween." She took a bite of the candy. *Mmm*, that was good.

He smirked. "So most of the candy's for you?"

The doorbell rang and they all jumped. "Excuse me," Paige said. She opened it to a dad in the company of a small firefighter and an even smaller child dressed as a Dalmatian.

"Trick or treat!" the children intoned.

"Oh, my goodness," Jessica squealed. "You guys are so cute."

As Paige dropped candy in their bags, the

firefighter squinted at Paige. "You look like a real fairy."

"She is," Dylan said seriously. "I found her in a garden."

Hmm. That was a little flirty, wasn't it? How was she supposed to respond to that? If she told him to stop, he'd probably deny it had meant anything. Maybe it hadn't. And she wasn't at all sure she wanted him to stop, either.

The child gave him a suspicious look. "Happy Halloween," Paige said, and the dad ushered the kids back down the walk.

When Paige turned away from the door, Dylan took a seat on the couch. "So you're only expecting a few more?"

"I didn't finish my story." Paige came over and sat down, and so did Jessica, although she nabbed a piece of candy first. "Harry said they only got a few trick-or-treaters, and I thought, how can I get more kids to come here? I decided I'd make it look like this magical Halloween house. I got tons of lights and I made the pumpkin patch, and I had it all lit up for a week beforehand. And on Halloween night, we had more than fifty kids."

"You think you lured them here with your decorations?"

"Two parents even told me they came here especially because it looked so great when they'd driven by earlier in the week." The doorbell rang again. "Excuse me."

She opened the door to three teenagers.

The girl wore an eye patch and a striped top in a vague attempt at a pirate costume, one of the boys had donned a black cape over his sweatshirt and jeans, and the other boy stood there in ordinary clothes. The girl giggled. "Hi, trick or treat?"

"Here you go." Paige smiled as she distributed candy. "Happy Halloween, you guys."

After she closed the door, Dylan said, "That was just wrong."

Paige blinked. "What?"

He spread his hands in a gesture of disbelief. "They're too old to be trick-or-treating."

"It's fun!" Paige protested. "I don't think there's an age limit. If I had senior citizens show up at my door, I'd think that was adorable. In fact, I'm going to make a note to myself to go trick-or-treating when I'm an old lady."

"You *will* be adorable," Jessica said. "Maybe we'll go together."

"Okay, yes, that would be adorable, like everything you do, but that's not the point," Dylan said to Paige. The offhand compliment gave Paige a small thrill, and Jessica raised her eyebrows. Dylan didn't seem to be aware of what he'd said. "They didn't even dress up."

Paige ignored her inner confusion and focused on the conversation. "Yes, they did."

"Not all of them. And those were the laziest costumes I ever saw in my life."

Jessica sighed. "I hate to say this, but I actually agree."

Dylan extended a hand to her. "Thank you."

Paige perched on the arm of the couch. "While this is my house, I welcome *all* trick-or-treaters. And here's the other thing I was going to tell you. Everyone who comes here hits the whole block. Including Harry's house." She pointed in its direction. "Since his wife Judy died, he's been very lonely."

A stricken look passed across Dylan's face, and he looked down at the floor. "It's got to be hard," he muttered.

She'd expected him to sympathize with Harry. After all, Dylan was a good guy in many ways, even if he was too stubborn to back away from buying the house she loved. But his heartfelt reaction threw her. Maybe he was more sensitive than she'd realized. Something niggled in the back of her mind, telling her there was more to it than that. But she couldn't imagine how to get to the bottom of it.

"It is hard," she said. "And he's far away from his daughter and his grandchildren, and he misses them. So he *loved* getting more trick-or-treaters. It made his night."

"You did a good thing there," he said.

She sighed. "If I move back into an apartment, I'm not going to have a yard to decorate and I'm not going to have any kids coming by."

"You know, you keep on talking about moving back into an apartment building," he said. "But maybe you could rent another little house somewhere."

"It's hard to find cheap houses for rent."

"But not impossible," he pressed. "You could still have your magical pumpkin patch and your trick-or-treaters."

Dang. He was right about that. Even Jessica tilted her head in acknowledgement of it, agreeing with him for the second time.

"But this place is special," she said.

"Yeah, I mean obviously I agree." He rubbed a hand over his mouth. "There's something I should tell you."

chapter fourteen

Dylan took a deep breath. This was his chance to explain to Paige that he'd spent a fair amount of his childhood there. She might not like it that he hadn't said something sooner, but with any luck, she'd forgive him, and understand that he wasn't insensitive to her love for the place. That even though he was set on buying it, he did feel for her...and he liked her.

The doorbell rang again and he jumped. "Oh!" Paige said, hopping up to answer it.

Jessica trailed behind her. They opened the door to a group of six children in the supervision of two moms. "Trick or treat!" they all sang out. As Paige dispensed candy, one of the moms inclined her head toward the other and said, "I told her she had to bring the kids to this house." Then she patted the smallest girl, dressed as a ladybug, on the shoulder. "Tell her what you told me, Isa."

The little girl said, "I like it that all your pumpkins are happy."

"Yay!" Paige said. "I'm so glad!"

Dylan felt he'd missed his moment for a heart-to-heart with Paige. He stood back and watched Paige demonstrate her absolute mastery in the field of giving children happy memories.

When he'd gotten out of his car and looked at the cabin, the sight had stunned him. The place had been transformed into a Halloween wonderland of twinkling orange and purple lights. And in the middle of a patch of smiling, glowing jack-o-lanterns, she stood, dressed as a fairy and looking so genuinely magical, it almost felt like a dream.

More than ever, he didn't like it that they weren't dating. No. He hated it. They could've enjoyed such a perfect night if they'd been not only together but really *together.*

Even as it was, watching her give out candy and coo over children's costumes was not, by a long shot, the worst way to spend an evening.

He kept looking for an opportunity to tell her about his history with the cabin. He really wanted to. But the steady stream of princesses, space fighters, princesses who were space fighters, and so on, made it hard to find an opening. Besides, the presence of her best friend Jessica made it all the more difficult. He didn't know why Jessica's fiancé hadn't showed, and didn't figure it was his business to ask. He was just grateful for the guy's absence. One suspicious friend of Paige's was enough. Though really, he couldn't help but like Jessica. She obviously adored Paige, and he admired that kind of loyalty.

He didn't have a good friend like that. Dee's husband Paul was probably the closest friend he had. Paige had mentioned hanging out with other coworkers, too—going to a baby shower, for instance—but he escaped the people at the office as soon as he could.

After an hour and a half had passed and they'd hit a trick-or-treater lull, he got up. "Well, this has been fun, but I should be going."

A look of disappointment crossed Paige's face. Why? Did she have something else to show him? Maybe plans to turn the cabin into a replica of Santa's village at the North Pole, come December? Nothing would surprise him.

"I'll walk out with you," she said. "I need to make sure none of the candles have gone out." Jessica gave her a curious look, but then shrugged and looked at her phone.

Outside, a nearly full moon shone in the dark sky above them, and dry leaves rustled slightly in the breeze. She didn't spare a glance at the jack-o-lanterns. "Well?" she asked.

"Well, what?"

Kiss her.

He pushed the insane impulse out of his head. He didn't know why she was looking up at him expectantly, as they stood close to one another on a beautiful autumn night, but it wasn't because of that.

"Don't you think I deserve the cabin?"

She had to be chilly in that sleeveless dress, making him want to wrap his arms around her and pull her close...

Stop it.

"See?" she said. "You can't deny it."

Deny what? Oh. The cabin. He wasn't going to tell her the truth now. It was a good thing he hadn't before. He needed to keep seeing her.

But he still felt the urge to make his case at least a little. "You have to admit I deserve it more than some people."

"Why?"

"Because I don't want to tear it down."

Slowly, she nodded. "I liked what you said about building on. But I still think it's not your kind of house."

"Here's the thing," he said. "I need a good place to come home to at the end of the day."

She straightened in affront. "You need that and I don't?"

"No, I mean—your work is fun, and mine isn't." She stared at him, and he continued. "You do the same things as you've been doing tonight. Talking to kids, talking to your best friend."

She glared at him. "I don't know why you keep thinking my job is so easy. I do all kinds of administrative nonsense, and some of the parents are difficult, and—"

"But you love it."

She exhaled. "You're right. The kids are amazing, and I think I'm...well, I'm not perfect, but I'm really good at parts of it."

The modesty of her bragging touched his heart. "Of course you are. And you love it," he repeated. "That's the difference between you and me."

"But you don't *hate* your job." Again, he didn't know what to say. "You flat-out hate your job?"

"Lots of people hate their jobs. That's why they have to pay you. Because you wouldn't do it for free." Why did she look so appalled? This was the way of the world. Sure, some people liked to pretend otherwise. They shared quotes like *Do what you love,* which had always struck him as not the key to happiness, but rather the key to being broke.

But Paige did what she loved, and she was doing all right. Not well enough to buy her little dream home, though...

"What's the name of your office?" she asked.

"Hammersmith Capital."

She snapped her fingers. "I've seen that building. They have the red tulips out front in the spring?"

Did they? "I guess so."

"Tulips are my favorite. Though I like them in all different colors."

"Of course you do."

She smiled at this recognition of her nature. "Is it really that bad there? You go into that fancy office, you go to meetings, you make PowerPoints…isn't that basically it?" Now she was teasing him.

"You're leaving out the million emails a day."

"So what? I bet nobody you work with has temper tantrums."

"That's not exactly true," he interjected.

"Or pees their pants."

Dylan recalled the time they'd been audited. "I wouldn't bet on that."

"You probably get free bagels." She said this as if it settled the argument.

"You probably get free apples."

She laughed. "I do, actually."

"Yeah, why'd you even come with us to the orchard?"

He was joking, but she looked hurt. "Because I liked you." Something twisted in his chest. While he tried to think of how to respond, she reverted to the safer subject. "*Do* you get free bagels?"

He nodded. "I get free dinner, too."

"Wow." She sounded genuinely impressed. "See? How bad can it be?"

"If you went there, you'd get it. There's this…fog of doom hanging over the place."

She scoffed. "Maybe that's your negative attitude."

"It's not." Possibly a little. But mostly no.

"I want to visit." He laughed at that. "You've got me curious now!" she insisted. "I get off at three forty-five. I could come by."

He shook his head. "We don't have a Take Your..." He only just stopped himself from saying, *Take Your Girlfriend to Work Day*. It was wildly inaccurate, and would've been even more wildly inappropriate. "Take Your Real Estate Rival to Work Day," he finished.

"I guess you could show me now, while nobody's there. If you can get in at night."

"Of course I can. And there's never nobody at the office."

Her eyes narrowed. "You mean to tell me that right now, on *Halloween night*, people are burrowed in your office like moles?"

"That's exactly what I'm telling you. But this wouldn't be the right time to go. You'd need to go tomorrow when everyone was there for the full gloom effect."

She laughed a little. "Fine." The idea of her at his office made him smile, though of course, she was only joking.

chapter fifteen

The next day, Paige felt a twinge of misgiving as she stood outside the modern
offices of Hammersmith Capital. Maybe she
shouldn't have invited herself for a visit. Now
that she thought about it, he hadn't even
seemed that enthusiastic. But she'd had to
come. He was simply being jaded about his
workplace, she was sure. That happened to
people: they got so accustomed to their familiar circumstances and surroundings that
they no longer saw the good in them. Maybe
she could teach him how to do the morning
gratitude ritual, like she did.

He probably wouldn't try it, though. She
could imagine him making some joke about it.
Not one that would hurt her feelings. He was
good at being funny without being mean, and
it always made her want to tease him right
back.

She went into the lobby and walked up

to the receptionist. "Hi, I'm here to see Dylan Cain?"

He nodded. "Sure. Do you know the number of your conference room?"

Conference room? "I, uh, I'm not in a meeting with him." The receptionist gave her a blank look. "I'm a friend. I'm just stopping by."

"What's your name?"

"Paige Reynolds."

Unease coiled in her belly. This was quite a bit more formal than she'd been expecting. Somehow, she'd imagined that someone would casually point in the direction of Dylan's office, and she'd go over and say hello.

The receptionist picked up the phone and dialed. In a moment he said, "Hey Dylan, Paige Reynolds is here, she wants to see you?" After a pause, he answered, "Yeah." What had Dylan asked him? "Okay." The man hung up the phone and opened a drawer. "Here's a visitor's badge. Dylan's office is on the left, three doors past the kitchen."

Paige went to the door and flashed the badge in front of the device next to it. Nothing happened.

"You have to swipe it," the receptionist said. "Then clip it on."

She let herself in, and as the door shut behind her, she considered where exactly to clip the ID. Her dress, the purple one with little orange pumpkins, had no pockets. She attached the badge to her purse strap.

A guy in the first cubicle looked up. "Can I help you?"

"I was dropping by to say hi to Dylan."

He raised his eyebrows. After a quick glance around him, he said in a quieter tone, "They don't exactly encourage visitors around here."

"Really? He said it would be okay. But I'll make it quick."

The guy shrugged and returned to whatever he was doing on the computer.

Paige bit her lip. *I've made a mistake.* If Dylan's workplace frowned on visitors, why had he agreed to her coming by? She hadn't known him that long, but he seemed like a consummate rule-follower.

Confused, she continued down the corridor. In one of the offices she passed, a man talking on the phone stared at her. A woman who passed her also gave her a curious look. Paige wouldn't have felt more out of place or conspicuous if she were wearing her Halloween costume.

Dylan appeared in the doorway of an office near the end of the corridor. "Hey, Paige."

He wore a navy suit and looked startlingly handsome. She flashed back to when she'd first seen him at the café. He'd been dressed for work then, too, but he hadn't had the same effect on her. Now, the sight of him in a tailored suit made her feel a little shaky. She still had a crush on him. Maybe even more than ever.

As she reached him, she smiled. "Hi."

He looked perplexed. "Come on in." Not liking his slightly formal tone, she obeyed, and he left the door ajar. His expression seemed to hover somewhere between amused and baffled. Quietly, he asked, "What are you doing here?"

All her remaining confidence drained out of her. "You said I should visit today, when everyone was here."

He gave a disbelieving laugh. "I thought we were kidding."

Her face burned with embarrassment. "I'm going to go."

His expression softened. "No, it's fine." He put his hand on her arm, and her heart gave a little leap. Immediately, he took it away again, as though touching her had been an accident. "I'm just surprised." Warmth kindled in his eyes. "I'm glad you're here. I could use the break."

"So this is the place of doom and gloom," she said, quietly so his coworkers wouldn't overhear. He had a huge desk, an expensive-looking black leather office chair, and another chair for visitors. The office didn't hold much else, though, besides his computer. If it hadn't been for a wire-mesh tray holding a stack of papers, it would've looked as though he'd started work there yesterday. "Homey."

"Isn't it?"

"It looks like you're in some kind of executive solitary confinement. You should bring

175

some stuff from home. Didn't you say you lived close to here?"

He nodded. "Just around the corner. Factory Lofts." He even lived in a place that sounded like work. She hated to admit it, but she could see why he'd want to buy a log cabin.

"You could bring in pictures, or knick-knacks, or..." She trailed off as she noticed the amused gleam in his eyes. "What?"

"Home looks pretty much like this. Give or take a basket of laundry."

Hmmm. What would be an easy way to give the office a little bit of soul, then? "You should at least get some plants." What else could go on those barren bulletin boards? "And a calendar."

"My computer has a calendar."

"But it doesn't have pictures of your favorite things. What *are* your favorite things?" He looked at her blankly. "If you were going to get a calendar, what would the theme be?" Maybe she could get him one. No, that wouldn't be right. They weren't in a gift-giving type of relationship.

"What would yours be?" he hedged.

"The one at home has classic children's book illustrations, and the one in my classroom has sparkly unicorns."

He gave a short laugh. "I feel like I could've guessed that."

"Oh, you think you know me that well?" she teased.

"You're the easiest person to get to know on the planet. You don't hide anything."

"Do you?" She didn't mean it as a serious question, but he looked pained. Maybe he didn't feel like he could be himself at work... which was exactly why the idea of bringing some personality to his office had captured her imagination. "What kind of calendar would you get?"

She expected him to make a joke. Instead, he said, "Probably national parks." He winced at his own answer. "It's boring, right?"

"No. Maybe you want to be closer to nature."

At the cabin, he would be. There was the pond out back, and the view of the mountains, and regular visits of rabbits... She pushed away the unwelcome thought.

"I was going to run a new marathon this month. It's a beautiful trail, national forest..." He shook his head. "I got too far behind on my training."

Why did he have to be so hard on himself all the time? "You could walk around in nature anytime. You don't have to make it into a job."

He tilted his head and raised his eyebrows in a nonverbal *touché*.

Speaking more softly again, because she saw a man coming their way, she asked, "Besides your unfortunate lack of décor, what's so bad about this place?"

Also looking at the man's direction, he

murmured, "Oh, I think you're about to find out."

The man came into Dylan's office without hesitating. "Hey, Cain. Who's your friend?" He looked Paige up and down in a way that was not, to her mind, exactly polite. He had very chapped lips and behind his stylish glasses, his eyes looked pale and cold.

"Hey, Mark," Dylan said. "This is my friend Paige. She was stopping by to say happy birthday." It was his birthday? No, he was probably lying, giving a reason for her unexpected presence, but he told the lie effortlessly. Did he often feel the need to tell lies at the office? Because if he did, that was probably a good sign the place wasn't for him. "Paige, this is Mark, my boss."

He hadn't made the best first impression on her, but she smiled brightly at him, anyway. "Hi, nice to meet you!"

"Hi." He returned his attention to Dylan. "There was an error in the Lionex pitch book."

Dylan's face fell. "The French translations?"

"Not exactly. Slide forty-four. One of the numbers didn't get converted to Canadian dollars in the second column."

Dylan sighed. "We had about a hundred corrections at the last minute." Seeing him dressed down right in front of her made her want to squirm. Wouldn't a normal human being wait to deliver criticism in private?

Paige couldn't help but say something. "So it was just a typo."

Mark looked at her with surprise, as if he'd thought she'd disappeared the moment he turned his attention away from her.

"Sorry, man," Dylan said. "Ice Media should go better. I went over those numbers again on Sunday."

His boss waved his hand in dismissal. "Yeah, that's cancelled. They got cold feet."

Paige laughed. Mark turned to her again, his eyes wide with impatience. She said, "It's funny. Ice Media, got cold feet." He didn't smile.

"That's too bad," Dylan said. "I thought things were moving along there."

"Elaine could've done more to grease the wheels. You're better with the clients." Was that professional, criticizing one employee to another? Mark added, "She's detail-oriented, though. Got to give her that." He licked his lips. "By the way, someone from Wakefield will be at the New York conference. Can you set up a meeting with them?"

A flash of dismay crossed Dylan's face, replaced with a bland mask. "Yeah, sure."

"Great. Hey, don't stay at the Dreighton if you can help it. That place is trash." Mark clapped Dylan on the shoulder before leaving. If Dylan's stiffness was any indication, he didn't appreciate it.

He shot Paige a droll look. "I always stay at

the Dreighton," he said in an undertone. "It's fine."

His conspiratorial banter made her feel better about the whole awkward scene, but she still regretted stopping by. "It sounds like you're really busy. I'll go. Like I said, I'm sorry I misunderstood."

Dylan frowned slightly and shook his head, a *don't worry about it* expression. "I'll walk you out."

Once they got outside, Paige felt her mood lighten. "You're right," she admitted. "It is gloomy there."

"Now you get it."

"What's your plan for leaving?"

He cocked his head. "Sorry, what?"

"Do you think you'll get another job like this, or try a different field...?"

"I'm not leaving," he said.

"Why not?"

He snorted. "I am this close to making VP. It's between me and Elaine, but it's probably going to be me."

Was he crazy? "But you hate it! There are probably lots of jobs you'd like. If you're good at numbers and at talking to people, you can do anything, right? You could...work for a nonprofit, maybe. Maybe something about nature or..." At the disbelieving expression on his face, she faltered.

"I'd make about a third of what I'm making at a nonprofit. I've been working toward this promotion for a while. I'm not going to just give up."

"It's okay to give up things you hate." Paige's frustration rose. He was miserable, and yet he refused to change it. How did that make any sense?

"But sometimes the things you hate get you the things you want," he said. "Like the cabin."

He'd hesitated for the barest moment before throwing that out there. And with good reason. It rankled her.

"Then you have to stop complaining," she said.

"Sorry?"

"If you refuse to do anything different, then you have nothing to complain about." She gestured toward the building. "This is your choice."

His mouth fell open. Then irritation flashed in his eyes. "Okay, that's great. Thanks for coming by."

Paige felt crushed. "Dylan—"

"Forget it. It's fine." Paige knew it wasn't. "I'll see you later, okay? I've got to go."

"Okay."

She watched him go back inside. Then she walked back to her car, got in, and sat in the driver's seat.

She'd expected to bring some lightness to his workplace, to help him see the good in it. Instead, her presence had been awkward, and then right after his boss had made him feel bad, she'd piled on. She hadn't even meant to. She really wanted him to be happier. Him bringing up the fact that it was easy for him to buy the cabin had riled her up, she had to admit. But still. She saw herself as someone who made people happier, not someone who criticized when it wasn't even her business. What had gotten into her?

I was right, though.

That was beside the point. He hadn't even invited her there. *Ugh.* The whole thing had been a disaster.

The next day, Jessica and Paige sat in the teacher's lounge eating the lunches they'd brought from home. Jessica said, "I know you're trying to convince him not to make a high offer. But I don't get it. Why did you go to his office? Other than you being secretly crazy about him."

Paige chose not to rise to that bait. "Because he'd been complaining about how dreary it was. And he was right, it was. But when I said he should either find something new or stop complaining, he got mad."

Jessica let out a laugh. "You told him that?"

Paige sighed. "I don't know what got into me."

"No, no, I like this side of you."

Linda Goff appeared next to their table. "Hey, Paige," she said. "I heard that cabin you're renting is for sale."

She had her back turned to Jessica, who bugged out her eyes and shook her head, indicating this information had by no means come from her. She didn't need to worry. Paige knew Jessica didn't go around telling people about her private business. The principal, whom Paige had told when she'd had to get out of bus duty to go to the bank, was apparently a different story.

"That's right," Paige said. "I might buy it."

Linda gave a look of exaggerated sympathy. "Real estate prices have gotten so crazy. I don't know how a single woman on a teacher's salary could do it." Paige had seen pictures of the sprawling ranch home Linda and her husband had bought last year. They owned a few acres and a barn with two horses.

"I haven't decided yet," Paige said.

"You've got to be careful with those older houses," she added. "They can really be a money pit. If you ever need someone to show you around, our agent was fantastic. She could find you a cute little condo somewhere."

"Thanks."

"Well, good luck!"

As Linda left the teacher's lounge, Jessica's face reflected outrage. "Did she just call you too poor to buy your house, *and* call your house a dump?"

"Uh, basically." It wasn't easy to insult

someone in two ways in under a minute, but that was Linda.

"I'm going to go talk to her." Jessica pushed away from the table.

"No!" Paige grabbed her arm. "What good would that do?"

"You're right, you're right," she muttered. "Just wait till you buy that cabin. You'll show her.–What were we talking about?"

"Um..."

"Oh yeah. Dylan. If he got mad because you gave him good advice, he was being stupid. Maybe I should go talk to him?"

Paige peered at her. "Why do you want to fight the world today?"

Jessica shook off the question. "I knew that guy was bad news from the start."

"You did not." Jessica had practically insisted they should start dating. "And I'm not surprised he got mad. It's rude to tell people to quit their jobs." Paige shook her head. "But I don't get it. With his experience, he could do anything. Why would he stay in a job he hates?"

"Guys have their identity all wrapped up in their jobs." Jessica lifted one shoulder in a shrug. "He has a high-status job, and it makes him feel like a superior human being."

There was some truth to this, no doubt. But still... "I don't think he's *that* bad. And I don't think that's true of all guys, either. Steve's not like that, is he?"

Jessica's big brown eyes welled up with tears.

"Honey, what's wrong?" Paige blurted out, although to her horror, a part of her already knew. *The wedding's off.*

"Steve and I broke up." Her voice shook, but she managed to keep it together.

"Oh, no!" Paige started to get up to hug her, but two other teachers had glanced in their direction. Not wanting to make a big scene, she settled for putting a hand on Jessica's arm. "What happened? Are you sure it's off?"

Jessica sniffled. "That's what my mom asked, too. I'm sure."

"Sorry," Paige said. She'd only asked because she could tell, even secondhand, that the wedding planning had been stressful. A petty quarrel might turn into a blowout when emotions ran high, and it would be a shame for that to ruin their future. But if Jessica said they were over, well, she of all people would know. "I'm just shocked. What happened?"

Jessica took a deep breath and let it out. "He said he couldn't do it. That he'd been faking being happy for weeks."

Paige sat silent for a moment, stunned. She was the least violent person she knew, but at the moment, she wanted to track Steve down and slap him.

Jessica shook her head. A tear clung to her eyelashes. She looked so beautiful and so sad that Paige's heart broke for her. "I was going to tell you later because I knew I'd get all emotional."

"When did he tell you this?"

"We had an appointment with the bakery to taste different wedding cake flavors. I was so excited about it. Best meeting in the world, right?" She gave a short, bitter laugh. "He didn't show up. And I tried to call him and he didn't answer the phone. Then later that night he sent me this long, long text about how he felt trapped and was having panic attacks."

"A *text*? He couldn't tell you before? In person?" Paige's voice rose to almost a squeak. "Sorry, sorry," she added quickly in a more hushed tone.

"It's fine," Jessica said wearily. "Everyone's going to know soon, anyway. The thought of being married to me gives people panic attacks!"

"Not people. Steve. Because Steve's stupid. You're gorgeous and nice and fun and smart and he's an idiot."

"He said he wanted to travel the world first." Jessica shook her head. "I told him I want to travel the world too! I even have a list of the top ten places I want to go in my lifetime. And he said that was the problem. My list."

Paige shook her head. "Why was that a problem?"

"I know! What's wrong with knowing what you want? I guess he...thinks I have everything planned out too much. But I sure didn't plan this." She pressed her fingers to the corners of her eyes as though to physically block the tears from falling.

Paige's blood simmered with rage. What kind of man would bail on her wonderful friend at the last minute? "There's something wrong with him. He's going to regret this when he's old and gray. But you're not. You're so much better off without him." She shook her head. "At least—" She cut herself off.

"No, you're right. At least it was before the wedding," Jessica said, correctly guessing what Paige had been going to say. "That's a lot better than him freaking out afterward."

"How can I help?"

"I don't know."

Paige racked her brain. "We could ritually burn things that remind you of Steve." She could put the fireplace to good use while she still had it.

Jessica snorted. "Yeah, right."

"I wasn't joking. Think about it. But what else can we do?"

"Nothing." Jessica took another morose bite of her sandwich. "Unless you want to go with me to try to return the wedding dress."

"Did you get alterations?" If she had, Paige didn't like her friend's chances at getting her money back. It made her sick to think of it, too. Those dresses Jessica had been considering hadn't been cheap.

"No, I finally found one that fit me pretty

187

well. I'm just..." Jessica gave Paige a wide-eyed look. "I'm going to be *mortified*."

No, no, no. Paige couldn't have her friend feeling like that. Steve should be mortified, but Jessica? Paige wasn't having it. "First of all, it happens all the time."

"You don't know that."

"Yes, I do. Because how could it not? And second of all, I'll be right there with you." She grinned. "I'll casually mention to the sales associate how you dumped the guy."

"You don't have to do that!" Jessica's big brown eyes still sparkled with tears, but she smiled. "You are the best friend."

"*You* are." Paige got up and hugged her. No matter what life threw their way, they could always rely on each other.

chapter sixteen

Dylan finished a longer-than-usual run on the treadmill at his gym. After work, he'd come straight there, not wanting to go home. He took out his earbuds and turned off the movie on his iPad. He couldn't stop thinking about Paige.

Honestly, her unexpected visit the day before had been a welcome surprise...until she'd taken it upon herself to lecture him. He rubbed his towel on his forehead and took a big swig of water from his sports bottle. Then he headed toward the door. He never showered at the gym.

It had seemed unlike her. Usually she was so upbeat and positive.

She was telling you how you could be positive, too. As he walked out to his car in the parking garage, he tried to brush the thought away, but it refused to budge. He started the car and backed out of the parking space.

He didn't even know why he'd been bad-mouthing his job lately. It wasn't like he'd never worked hard before. Hammersmith Capital didn't compare to the grueling labor at the cannery, that one summer in Alaska. He hadn't whined about that, and yes, he'd been younger then, but he was still young. Honestly, she'd been right to tell him to stop complaining.

He pulled back in, turned the car off again, got out his phone, and called her.

"Dylan," she said after picking up.

"Hey Paige. I was calling to..." He didn't know how to finish the sentence. What *was* he doing, actually? He probably should've figured that out before dialing. "We uh, weren't on the same page earlier." *Weren't on the same page?* Corporate-speak again. And since her name was Paige, it sounded especially awkward.

"It's my fault." Regret filled her voice. "I accidentally surprised you and it was weird. I'm sorry I came."

"I'm not." He wasn't sure what he wanted to say next, either, but he didn't think he wanted to say it over the phone. "Hey, is it okay if I stop by for a few minutes?" One second of silence on her end made him scramble to add, "I know it's late, so if—"

"No, come by," she said.

"It'll be about twenty minutes."

"I'll make some tea."

It made him smile. "You know I don't actually drink tea, right?"

"You know I do, right?" she parried, and

suddenly he felt like everything was okay between them again.

"Be careful," he said, meaning it.

She laughed. "I was making tea for many
years before I met you, Dylan Cain."

"And were you burning yourself?"

"Only once in a while." He could hear the
smile in his voice. "See you in a bit."

When Paige answered the door, she said, "I'm
in my pajamas."

They were a matching set in pink flannel,
and Dylan took note of the pattern as he came
in. "Are those monkeys?"

"Yes. And look, I have matching slippers."
She pointed down, and Dylan laughed. They
were, indeed, monkey slippers, with smiling
simian faces on the toes. The ends of her hair
were damp and she smelled as though she'd
just gotten out of the shower. He felt a strong
urge to hug her, feel her wet hair next to his
skin, and breathe in the scent of the fruity-
floral soap or body wash she'd used.

Belatedly, he recalled that he hadn't taken
a shower at all. "Sorry I'm sweaty," he said,
putting another inch or two between them. "I
came from the gym."

"Oh, I don't care," she said, so offhandedly
that he believed her. "Sit down." She curled up
on the sofa in the spot nearest to the fireplace,

where embers of a fire glowed, and wrapped her arms around her knees. She looked impossibly cute. As he sat down next to her, he noticed the cup of tea on the little table next to her. Had she been sitting there, waiting for him? The thought stirred something inside him.

"I'm glad you called," she said. "I think I got mad when you said—you know, that you could buy this place and I couldn't." She gave a wistful look around them. "I know I'll probably need to deal with not living here anymore."

A crackle and snap from the fireplace took him back to when he'd been a boy in this house. It had been such a cozy place then, and it was now, here with Paige. Would it feel that way when he was here by himself? This hadn't occurred to him before. Every time he imagined living here, he envisioned Connor and Noah visiting. But most of the time, he'd be alone. All his experiences with the place had included laughter and being with people he loved. It might feel very different when he was alone. Why did he want it so badly, then? What did he *really* want?

"I don't have any right to tell you what you can and can't complain about," she said. "Besides, everyone complains sometimes."

Dylan had to smile at hearing her express some of his very own sentiments from earlier in the day. "You had a point," he conceded.

Her expression brightened. "You might leave that job?"

"No. I might stop complaining about it."

She groaned and briefly buried her forehead in the sofa cushion. "But your boss is the *worst*."

He so rarely heard Paige say anything bad about anyone that it made him laugh out loud. "You noticed that, did you?"

"I'm sorry, but he is."

"Don't be sorry." Dylan shrugged. "Maybe I'll outlast him there."

He didn't hate Hammersmith because of the long hours, he realized suddenly, but because he didn't respect Mark. Oh, and he didn't like a few of his other coworkers, either. And some of the clients lacked scruples. Somehow, he'd accepted these things instead of asking himself whether it was worth it.

But it was. No job was perfect, and Dylan had put too much into this one to give up now, right before his promotion. But it made him feel better to admit his feelings to himself. Maybe after making VP, he'd discreetly look around for some new opportunity.

"I think—" She cut herself off, holding up her hands. "Sorry, I'm done giving you advice. I'm going to get some more tea. I'll be right back."

As she went into the other room, Dylan looked down at the cluttered coffee table. Math tests, spelling homework, a couple of children's books, and...

Paige's journal. Lying wide open, filled with her handwriting and drawings.

Dylan peered closer at the pages. A princess lived in the cabin. And a giant bull and a knight were kicking her out of her home. What Paige had said in the costume shop came back to him. *I could see you as a knight.*

A bad knight, apparently. He'd always seen her as open and honest, but she was writing stories about him behind his back, with him as the villain. It stung.

She came back into the room and stopped dead in her tracks when she saw him looking at her work.

"It was open," he said. Under the circumstances, he hardly needed to defend himself. "What is this? A kid's story?"

She looked mortified, and that took the edge off his hurt. Her cheeks flushed pink. Not for the first time, he noticed how pretty she was when she blushed. "It's just this silly thing I'm reading to my class."

Dylan read from the page. "'And then the fairy knew the knight was the worst knight in all the land.'" Seriously? "You read stories to your kids about how I'm the worst?"

Misery clouded her features. "I'm sorry. It's not really you, I swear."

"You *drew* me." Amusement at her absurd denial mingled with his affront. He pointed to the picture. "I can tell it's me. You're not a bad artist."

She came over and pulled the journal away from him, shutting it. "I'm so, so sorry." Her eyes pleaded with him. Okay, well. He had no chance of staying mad at her if she was going to look at him like that. "I wrote that right after you came to the open house."

Hmm. He could understand that. Especially since she wouldn't have been mad at him if he'd leveled with her about why he wanted the cabin. That was on him.

She stood next to the table holding the journal to her chest. He couldn't help but see the humor in the situation. "Come on," he protested. "You've gotta let me know what happens next."

"No, this one's too silly. It's just for me and the kids."

"I have the right to know," he grumbled, and then considered her phrasing. "What do you mean, 'this one'?"

She blinked. "What?"

"You said this one was for you and the kids. What are the other ones, and what are they for?"

She squirmed, spiking his curiosity even more. "I...I've written other children's books that I'm trying to get published. I have an agent and she's been shopping them around."

"Wow. That's so cool." He'd never met anyone who did that kind of thing. "How come you never told me?"

She sat down next to him again. "I don't know. It isn't going well."

"It must be going well if you have an agent." He knew almost nothing about this kind of thing, but still.

"It took forever to get one," she admitted. "And when I finally did, I was so excited. I thought I was going to get published right away. So I told everyone. I announced it on Facebook with all of these exclamation points. I mean, I did everything but rent a billboard."

Even though she winced with shame, Dylan could imagine what it would've been like to see her so thrilled, and to maybe share in her joy. Deep down, he wanted to celebrate the good things with her, big and small, and to comfort her in the rocky times.

She sighed, staring down at the closed journal on the table. "Turns out that getting an agent doesn't mean you'll get published right away. Or at all. But now I might, and I'm waiting to hear, and it's driving me crazy."

Something clicked in his mind. "This is why you might get the money for the down payment. If you sell the book."

She nodded. "There's one publisher that's interested now, but it's not for sure yet."

"That's amazing." He decided that for the moment, he wouldn't think about what that would mean regarding the cabin. She didn't smile, and her shoulders were hunched. "Why aren't you more excited?" The girl got excited about going to the library. One would think a possible publishing deal would make her euphoric.

"It's been rejected eleven times." *Ouch.* Dylan had been turned down by prospective clients before, and while it had been rough, it had just been business. For Paige, it had to be personal. She put her heart and soul into everything she did. "The publishers have been saying they're too traditional. They all wanted something quirkier. So I don't know."

"What are the books about?"

"There's this rabbit named Muffy and a squirrel named Kerfuffle, and..." She laughed. "I don't know, they have adventures?"

"I bet I'd like them. I always wondered what you were writing in that journal. When I first met you at the café, I saw your drawing of the cabin, and it reminded me of this place."

Her mouth parted. "Really?"

"It was one of the things that got me curious about you. Besides, you know..."

"Besides what?"

Besides everything else about you. Your voice. The way you dress. The way you like Mondays. The way you care so much about people. Everything.

He couldn't say any of this. She'd already said they couldn't date if he was making an offer on the house. He still wanted the place. And he understood what the word "no" meant.

He asked, "Can I see the whole story?"

She hesitated, and then pushed the journal toward him. "The knight gets better later on."

Dylan read through the story. It pleased him to see the knight didn't turn out to be so bad, after all, and the whimsical details made him smile. "It's so random."

"That's just the first draft," she said. "I typed it up and I made a lot of changes." She shook her head. "It's still kind of bananas, though."

"If they've been saying your other story is too traditional, why don't you send your agent this?"

"No, it's ridiculous."

"Aren't a lot of kids' books ridiculous? Like on purpose?" He'd read some to Connor and Noah when they'd been younger. "What have you got to lose?"

"My pride?"

He didn't know a lot about books, but he did know about deals. "No, you're thinking about this the wrong way. I've pitched to clients who were way out of our league, right? We're not the biggest firm in the world. But there's me, in person, in my suit, convincing them they need to work with me. You have to be confident." She looked anything but. "Other people publish crazy stories. Why not you?" He pushed the pen and journal toward her. "Why don't you go ahead and write out what you'll say in the email?"

"I'm not sending her this anytime soon."

"C'mon," he urged. "Then I can take a look at it and, you know, plus it up."

"Plus it up," she echoed. "Well...I guess it wouldn't hurt."

She picked up the pen. After a few moments of thinking, she wrote out a message.

Then she pushed it back toward him. "There. It's nice and casual."

Dylan read aloud. "'Dear Alexis, how are you?'" He used a slightly higher register of voice, filled with chipper enthusiasm.

She laughed. "I do not sound like that!"

"Oh, you do," he lied, grinning. "It's uncanny, really." He continued reading in the silly Paige-voice. "'I've been thinking a lot about what you said about needing to be edgier and quirkier in my writing. I'm attaching a story that's still a little rough. I know you're really busy, so...'" He stopped and looked up at Paige with disbelief.

"What do you think I should change?"

"Everything," he said gently. "This is terrible."

"What? It's not that bad."

"No, it really is."

"Wow." She shook her head. "Well, so what? I want to be a good children's book writer, not a good email writer."

"But one thing could get you to the other." He looked down at the wishy-washy email draft again. "I don't get it. When you're talking to me about the cabin, you're *very* persuasive. Why can't you be the same way here?"

"It's different when it's about my writing."

"It doesn't have to be. Here. Let me try." He gestured for the journal.

"Fine." She gave it to him. "It's not as easy as you think."

He wrote furiously as she watched. In half

a minute, he said, "Okay, I've got it." He held up the journal and read aloud in the Paige voice. "'Dear Alexis, I want to thank you again for your recent helpful feedback. I've attached *Log Cabin Princess*, a quirkier and edgier story—'"

"I can't say it point blank like that," she protested.

"Why not?"

"Because it's bragging."

He shook his head and continued. "'...a quirkier and edgier story I've been working on for a while.'"

"I haven't been working on it long at all."

"'A while' is very vague," Dylan pointed out, and then finished reading. "'I think publishers are going to love it! Kind regards, Paige.'"

"I don't know."

"Well, think about it." Dylan knew when to stop talking. It was one of his key workplace skills. He didn't have to do all the work of convincing someone of something. He just had to give them enough so that they could convince themselves. Deliberately changing the subject, he asked, "I really can't see the other stories?"

She tilted her head. "I guess I could send them to you."

He felt a small surge of triumph. "I'll give you my email." He jotted it at the bottom of the page. "Here. Don't forget."

She gave a rueful laugh. "I wish editors were that eager to get my stories."

"When are you going to hear back from the one who's interested?"

"Oh, you never know." She shook her head. "It probably won't be in time. This place will be yours."

Her voice carried no bitterness, but Dylan's heart went out to her. "You know, if it were any other house, I wouldn't buy it. The thing is…" He pushed through the reluctance. He'd gone way too long already without telling her. "I grew up here."

chapter seventeen

Paige's mind reeled. What in the world was he saying?

His expression was serious. He was telling her the truth. Still, when she managed to speak, all she could say was, "*What*?"

"It was my grandparents' house. My sister Deidre and I spent a few...five summers here, when we were growing up. And a lot of weekends, and we'd come here with Dad every Christmas."

Humiliation washed over Paige...followed by indignation. She felt like the victim of an elaborate practical joke. "Why didn't you *tell* me?"

He raised his palms up in defense. "I know, I should've. I—"

"You let me show you around, try to prove to you I deserve it." Her voice rose. "Ugh. This is just like Steve."

"Who's Steve?" His voice took on a jealous edge. Paige wasn't sorry to hear it.

"Jessica's ex-fiancé. He didn't tell her until right before the wedding that he didn't want to be married."

"That's...terrible." He looked sincerely concerned, which was to his credit, especially considering Jessica hadn't been completely friendly to him. "But what does it have to do with me?"

"You didn't tell me what was really going on," she said. "I made a fool of myself!"

"No, no you didn't. I'm the one who's been dumb here." The unqualified apology and the way he was looking at her, sincere, completely unguarded, weakened her defenses.

"But why didn't you say anything?"

"Because it was too personal, and..." He sighed. "Because I wanted to spend time with you. A lot of time."

Paige melted. The truth was, she loved being with him, too. If Dylan had told her right away that he'd spent a lot of his childhood here, she would've given up immediately on making her case. But would she have gone on another date with him? She didn't know. The shock of probably losing her home had still been fresh. It would've been awkward.

She looked around them. How strange that Dylan had been here as a boy. Now that she thought about it, he hadn't said anything about his childhood when they'd gone to brunch on that first date, even though she'd told him all about hers. She grew more curious.

"Why were you with your grandparents so much?"

He frowned. "My mom died when I was little."

She pressed her fingers to her lips, stricken. "You never told me that." Could there be anything sadder than a child losing a parent?

"I don't remember her very well. I was too young." Still. He'd grown up without a mother, and that struck her as unbearably sad.

He fixed his gaze on the floor. "Dee says Dad was different before Mom died, but all I remember is him...not paying much attention to us. You know how when I first met you, and you were buying the cupcakes for that kid? Because his parents probably wouldn't send any with him?" He glanced up, and she nodded. "That kid was me. That was me and Dee. He forgot our birthdays a few times. We'd have to remind him to buy school supplies, to take us clothes shopping. He'd almost never ask, 'How was school?' Things like that. Like I say, it was no big deal." He shrugged.

Paige's heart hurt. "What do you mean, no big deal? You were neglected."

He shook his head. "No, I mean, we always had enough to eat, he got medicine when we were sick, he didn't yell at us or anything. He was just..."

"Depressed." Paige could only imagine how one of her parents would feel if they lost the other. Their lives were so entwined that it would be like losing part of themselves.

"Yeah, I guess. I mean…it kind of made me mad. Like, *I know you're sad, but what about us?* You know?" He shrugged again.

"Of course it did." She couldn't stand it, him acting like this was nothing. "You were a *child.* You wanted someone to pay attention to you."

He looked away with a dismissive chuckle. "I didn't want to go into this. He's really good as a grandpa."

"You get along with him now?" She hoped so.

"I was just trying to say that…Grandma and Grandpa knew he was struggling. So they'd take us sometimes."

He hadn't answered her question, she noticed. "They were your dad's parents?"

"No, my mom's."

"It probably helped them to have kids around, too."

He let out a little huff of realization. "I never thought of that. I know they missed her a lot. But we'd have so much fun." He had a faraway look in his eyes. "Then I'd worry about my dad being alone, so I'd be glad when we went back, too."

She could imagine him as a boy, basking in the attention of his grandparents, worrying about a father who was often absent even when he was there. "You make me want to hug you a hundred times."

He looked profoundly uncomfortable. "A

lot of people go through terrible things. This is nothing."

"Stop saying that." He straightened; her no-nonsense voice had gotten his attention. "It's not nothing," she added gently. "What was it like, when you and your sister were here? Has the place changed a lot?"

"Not much. Though there used to be a Scotch pine tree in back, and I'd climb it and get on the roof—"

"Oh, my gosh," she said. "Harry cut that tree down. The ice storm damaged it. But it was here when I moved in." She cocked her head. "What kind of tree did you say?"

"Scotch pine?" He sounded as though that were obvious.

"How did you know what kind it was?"

He shrugged. "When I was a kid, I liked trees."

The revelation secretly delighted her. Then she clicked her tongue, remembering their time at the orchard. "And you told me you'd never climbed one in your life."

The corner of his mouth twitched upward. "I don't think I said that. You're remembering wrong." He always got a mischievous spark in his eyes when he teased her, and she found it ridiculously charming.

"Oh, that must be it," she said.

"And my grandpa taught us how to play card games. Right here at this kitchen table."

She laughed. "That's awesome." Then she sobered. "Are your grandparents…"

"My grandpa died about ten years ago. My grandma went into assisted living then…that's when she sold this place to Mr. Burke. But she died a couple years after."

"I'm sorry." He'd lost so much.

"Thanks. I have such great memories of them, though. Every Sunday, my grandma would make these muffins with maple syrup and pecans—"

"Oh, my gosh!" Paige sat bolt upright. "The Sunday muffins!"

Dylan blinked. "What?"

She jumped out of her chair. "I have her recipe!" She opened the drawer, pulled out the sheet of stationery with the spidery handwriting, and thrust it toward him. "I found it a few weeks ago."

He took it and stared at the handwriting. "Oh, man," he breathed. "Dee's going to love this."

Paige felt a bright bubble of joy rise up inside of her. "I'm so glad I found it. Wait—do you mind if I take a picture of it first, so I can have the recipe too?"

"No, go ahead." She fished her phone out of her purse, and he lay it flat on the table so she could snap the photo. He said, "That cedar chest in the bedroom—Dee always wished she'd gotten that."

"That was your grandma's." She winced. "I'm sorry I got mad at you for opening it."

He looked embarrassed. "I didn't blame

207

you. I guess Grandma had a couple of things from her wedding in there."

"Yes." Paige grabbed his hand and pulled him out of the chair. "I wondered what the story was behind those!" She led him to the bedroom, knelt down in front of the cedar chest, and opened the lid. Shoving the blankets aside, she explained, "They're at the bottom. I couldn't throw them away." She took out the bridal veil with the silk flower headband and a silver coin. "Is this it?"

"*Yes*. Oh, wow." He kneeled next to her and she handed the items to him. "I don't know what the coin is about, but Dee mentioned it."

"It's for good luck." He gave her a blank look. "'Something old, something new, something borrowed, something blue, and a sixpence in her shoe.'"

"How did you know that?"

She lifted a shoulder in a half shrug. "I'm a teacher. I'm a font of knowledge."

He stood up again. "I can't wait to take these to Dee."

She could go ahead and tell him the other thing about the cabin. "A week after I moved in here, I saw a rabbit and a squirrel in the backyard. And...I know this is going to sound crazy, but I could've sworn they were playing together. All at once, I got this story in my head, and that's where *Muffy and Kerfuffle* came from. I was so inspired. I wrote those three books my agent has...They came so easily. It's like this is the perfect place to be creative." He frowned, but didn't argue with her. "I guess I was afraid if I moved out, I'd go back to being stuck in my writing."

"You're a creative person. You could write in a pup tent if you had to."

The words made her emotional, and she covered it with a laugh. "What's a pup tent? A tent for puppies? Because that sounds adorable."

"Yes," he said. "That's exactly what it is."

She sighed. "Maybe you're right. Thanks."

He nodded. "Thanks for listening." It hadn't been easy for him to disclose all that, she knew, but he'd trusted her, and that meant a lot to her. Impulsively, she reached over to give him a hug.

He stiffened and didn't hug her back. For a terrifying second, Paige believed she'd made a mistake. Then he wrapped his arms around her, and she got a warm feeling inside, as sweet as a pumpkin spice latte with all the whipped cream.

"I'm still sweaty," he said by way of explanation as she pulled back again.

"You are," she admitted. "I don't mind."

He cleared his throat. "I really should go home and take a shower, though."

"Okay." Of course he wanted to get home. It was late, and he probably felt talked out. But when would she get to see him again? She hated to let him leave without making plans. "Hey, do you want to come over again on Sunday morning?"

"Um. Sure."

"I thought I'd make some Sunday muffins."

His face broke into a smile. "I would love that."

Oh, shoot. The wedding dress shop. "You'll have to leave by eleven-thirty, though."

"Who's your other date?" he asked lightly.

"Jessica." He raised an eyebrow, and she laughed. "Not really a date. I just promised to go with her. She's going to try to return a wedding gown, and I'm there for moral support."

"Ah, that makes sense."

After he left, she sat for a minute pondering Dylan's story. She'd already figured out that he was close to his sister, which she'd thought was nice. And it was, but now she suspected that what they'd gone through—the tragedy of a lost parent, the neglect of another—had led them to rely on one another more.

Dylan had done so much in his adult life to succeed and to make sure he wanted for nothing. Was it because he'd lacked attention as a child? These things were never so simple. Still, she couldn't help but wonder. He was good at getting what he needed. Just his quick rewrite of her email had proved that.

She picked up her journal, re-read her attempt at the message to her agent, and cringed. Dylan had been right: it sounded a bit pathetic. When it came to her work, she suddenly lost all her nerve. Dylan's draft rang crisp and confident.

Well, she wasn't going to send it yet, since

she was seeing Alexis tomorrow. Who knew? Her agent might have good news for her.

The next day, Paige sat at the bar at the big hotel, looking at the time on her phone. Was it possible she and Alexis had somehow missed one another? Surely Paige would've spotted her. Alexis's red hair, arranged in a sleek bob, made her stand out. Did Alexis even remember what Paige looked like?

All around her, men and women wearing badges for the writing conference clustered in small groups or paired off, all caught up in intense conversation. Paige looked down at her fingers to make sure she'd washed off all the glitter and glue after the art project that day. *Every single person here knows what they're doing except me.*

She brushed off the thought and got out her phone to text Jessica when she saw Alexis striding toward her table. Her agent wore a gray dress and pumps with no tights or hose, despite the chilly weather. Paige could never tell how old the woman was—in her forties, or fifties? Paige got up from her seat. Alexis gave her a quick, businesslike hug.

"I'm late," Alexis acknowledged. "I was on a panel and the Q&A went long."

"That's okay. What were you talking about?"

"Oh, changes in the industry." Alexis settled herself down in a chair as the server returned to their table.

"What can I get you two ladies?" he asked.

Alexis said, "Manhattan with your best rye, neat."

"Yes, ma'am." He asked Paige, "Another Earl Grey?"

"Yes, thanks."

When he retreated, Alexis made small talk, asking about Paige's teaching and telling her about a recent trip to a book fair in Frankfurt. After the server had returned with the drinks, Alexis's tone changed. "Well, I wanted to meet you in person and talk about how things are going."

"Right."

"And unfortunately, they're *not* going. I heard back from Vandergast Books today. They declined."

"Oh."

It felt like a kick to the stomach, even though Paige should've been used to it by now. She'd gotten her hopes up about the medium-sized publisher, convincing herself that they would be the right home for her books. Of course, she'd believed the same about the big publishers who'd already passed. Alexis always said *declined* or *passed*. She never said *rejected*. It showed tact, but the words all meant the same thing.

Alexis took a sip of her cocktail. "They said the same thing as Crofton. It's too traditional for them. Old-fashioned."

Even though Paige had heard this before, her scalp prickled with shame and indignation. "People *like* old-fashioned. They still read *Winnie the Pooh* and Beatrix Potter." Personally, she always imagined someone reading her rabbit and squirrel stories and then describing her as a modern-day Beatrix Potter. No one had done so yet.

"It's not what publishers are buying right now. They want something edgier." Children's books needed to be edgy? Sympathy tinged Alexis's voice. "I always think it's best to be open and honest. I'm going to send it out one more time, to Butterfly Books. But if that's a no, I'm not going to pursue it any further."

Paige couldn't think of what to say. Her throat constricted; it would've been difficult to get the words out, anyway.

"I'm sorry," Alexis said into the silence. "It's a tough business, and you can't take it personally. We'll see how it goes."

Maybe there was a way to not lose her as an agent, even if she was giving up on the rabbit-and-squirrel stories. "I'm um, I'm actually working on something new they might like better. We can try with the next story once I'm done, right?"

"I just don't think you're aligned with where the agency is headed. It's not about the talent; it's about the market." Alexis's voice was smooth. Paige suspected Alexis had given this exact same speech before—maybe dozens of times. "I wanted to talk about it now so you can start thinking about what you'll do next."

What I'll do next? How about cry? Except Paige wasn't going to do that, of course. Instead she said, "I appreciate your time."

chapter eighteen

Someone knocked on Dylan's office door, and he looked up to see his coworker Josh. "Hey, Cain. McGreevy and I are headed out to Q. You want to come?"

Dylan knew of the club, on a block of clubs and bars. They'd no doubt hit a few of them before they'd call it a night, which would be when the sun was coming up. That's how it had gone the one time he'd joined them.

"Nah, thanks anyway," he said. He was friendly with them every day and joked around with them, but he didn't actually like them that much. When they were drunk, their jokes got louder and ruder, and he liked them even less.

"C'mon," Josh urged. "If we're going to work on Saturday, we should treat ourselves afterward."

Kyle came up behind Josh. "You should see the new girl bartending at Dirtbags." He looked to Josh. "We're going there, too, right?"

"Totally."

Dylan, not for the first time, tried to think of a more obnoxious name for a club than *Dirtbags*. Again, his imagination failed him. The fact that the place served some of the most expensive cocktails in town made it even worse. "Maybe next time," he said, a bald lie. "Have fun."

"I'll go," Brian piped up from his cubicle. Josh and Kyle showed no signs of hearing him.

Dylan zipped his laptop into his bag and put on his coat.

When he exited his office, Brian intercepted him by saying, "Hey, I still didn't get to ask you. That girl who came in the other day—was that your girlfriend?"

He shook his head. "She's a friend." Even if he'd been dating Paige, he wouldn't have told the guy. It wasn't any of his business—or the rest of the office's business, either, and Brian loved to gossip.

"Oh," Brian said. "Well, she's hilarious. Think you could introduce me?"

"*No.*" Dylan immediately regretted his tone of voice. The idea of Brian hitting on Paige had sent a flare of pure anger through him.

"Dude. Why not?"

"Aren't you dating someone?" He tried to remember. "Did that other girl ever call?"

Brian scoffed. "No. And I never called her." Dylan had told him not to. "C'mon," Brian wheedled. "What was her name? Paige?"

"No." Dylan shook his head and walked away.

He'd told Dee he was going to stop by, and when he came to the door, Connor answered it. "Uncle Dylan, guess what?" he blurted out. "I'm going to be in a talent show!"

"Really? That's awesome." Dylan tried to imagine what his nephew might do in a talent show, and came up with nothing. Connor didn't sing, dance, act, or play a musical instrument. As far as he knew, the kid didn't do any magic tricks, either. He played soccer and videogames. As Dylan came into the house and nodded hi at his sister, Connor said, "It's on Friday the ninth. You'll come see me, won't you?"

"Honey, your uncle's really busy with work," Dee interceded.

"No, I'll be there," Dylan said. He'd be back from New York by then. No one expected uncles to show up to those kinds of things, he knew. That was a father's job. For relatives, it was merely an option. But it didn't matter. He wanted to be a part of the boys' lives. He was sticking with his job at Hammersmith, but he wasn't going to let it stop him from committing to a family event. He added, "Maybe we can celebrate me buying the cabin."

"Oh my gosh, that's right," Dee said.

"Hey Connor, go tell your dad I'm here," Dylan suggested. Once the boy had trotted off, he asked Dee quietly, "What's his talent, exactly?"

"I have no idea. He wants it to be a surprise. He keeps telling me it's going to be epic." She cringed. "I'm worried."

Paul emerged from his office, Connor and Noah trailing after him. "Hey, how's it going?" he greeted Dylan as he joined them. "You want a beer?"

"Nah, I'm good."

"What did you want to show us?" Dee asked as they sat down. "I've been wondering all day." Dylan handed her a bag that had held last night's takeout from Jade Palace. She reached inside and pulled out the bridal veil.

She gasped and her hand flew to her heart. "Oh, my gosh." Dylan had expected her to react like this, he enjoyed it.

"What is it?" Connor demanded.

"It was your great-grandma's bridal veil," Paul said, and turned to Dylan. "Am I right? She's told me a dozen times about playing with that." Dylan nodded.

"How did you get this?" she demanded. "Was it during the home inspection?"

He should've prepared for that question. "No. Uh..." He had no reason not to tell her the truth. "I was over there last night, and Paige gave it to me."

"You were with Miss Reynolds?" Connor

demanded. From the look on Dee's face, she shared his surprise.

Noah snatched the veil from his mother's hands and put it on his head. "La, la, la," he sang, inventing a melody as he danced away from her.

"Noah, you be careful with that," Dee said, but she didn't stop him. She turned back to Dylan. "Are you dating her again?"

Connor interjected with some singing of his own. "Dylan and Miss Reynolds sittin' in a tree, K-I-S-S—"

"No. Stop," Dylan said. He added to Paul, "I can't believe kids still sing that."

"You'd be surprised what's still around," Paul said.

Dee still appeared to be waiting for an explanation. Dylan said, "We're not dating." *Though we would be if it were up to me.* Maybe it would be possible, now that Paige knew the truth. He squirmed every time he recalled how he'd told her his life story, and her sympathy had made him even more uncomfortable. At the same time, it had meant a lot to him. "We've been talking."

Noah took the veil off and set it on the coffee table. Dee picked it up again. She asked Dylan, "Is she trying to talk you out of buying the cabin?"

"No, no." After a pause he said, "I mean, yeah, she was."

"But you've got history with the place. How can she expect you to not make an offer?"

He didn't feel like getting into this, but on the other hand, he didn't want Dee to think badly of Paige. "She didn't know. I just told her the other night."

She looked at him as if he'd lost his mind. "Why didn't you tell her sooner?"

"It was personal," he said defensively.

"Have you told Dad about buying it? I almost said something the other day, but I figured you wanted to tell him."

He'd barely even thought about it. Dee talked to their father more regularly than he did. For the most part, Dylan only saw him at Dee's house. "Do you think he'll like the idea?"

"Yes. He loved it there."

"How do you know?"

"A couple of times in the past few years, he's brought it up," she said. "How Mom brought him home to meet Grandma and Grandpa, when they were first dating, and he thought it was so cute that she grew up in a log cabin."

"Really?"

She nodded. "You should tell him soon. November ninth is coming right up."

chapter nineteen

When Paige woke up Sunday morning, even before she opened her eyes, she remembered being sad. Why? She waited a moment, and it hit her. Oh, yeah. Her meeting with Alexis, who was about to drop her.

She'd wallowed the night before, calling her mom and dad, texting Jessica and watching TV. That had been fine, but she needed to snap out of it. She swung her bare feet down off the bed. They connected with a cold, hard floor.

At least Dylan was coming over.

She found her phone and checked the screen: a few minutes after eight. She'd overslept. Still, she had plenty of time to make the muffins and some coffee. She padded out to the back door and stepped outside.

Of course, the sunrise had long passed. It had given way to an uninspired gray sky. Oh, well. Paige began.

"I'm thankful for this day." Rebellion

streaked through her. "But I'm not thankful that nobody wants my books."

Weirdly, the top of her head tingled, as though someone had touched her lightly there. She thought she felt a patient, loving presence. "Sorry," she muttered. Time to get over herself. Hadn't she chastised Dylan for complaining?

Many people could hardly dream of the advantages she had. When she'd been hired at Jefferson Elementary, she'd been over the moon. Why not still be over the moon about it? She could if she wanted to. Her close relationship with her parents was a blessing, too. Not everyone had that. Dylan had lost his mother when he'd been small, and he was distant from his father.

But he could probably be closer to his father now if he wanted to.

Well, that was another issue. In any event, she had plenty of reasons to be grateful.

"I'm thankful for this day," she murmured. "For my parents. And for Jessica. And for my wonderful job." Inspiration hit her. "I'm thankful that even if I lose this home, it'll go to someone who loves it, and that I don't have to worry about being homeless. I'm thankful that even if nobody wants to publish these books, I know children who like them, and I have the creativity to write more." As she said those words aloud, a wave of optimism overcame her. One more blessing nudged at her spirit, demanding acknowledgement, although she'd never counted it before. "And I'm thankful for Dylan," she added quietly. "Amen."

She'd miss doing this here, like she'd miss everything about the cabin.

Or maybe she'd get to spend at least some time here, because she'd be visiting him.

Oh, boy. She needed to stay away from those thoughts. She'd always believed in the power of hope, but she couldn't deny that hope had slapped her around a couple of times lately. She'd do better to take each day as it came for a while. He was coming over this morning, and it would be fun. Out loud, she said, "Let's go make some muffins."

As she measured and mixed the ingredients, she thought again about how Dylan had urged her to send Alexis the log cabin story. Was it really such a bad idea? She got the shortening out of the cupboard and greased the muffin tins.

Why shouldn't she? She had nothing to lose, after all. *You want quirky? I'll give you quirky. I am quirky.*

After putting the muffins in the oven, she booted up her laptop, pulled up the story, and scanned it, making a couple more tweaks. She read through the whole thing again. Then she opened her email, flipped through her journal to Dylan's handwriting, and began. *Dear Alexis...* She typed out the whole message exactly as he'd written it, attached the story, and before she could second-guess herself, she hit *Send.*

An ungodly, ear-splitting screech almost made her jump out of her skin. Her heart lurched into a panicked pace.

The smoke alarm. "Nooo." She launched herself from the chair and rushed the three steps to the oven. When she opened it, billows of smoke escaped along with the all-too-familiar smell of burning baked goods.

"No, no, no." She grabbed a potholder in one hand while waving away the smoke with the other and yanked the tin out of the oven. After slamming the oven door shut, she set the muffins on top of the stove. Maybe she could trim off the burned edges... No. The tops of them were black circles with less-burned parts in the center. They were toast. Except toast would've been better. It would've at least been edible.

A knock sounded at the door. Paige covered her face with her hands. It shouldn't matter. Things happened. But she felt crushed.

Well, she had to let him in. She crossed the living room and opened the door.

"Good morning." The corners of his eyes crinkled when he smiled. She liked that.

"Hi." She gestured for him to come inside.

When he did, he sniffed. "Um..."

"I burned the muffins," she blurted out. "I'm sorry."

She thought he'd make fun of her. He did laugh, but in the next breath he said, "No big deal." Then she noticed the bunch of tulips in his hand. He held them out to her. "Oh yeah, these are for you. You said they were your favorite."

"Oh, my gosh. That's so nice." As she took them, she felt even worse.

"Hey, hey." His hand came to rest on her upper arm. "What's the matter?"

"You haven't had those muffins since you were a kid, and—"

"We can make them again sometime," he said. Even in her embarrassment, she noticed how he said *we*. "We can make them as many times as we want. That's how recipes work."

She gave a shaky and grateful laugh. "I feel so stupid. I was sitting in the kitchen! What is wrong with me?"

He pursed his lips thoughtfully. "What were you doing?"

"I was making more changes to the cabin story. And sending it to my agent, like you said."

"Good! And I knew it would be something like that." His eyes glinted with affection and amusement. "You're not stupid, you're creative. There's a difference."

That was such an understanding way to look at it. Some of the tension eased out of her shoulders. "I wanted this to be this special breakfast."

"It is." What did he mean by that? He headed into the kitchen. "Come on. We'll make another batch."

Paige followed him, tulips in hand. "We can't. I don't have more pecans."

"Then we'll make something else." As he opened the fridge and inspected the contents, she found a vase and put the tulips in water. Then she grabbed a spoon, picked up the pan, and began dislodging its charred contents into the trash.

In the end, Dylan decided to make omelets with bell peppers, onion, and cheese.

"Do you cook a lot?" she asked, watching him.

"I haven't in a while." He slid the second omelet onto a plate. "There you go. Denver omelet. Named after our city."

"Denver omelets have ham," she pointed out as she carried her plate to the table.

"True. This is like a Boulder omelet."

"How do you figure?"

"They've got a lot of vegetarians in Boulder."

"I think you're right." She sat down and studied his creation. "This looks so professional."

He shrugged. "I've never been a short-order cook. I've bussed tables, though."

"Really?"

"Oh, yeah. My first job in high school."

She took a bite. Delicious. Suddenly she realized how hungry she was. "What other jobs have you done?"

"Ha, what haven't I done?" Interesting. Paige had never imagined him in a work environment other than an office. He began listing them off on his fingers. "I've worked in a warehouse, I've cleaned buildings as part of a night crew—"

"When did you do that?"

"College."

"You went to classes during the day and cleaned at night?"

He nodded. *Good heavens.* That sounded exhausting. But she knew by now that he pushed himself hard. He continued. "I've worked in a cannery in Alaska."

She'd heard about that kind of work before. "I bet that was your worst job."

He shook his head. "Telemarketer was my worst job. By far. But it made me tougher, for sure. And I had an accounting job before I started at Hammersmith."

"Do you ever get tired of working so hard?"

He paused. "Yeah. I really do." A moment of silence hung between them. Then he said, "Hey, I wanted to ask you something, but now might be a bad time."

Oh no. She didn't like the sound of that at all. "Well, you can't not ask *now.*"

He gave a crooked smile. "I guess not. I was going to talk to Mr. Burke about something in the inspection report, but is that going to make you feel weird if I go over there after this?"

Relief washed through her. It was a question about the house. Not a question about *them.*

"I don't mind, really. But that's nice of you

to ask." A question pricked her mind. "Why do you call him 'Mr. Burke'?"

"Because that's what we called him when we were kids."

"Oh my gosh, of course." Somehow, she hadn't considered the fact that Dylan and Harry would've known each other then. "Did you tell him who you were?"

Dylan shook his head. "There were a bunch of people at the open house, and I didn't want to get into it." That didn't surprise her at all. He could be so private. "And then I hadn't told *you*, so it would've been weird to tell him."

"I'm surprised he didn't recognize you," she mused. Or maybe, on some level, he had. Harry had decided right away that Dylan would be a good future owner of the cabin. Maybe, subconsciously, Harry had remembered the little boy Dylan had been.

"I guess I've changed since I was ten." He pointed at her barely touched omelet with his fork. "You don't like it?"

Apparently, the mild anxiety of cooking for another person, someone you liked, went both ways. "No, I do. It's delicious." She took another bite. "Where *did* you learn to make them like this?"

He looked uncomfortable. "Ah..."

"What?" She'd only meant it as a compliment.

"My ex-girlfriend taught me," he admitted.

"Oh." Though he'd said it had been a while

since he'd dated, she'd never asked him about his romantic past before. "She must've been a very good cook." *The opposite of me!* she thought brightly. *Yay.*

"I guess. We went out most of the time, though. She was at Hammersmith, so we'd get off late and go to dinner."

"You two had a lot in common." Paige fiddled with her fork. "Why did you break up?"

"She got a job in New York." Dylan fixed her with a look. "Honestly, I didn't come here to talk about her."

Paige's heart skipped faster. "Why did you come here?" she dared to ask, softly.

He gave a short laugh and ducked his head. *Ooh.* Whatever that unspoken answer was, she liked it. Then he said, "I wanted to see how your week was.—How was your week?"

"Um...it was bad, actually," she admitted, smiling.

His features immediately reflected concern. "How come? What happened?"

"Oh, I met with my agent, and that deal didn't go through. And then she told me she was giving up on it." Paige kept her voice light. Already, she was getting over it. That was what she did.

But Dylan looked struck to the heart. "That's why you sent her the new story."

She nodded. "Last-ditch effort."

"Maybe it'll work. But I'm sorry. She's an

idiot for giving up on those stories. I should've told you sooner, but I read them."

Paige's spirits lifted. "You did?"

"I thought they were great. I read them to Connor and Noah. They loved them, too. Well, Connor said he'd heard you read part of them before, when he was still in your class, but he got into it." Dylan's phone rang. He moved reflexively as though to grab it, then stopped himself.

"Oh, you can get it," she said. She appreciated his politeness, but she truly didn't mind.

He took out the ringing phone, glanced at the screen, and then set it down again as it stopped ringing. "It's just my dad."

"Why didn't you pick up?"

"It's nothing important. He's been asking lately if I want to come over to watch Monday Night Football. And Monday nights are always bad for me."

Paige paused before asking, "Is he nice to you? Now that you're a grown-up?"

Dylan looked impatient. "It wasn't like he was ever *mean*."

Paige didn't want to interfere. Really, she didn't.

"What?" Dylan asked.

"I didn't say anything."

He gave an ironic laugh. "Don't ever take up poker, Paige. You'll lose everything you've got."

Well, fine. He'd asked for it. "He wants to spend more time with you. Maybe you should."

His features arranged themselves in an exaggerated expression of patience. "I appreciate the concern, but we don't have a lot in common."

They'd have more in common if they spent time together. He was an adult. He must've known this. "I get that you're still mad at him—"

"I'm not," he said immediately. "I told you, it was no big deal. And it was a long time ago."

"I guess if you don't admit you're mad, you never have to forgive him."

Dylan rolled his eyes. "He and I get along fine. Don't worry so much, okay?"

She still couldn't help but think that Dylan deserved a dad. "What does he think about you buying this place?"

"I haven't told him yet." He cut off her exclamation of disbelief. "Hey, until this morning, I thought you were probably buying it."

That made sense. "I'm glad you are, though."

"Really?" He studied her face. "Maybe you can come over for omelets sometimes."

Her heart lifted. "Or I can come over and make muffins and not burn them." A thought occurred to her. "You know, if I were better at baking, I never would've met you."

"How do you figure?"

"That morning at the café," she explained. "I tried to bake cupcakes, but I ruined them. So I went into the café to buy some."

"Oh, okay," he said, smiling. "Wow, you're terrible in the kitchen."

"One time I invited Jessica over for dinner, and I accidentally set the spaghetti I was boiling on fire. She never let me forget that one."

He looked adorably incredulous. "How is that even possible?"

"Hey, it's easier than you think!" She sighed. "I keep thinking I'm going to get better, but I always get distracted."

"Did you burn the cupcakes because you were writing?"

"No. Actually, I was..." She thought of the tulips she'd planted. "You know, I should show you something. Because it's kind of my housewarming gift to you. Though that wasn't my plan at the time."

"What are you talking about?"

"Come on." She got up and beckoned him to do the same. He followed her out the back door.

"Look." She pointed her toe toward the row of fresh dirt where she'd done the planting. "Guess what this is?"

He peered at it. "A grave for your pet python?"

She laughed. "I planted a bunch of tulips out here. There's pink, purple, yellow, orange...they'll come up in the spring, year after year."

"Wow. You really expected to be here a while."

There was no point thinking about her thwarted plans now. It was troubled water under the bridge, or something. She looked out over the backyard and the pond. As long as she was still here, she'd enjoy the view. After that, she'd be happy that Dylan could enjoy it again, since it had been a part of his childhood. "Isn't this back patio the perfect place to watch the sun rise?"

He raised his eyebrows. "I guess?"

"Didn't you ever watch the sun come up from here? You must've seen it dozens of times."

He squinted as though looking more carefully into his past. "I didn't get up early in the summer. Only a couple of times, when Grandpa took me fishing at the reservoir. But I don't remember ever seeing the sunrise."

"Well, you were missing out. I watch it almost every morning."

"Huh. Why does that not surprise me about you?"

"And..." This was close to her heart, and personal, but something told her it would be good for Dylan to hear it, so she forged ahead anyway. "I say out loud all the things I'm grateful for."

"Really." He looked amazed. "Is that something you've always done?"

She shook her head. "I started doing it not too long after I moved in."

He stared at her. "I wish you could buy this place."

chapter twenty

Paige's mouth fell open. "Seriously?"

Dylan hadn't expected her to be so surprised, but it gratified him. "Yeah. If you could, I wouldn't make a counteroffer."

She shook her head. "What made you change your mind?"

"You love it here. Maybe I don't even want a different house. Maybe I want a different *life*."

To him, the cabin had been more than a place. It had meant taking time to enjoy life... and closeness, and sharing. It had meant love. He could live a completely different kind of existence, if he chose, without even moving from his loft. And it would've been possible for him to buy the cabin without changing much else in his life.

She nodded. "I can see that."

"Besides." He couldn't help but smile. "You'd let me visit."

"Oh, you think so, do you?"

"I know so," he teased, being cocky. "I think you'd have me over every day."

"Every day?"

"Yeah," he said, still in a joking tone. "You're crazy about me."

Paige swallowed. "I am crazy about you." She wasn't joking at all. Her blue eyes were wide with an aching vulnerability that went straight to his heart.

Slowly, deliberately, he took her hand, watching her to see if she objected. She didn't, but he could feel a slight tremble in her cool fingers as she wrapped them around his. They were so much smaller than his own. "My hand's cold," she murmured, sounding mildly embarrassed.

He covered it with his other hand. "I'll warm it up." He wanted to wrap his whole self around her, caring for her, appreciating her. He looked down at their joined hands. "Thank you."

"For what?"

"For telling me all about yourself." She wrinkled her brow in sweet bemusement. "No, listen." This had crossed his mind a few times now. "Hearing about your life has been one of the best parts of mine."

She ducked her head. "It's been one of the best parts of my life, too. Being with you."

No one had ever made him feel this kind of longing. What he felt for her belonged to a whole other world entirely, like one of the old stories he'd read as a boy, about noble knights and the ladies they loved. He'd read those stories right here, in this house. It felt like everything in his life had led up to this moment, and everything else had just been marking time.

With as much gentleness as he could possibly manage, he cupped her face in his hands. He traced the pad of his thumb beneath her cheekbone and buried his fingertips into her soft hair. Then he covered her lips with his own.

She returned his kiss, tender, soul-stirring, and wrapped her arms around him. This was happening. He was going to remember it forever.

When he pulled back, she buried her face in his chest, as though she needed a moment, still holding onto him tightly. Could she feel the pounding of his heart? She raised her head and whispered, "That was, uh..."

"Yeah." He restrained himself from immediately kissing her again, although he wanted to do it all day. Something deep inside told him that everything was going to change for him, and he was ready for it all.

Then she froze and her eyes widened. "Oh, my gosh."

"What's wrong?"

"Jessica. I've got to meet her at the bridal shop."

Right. She'd mentioned before that she'd promised to lend her friend moral support. No doubt, scorched baked goods and kissing on the back patio hadn't been part of her morning plans.

She dug out her phone and looked at the time. "Nine-forty. Okay. I can make it if I leave right now."

"Come on. I'll walk out with you." He put a hand on her shoulder. Once they were inside, though, she looked around wildly. "Purse, purse, purse," she muttered, stalking toward the bedroom.

He'd just seen it...where? There, on the bookshelf. "It's in here," he called to her, and when she jogged back into the living room, he pointed.

She grabbed it. "Thank you."

Once she'd locked the front door behind them, she turned to him, a little breathless. "We, um, we need to talk more."

"A lot more," he agreed.

She took a few quick steps toward her car. Then she turned back again. What else had she forgotten? Her wallet, maybe.

She came right up and kissed him again. *Yes.* Her soft lips under his...the sensation overwhelmed him. Dylan wrapped his arm around her waist, wanting more of that, but she shook her head. "No really, I've got to go."

He closed his eyes briefly. "Yeah."

"I'm sorry to rush off."

"It's fine, go," he assured her.

But as she reached her car, she turned around again.

"So, are we, uh...are you my..."

"Your boyfriend?" he ventured. She nodded, uncertainty in her expression. "Yeah."

The sunshine returned to her face.

Mr. Burke answered his door almost immediately. Dylan said, "Hi, Mr. Burke. I—"

"I've told you it's Harry," he interrupted.
"Hello, there. Come on in."

"I won't stay too long," Dylan promised as
he came inside.

"Oh, that's fine. I was just reading a soup
cookbook."

Dylan did a double take. "You were reading
a cookbook?"

"Oh, yeah." Mr. Burke's eyes twinkled. "It
was a potboiler."

It took Dylan a moment to get it. Soup. Pot
boiling. "Ah," he said and laughed, more at
the awkwardness of the joke than the humor
of it. When he and Dee had been children, Mr.
Burke had told them endless knock-knock
jokes.

The older man asked, "Sit down, why don't
you?"

Dylan hadn't planned to stay long, but he
acquiesced, taking a seat on the couch. Mr.
Burke eased into a burgundy faux leather
recliner that looked outdated and incredibly
comfortable.

"I wanted to ask you about the downstairs windows in the cabin," Dylan said.

"Yeah, I saw the inspection report. I'm afraid I'm not coming down on price because of that."

"I wasn't going to ask. My brother-in-law knows a guy who's free right before Thanksgiving. He's got two spare brand-new windows from another job that got cancelled or something. If you want, he could go ahead and replace the old windows for a lot less than we were thinking."

"If he's got good references, I'm game. It's still possible my tenant will buy the house, though. She's got another week."

"If she does, she might want those windows fixed, anyway," he said. "But it's not looking likely for her."

The older man leaned forward. "Is that right? Maybe you know something I don't."

"Yeah, she got some bad news. I feel for her. She really loves the place."

"She does," Mr. Burke agreed.

"But she doesn't have the history with it that I do." Dylan wanted the man to like him. He had, long ago. Any time Mr. Burke had been in his backyard, trimming the bushes or setting up the sprinkler to water the lawn, he and Dee had waved at him and yelled hello, and Mr. Burke had waved back. Now and again—not that often, but enough to stick in his memory—he and his wife, a woman with a loud laugh and a perpetual bright red manicure, had come over to eat grilled steaks and his grandma's scalloped potatoes while telling stories about their daughter at college.

"What do you mean?"

"Mr. Burke, do you remember—"

"Now why do you keep calling me that?" the man interrupted with cantankerous good humor. "I just told you to call me Harry."

"I'm getting to that," Dylan said. "You were friends with the people you bought this place from."

"Sure. Jerry and Leona Williams. Sometimes I wish we'd spent more time with them."

"I'm their grandson." Saying this made him feel strangely exposed. "My sister Dee and I spent a few summers here."

Mr. Burke stared at him, no doubt reconciling Dylan's adult self with an image of the boy he'd been.

Then he smacked his hand down on the cushy arm of the chair. "I knew it! I knew I recognized you. There was something about you I just liked. Dylan Cain."

He gave an awkward laugh. "Yeah, it's me."

"Some things I can remember clear as a bell. Like you and your sister with those sparklers on the Fourth of July." The memory hit Dylan like an actual stray spark on bare skin. He hadn't thought of that, himself, in twenty-five years. Him lighting three sparklers at once. Dee trying to twirl hers like a baton.

"I didn't remember your names," Mr. Burke said. "My memory isn't what it used to be."

"It's probably as good as mine is," Dylan said honestly. "I, um...I heard about your wife. I'm so sorry for your loss."

"Thank you." Mr. Burke cleared his throat.

Dylan's heart wrenched. "I remember she used to leave the gate to the backyard open so we could go jump in those piles of maple leaves."

Mr. Burke laughed. "I told her not to do that, because I had to rake them all up again later."

This hadn't occurred to Dylan. "That does sound annoying."

"I think of a lot of things that annoyed me, like...oh, she'd turn the thermostat way up, and...she'd repeat herself a lot. I'd cut her off and say, 'Yeah, you told me.'" Dylan had meant to suggest that he and Dee had been annoying, not Mrs. Burke, but the conversation had turned quickly to the older man's regrets.

"If I could have it back now..." Mr. Burke shook his head. "She could tell me a story about one of the girls at the office for the third time, and the heat would be cranked up to eighty, and I'd just sit here in my undershirt with a big dumb smile on my face."

Wow. Dylan tried to imagine that. Missing someone so much you miss the annoying parts.

That's how Dad felt.

That's how he still feels. The realization

struck him to the core. Why hadn't his dad explained it, though?

Because he hadn't wanted to make his motherless children even sadder, no doubt. He could've talked more about it now that Dylan was an adult, but who was Dylan to judge? He wasn't exactly great at talking about private things, himself. Maybe he'd gotten that from his dad, come to think of it.

And his father wasn't going to be around forever, either. Would Dylan have regrets of his own, someday?

"Didn't mean to bring you down," Mr. Burke said, and Dylan realized he hadn't even responded.

"No, you didn't," he said quickly.

"Well, Judy really was fond of you and your sister. I'm sorry, what was her name again?"

"Deidre. Everyone called her Dee."

"That's right, that's right." Mr. Burke nodded. "How is she doing? Does she still live around here?"

"Yeah, she's still in Denver. She's doing great. She's married, and she's got two boys."

"Oh, that's nice," Mr. Burke said with genuine pleasure.

"She's the one who told me this place was for sale. She likes the idea of her boys spending time here."

Mr. Burke nodded slowly. "I take it you've done pretty well for yourself, Dylan."

"I have."

"Well, that's a fine thing. I'm glad to hear

it." He leaned back in his chair. "You could probably get a much nicer house than that cabin."

"It depends on your definition of 'nice.'"

"That's true." Mr. Burke fixed him in his gaze. "But listen. Girls like Paige don't come along every day."

Dylan felt like the man could see right through him. "She's great."

"Yes. She is."

Mr. Burke got out of the recliner, with some difficulty. Dylan got to his feet and pretended not to notice that it took the older man longer to do so.

"It's good to talk to you," Mr. Burke said, proffering his hand, and Dylan shook it. "We'll be in touch."

chapter twenty-one

Paige stood outside the bridal shop, *Love and Lace.* She'd beat Jessica there by ten minutes and counting. This was new. Super-organized Jessica arrived five minutes early to everything, which had been one of the reasons Paige hadn't wanted to be late.

The wait gave Paige a chance to process what had happened. It hadn't only been the kisses...although, oh my goodness, who would've guessed a banker could kiss like that? The way he'd looked at her, the way he'd said she'd been one of the best parts of his life, and that he wished she could have the cabin...in every way, he'd overwhelmed her. It had melted her like gold and made her into something new.

A car door slammed, shaking her out of her reverie. Jessica went around to the passenger side of her car to extract the white floofy dress, encased in clear plastic. Paige trotted over to her.

"Sorry I'm late," Jessica said, a bit breathless, as she gathered up the garment that appeared to be larger than she was. "My family's in town, and the time got away from me."

"They came up from San Antonio?"

"Yeah." Jessica slammed the car door shut and rearranged her bundle in her arms. "My mom, my stepdad, and my sister. They took me to a concert last night and my mom made a big breakfast this morning. I think they're trying to keep me too busy to feel sad."

It sounded like a good strategy. "I'm so glad they could come see you," Paige said as they walked back to the shop. Jessica's family had always been very involved, and right now, that sounded like a very good thing. "Here, I'll take that." She reached for the dress. It would be easier for her to carry since she was taller.

"You don't need to."

"I insist. Maid of honor duties."

Jessica handed it over. "You're not a maid of honor any more. That's kind of the whole point of this."

"I still have plenty of honor," Paige teased. "No, I'm a bridesmaid until you fire me. Maybe your wedding's just a little further in the future."

Jessica looked at her askance. "You're assuming I ever trust a man again, ever."

"You will." Paige hoped so, anyway. She hated to think of her friend swearing them off forever. Some men were wonderful. Of course, given the morning she'd shared with Dylan, she was biased.

She couldn't tell Jessica about that today. The timing would be terrible.

Jessica held the door open for Paige, who had to smush the dress a little to make sure it didn't snag on the door. What was it made of, cotton candy?

They stepped into a little world of ivory and white, with a chandelier hanging from the ceiling and a few tufted ottomans. For all of her daydreaming, Paige had never spent much time imagining her own future wedding, the way many young girls and grown women did, even before there was a groom in the picture.

A lavish wedding that cost tens of thousands of dollars wouldn't be for her. She didn't judge; she just wasn't a formal person, herself. But for the first time, she could imagine the pleasure of planning a sweet little ceremony. Ordering flowers for a bouquet. Sending hand-written invitations to a handful of friends and family members. Choosing a venue—somewhere outside, maybe. She and Dylan would both like that...

Good heavens. Why did that pop into her head? They'd only kissed for the first time. One kiss didn't lead to marriage. Life wasn't a fairy tale.

And Jessica hadn't gotten her storybook ending. She was here for her friend, and she needed to stay focused on her mission. Since Paige already had Jessica's gown in hand, she went up to the counter and told the sales associate at the cash register, "My friend needs to return this dress."

"I'm sorry," the woman said. "We have a no-returns policy."

Behind her, Jessica looked like a sad little girl. "Okay," she said quietly.

No, no, no. They couldn't give up that easily. Paige said, "She's never worn it."

The woman shook her head. "No offense. But you know how many times I hear that? Brides walk down the aisle, and the next day, they want to return the dress. If we had returns, we'd be out of business in a month."

"Okay, I get that. But she didn't walk down the aisle. And I can prove it to you." Paige rifled through her purse. "Here!" She pulled out a thick, slightly bent-up ivory envelope and thrust it at the cashier. "That's her invitation. Take a look at the date. Still in the future."

As the woman inspected it, Jessica asked, "Why do you still have that?"

"In case you wanted to do, you know, the ritual burning thing," Paige said. She turned back to the sales associate. "See?"

"You've got a point." Her gaze flicked to Jessica with a measure of sympathy. "What did he do?"

Jessica stared at the floor. "I don't want to talk about it."

The woman nodded slowly. "Now I'm convinced. Do you happen to have the credit card you used?"

After Jessica and Paige had stepped out of the doors of the shop, Jessica said, "Oh, my gosh. Thank you. You saved me two thousand dollars."

Paige stopped in her tracks. "Seriously?"

"That's normal for a wedding gown," Jessica defended herself.

"Oh, I'm sure," Paige said quickly. It made her feel a lot better about the money she spent on sewing, though.

Her phone vibrated in a text alert. She looked down. It was from Dylan. *Hey, I'll stop by tonight, okay?*

He'd never texted her before. And now he was doing it even though they'd just seen one another. A smile spread across her face. She texted back, *Sounds good*, and added a heart emoji. Wait. Was that over the top?

"Who are you texting with?" Jessica asked.

"Uh, no one."

Jessica peered over her shoulder. Paige pulled the phone close to her and turned away.

"Is that from who I think it is?" Jessica demanded. *Rats.* Paige hadn't moved fast enough. Her friend looked her in the eye. "You're texting now?"

"Yeah."

"How long has this been going on?"

She couldn't hide anything from Jessica for long, so she might as well fess up. "I invited him over for muffins this morning, and he kissed me."

Jessica's brown eyes got even wider. "Those must've been some good muffins!"

"I burned them."

She shook her head. "That's my girl." No doubt she was recalling the uncooked spaghetti flambé. "I could tell on Halloween he liked you. Obviously. But why didn't you tell me right away about the kissing?"

"You know." Paige gestured vaguely back toward the bridal shop.

"Just because I'm sad doesn't mean I can't be happy for you. I can multitask. What did he *say* before he kissed you? I want details!"

"Um, that...hanging out with me was one of the best things in his life, and that if I did get the money for the cabin, he wouldn't try to outbid me." Jessica gave her a little shove. "Hey," Paige protested mildly.

"I can't believe you didn't tell me!"

Paige blushed. "He did say I could tell you I had a new boyfriend."

Jessica squealed. "He called himself your boyfriend! This is serious. And you could get that cabin!"

"I can't." She hadn't even had the chance to tell Jessica about this yet. "You know how I met with my agent?"

"Yeah...?"

"It got rejected again. My agent's waiting to

hear from one last place, and then she's giving up on me."

"What?" Paige had expected her to look sympathetic. Instead, she looked incensed. "What is she thinking?" She grabbed Paige's arm. "You listen to me. She's wrong. You are the best kids' writer around."

"Thank you. I appreciate that."

Jessica frowned. "Maybe you'll get the money another way." When Paige shook her head, she said, "Hey, aren't you supposed to be Ms. Positive? Something could still happen."

"Thanks. I don't think so, though."

"You never know." Jessica gave her a hug, and Paige squeezed her back. "Hang in there."

Once Paige got into her car, she looked at her phone again. No response. Well, sure. He was busy. The busiest person she knew, honestly. He wasn't sitting around waiting for her...

Wiggly dots appeared on her screen, a delightful indication that he was texting her back. And then they stopped. What the heck? He'd been going to say something, and then he'd changed his mind?

A couple more wiggly dots, and then no words: just a heart emoji.

Yay.

That night, at her kitchen table, Paige was staring at her phone again. This time, she was trying to choose a song to assign to Dylan's phone number. She'd been working ahead on a lesson plan, but had gotten engrossed with this instead. Sometimes Paige felt like her brain had only had two modes: indifference and complete obsession. She tried out about two dozen different songs.

The doorbell rang and she almost jumped out of her skin, tossing the phone into the air. She fumbled to catch it before it smacked down on the table. Laughing at her own foolishness, she went to let Dylan in. "Hey," she greeted him.

"Hey there." Affection warmed his voice. She could've wrapped up in it like a blanket. "You sound like you're in a good mood."

"I am, actually."

As he stepped inside, he frowned. "It's cold in here."

"I know. It's drafty." She wasn't wearing a giant wool cardigan over her dress, and leggings beneath it, for nothing. "Good thing you're going to replace the windows. I'll build a fire."

"Mm, you better not do that," he warned her, striding over to the hearth as though he owned it already. It surprised her that she didn't resent it. "You're not safe around hot things."

"I'll have you know I've built a million fires in there without burning the place down."

"A million?" He crouched down and grabbed split logs from the firewood rack.

"Yes. I counted."

Over his shoulder, he gave her a teasing grin. "Hmm. And they let you teach math at that school?" He arranged the logs in an overlapping square and found the kindling in the basket. After balling up several pages of newspaper and putting them in the center of the logs, he constructed a little pyramid of fatwood over it. Then he struck a match and set fire to the newspaper. He straightened as the kindling sparked.

"You do have impressive technique," she admitted.

"We don't want you getting cold." He settled in one of the armchairs. "How did things go with the wedding gown?"

"Great!" She sat down opposite him. It seemed so natural and comfortable, sitting with him by a cozy fire. As if it were old habit. "I talked them into letting Jessica return it."

"Doesn't surprise me. You're very persuasive."

The way he said it was definitely flirty, and she loved it. "That's a very nice compliment." He'd said a lot of nice things about her in the past couple of weeks. "That gives me an idea. I should do a unit on compliments."

"Excuse me?"

"Oh, sorry." Sometimes her train of thought took some hairpin turns. "I was trying to think of a weekly lesson plan around

World Kindness Day. You know, on November thirteenth?"

"My favorite holiday," he deadpanned.

"It actually is one of my favorites! Last year I did two random acts of kindness for it."

"What did you do?"

"I put extra quarters in an expired parking meter, and I gave blood."

He raised his eyebrows. "That's above and beyond."

"They give you free juice. It's win-win," she quipped. "But anyway, I wanted to do something with the kids for Kindness Day. We could learn new words that are compliments. Positive adjectives, like *persuasive*."

"That might be a tough one for first graders," Dylan pointed out.

"Not for a couple of them, but yeah," Paige agreed. "We could do funny." Hmm, that one applied to him. She gave him a look. "Or *handsome*."

"Or *beautiful,* or *creative,*" he suggested. Her spirits lifted even higher, light as a balloon. He said, "Hey, did you hear back from that agent?"

That brought her back down closer to earth. "No."

"That's rude."

She curled up in the armchair, wrapping her arms around her knees. "I figure she's either going to call me and tell me not to contact her again, or just not email back forever."

"Then send the story to a new agent."

Huh. She hadn't even considered that. It was probably a better alternative than the one she'd had in mind, which had been to delete the file, throw the journal away, and get a new one to start over.

"Maybe I will," she said. "So what's your week going to be like?"

"I wanted to talk to you about that." The seriousness in his voice set off warning bells in her head, as if he were about to say, *Let's just be friends.* "I'm heading out tomorrow to New York for a few days, but after I'm back, we should go out again."

Whew. "I'd like that. What's in New York?"

"A horrible conference," he said, and then added quickly, "but I'm not complaining."

She laughed. "I've never been to New York. Do you like it?"

He shrugged. "I probably would if I wasn't working. I'll be back on Thursday. Maybe we could go out that night."

"You'll be tired from your trip. Wouldn't Friday be better?"

"I have a family thing on Friday...but you might be going to that, too. A talent show? Connor's in it."

"Oh, yeah, I forgot! I'll be there." She'd seen a list of all the kids' acts. "He's going to do kung fu. That's going to be awesome."

Dylan leaned in closer. "He's doing what now?"

"Kung fu," she repeated. "How long has he been taking lessons?"

His eyes widened. "Zero days."

"What?"

"He's never taken a lesson. He doesn't know kung fu."

Paige laughed at the dismay in his voice. "Maybe he's a natural or something?"

He rubbed the bridge of his nose. "Oh, man. I better warn Dee."

"I wouldn't worry about it," she said. "They're kids. Whatever he does will be fine. But what do you want to do Thursday night?"

"Dinner, and maybe that art crawl thing they have downtown?"

Interesting. "Do you like art?"

"Uhh, maybe?" He sounded so uncertain that she had to laugh again. "I've never done it before. I thought you might like it."

"I do, actually. And I haven't been in for-ever." It touched her that he'd gone to the trouble of coming up with something she'd enjoy. She'd only been away from him for a matter of hours. He must've started thinking of their next date immediately. She was so used to preparing and arranging things for her classroom and for her own life that it felt nice to have someone else make a plan.

"Then it's a date. Write it on your calendar, Paige." He said her name a lot, as though he liked the sound of it. She did, when he was the one saying it.

"I will." The fire gave a loud crackle, blazing brightly now.

When it had burned down to glowing

embers, they were still talking. They'd only stopped once, to make popcorn. Paige had told him about all kinds of work stuff, including the next parent-teacher conferences and some of the funniest ones she'd had in the past, and the semester in college when she'd actually forgotten she'd signed up for beginning astronomy and had managed to drop it just in time before the class would've counted toward her grade point average, which had led to nonstop jokes about her being spacey for the rest of the year. Dylan had pointed out that he'd had a nightmare of a forgotten college course often, but for her, it had actually been true.

She didn't know how she'd gotten on that topic, but it had gotten Dylan talking about the Griffith Observatory, which he'd visited on spring break in college once, taking a Greyhound bus to Los Angeles because he'd never seen the ocean before, and how he'd suggested taking a vacation to L.A. with his ex-girlfriend Lauren, but they'd kept putting it off. Paige told him about going to Disneyland with her parents, and how she wanted to go back someday.

They'd talked long enough that she felt comfortable asking, "What was your mom like? You must've heard about her from other people."

He still looked relaxed. "My dad didn't talk about her at all. But my sister and my grandma did. Mom worked part-time for a charity, a conservation foundation. My dad was in insurance." He stared at the flames thoughtfully. "Dee says she loved taking long walks."

"She sounds really special."

"I remember a few things. Like…cuddling with her on the couch, with her reading me a book.—I was barely three," he added quickly.

"I think it's great that you remember."

"And I remember sitting next to her at church. Her singing."

Paige's heart went out to the innocent little boy he'd been. "I didn't know you went to church."

"We stopped after she died." He gave her a curious look. "Do you?"

"I still go with my parents on most Sundays."

They talked for a long time. When she gave a huge yawn, Dylan said, "I should really get going."

She looked up at the clock. "I should get to *bed*."

"You should," he agreed, getting up and moving to the door. "Or you'll sleep right through the sunrise in the morning."

At the door, she said, "I'll miss you."

He leaned forward and kissed her. Warmth spread through her, all the way down to her toes.

"Yeah," he said. "I'll miss you, too."

chapter twenty-two

On Monday morning, Dylan put his carry-on suitcase in the car and left long before he needed to head to the airport. He drove to his father's townhouse first.

His dad, in sweatpants and a sweatshirt, opened the door. "Dylan." He frowned. "Is something wrong?"

Dylan winced inwardly. The question only proved how rarely he visited his dad. "No, no. I was stopping by to say hey. Unless it's a bad time."

"No, this is fine." His father waved him inside. From the TV, sports announcers blustered. "Hang on, let me find the remote." He went around the sofa and dug between the cushions. "There we go." When he muted the program, the announcers still gesticulated, making the silence even more dramatic. "You want a coffee? Or something to eat? I've got some bagels."

"No, I'm fine." Dylan sat down and his father followed suit.

An empty water glass sat on the table, and a flattened shipping box leaned against a wall, but overall, the room was neater than Dylan would've expected. The house where he and Dee had grown up had always been a mess. On the mantel above the gas fireplace of faux stone, a row of framed pictures caught Dylan's eye. Two were old, and it took him a moment to identify them: his father and mother on their wedding day, and Dee as a little girl, sitting on a couch holding a baby Dylan. He'd never seen those before. They sat next to Connor's and Noah's school pictures. Noah smiled angelically, and Connor looked like he was up to something.

"It's getting chilly outside," his dad said. "I heard high of forty-five."

"Yeah, that's about what it felt like," Dylan said.

"How's work? Busy as ever?"

Dylan never wanted to discuss work again. He was sick of hearing himself talk about it. Everyone else probably was, too, even if they asked about it to be polite. Instead, he cut to the chase. "The cabin's for sale. Grandma and Grandpa's."

"Yeah, Dee told me. And then I saw it in the newspaper the other day."

"Do you still read the entire newspaper?" His father had always done this, every day, when Dylan was growing up: the main stories and the weather in the morning, and everything else in the evening, including advertisements and obituaries.

"I do. I've got more time than ever," his dad said with forced good humor.

He's lonely. Lonely and bored.

His father went on to say, "I thought about buying the place, if you can believe it. But I don't need to be taking on a new mortgage, at my age. And it would need a lot of upkeep. But your mom loved growing up there."

"I'm going to buy it."

His dad straightened, clearly taken aback. "Really? I thought you loved living downtown."

"It's convenient," Dylan said. That was a different thing than loving it.

"Does Dee know? Oh, you must've told her."

Dylan didn't know how to address the plain acknowledgement that he was much closer to his sister than to his dad. "Yeah. She likes the idea of the boys spending time there."

"I'll bet." His father nodded slowly. "I almost went to the open house." Dylan recalled the confusion of that day, right after his amazing date with Paige, and her outrage at the idea of him buying it. He couldn't imagine how much stranger that day would've been if his dad had turned up, too.

"That's where I proposed to your mother. Right in that living room."

Dylan straightened in surprise. "I never knew that."

"Doesn't even seem like that long time ago. It was before Sunday dinner. Leona was in the kitchen, and Jerry was out back grilling steaks. I'd been trying to get up the courage for a while, and I blurted it out." He chuckled. "I see all these romantic ways to propose now, on the internet. I sure didn't do a good job."

"You must've done all right. She said yes."

"Yeah, I'd say I did all right." He shook his head. "For a long time, I hardly wanted to go over there. When I took you kids, I didn't want to stay long. But now...it would be something to stand in that house again."

"It was for me." The awareness of a missed opportunity was too strong for Dylan to ignore. He could've told his father sooner. His dad could've gone with him when he went over there for the inspection. They would've discussed possible projects and needed repairs. That was the kind of experience fathers and sons shared, the kind of thing that was so ordinary, but that they enjoyed and remembered later. Regret gave him a hollow feeling inside.

"I have a lot of good memories of that place," his father said. "Time can go by so fast."

"Now isn't a bad time, though," Dylan ventured. "You've got your grandkids."

"Those boys are the light of my life. I don't know if you'll ever get married and start a family—I know for you, it's all about career—

but if you did have kids, I'd be a good grandpa for them, too."

"I know you would." Dylan felt a small measure of relief at saying something nice to his father.

"It's just too bad I wasn't that way with you, huh?"

"Uh." Dylan had a strong urge to run from this conversation—even though, for years, he'd been tempted to have it.

He'd imagined asking his father why he couldn't have paid more attention to them when he was growing up. Why couldn't he act happier about good report cards? Why had he relied on other parents to drive Dylan to cross-country meets so he could run his heart out and collapse at the end in a mess of sweat and snot, with no mother or father to cheer for him? Why couldn't his father even act like he was interested when Dylan had told him about a victory afterward?

"There's a lot I would do over," his father said.

For so long, Dylan had resented these things. But now, seeing his lonely dad sitting on the couch, he almost felt petty for holding on to that bitterness.

His dad went on to say, "Your mom died, and I was just going through the motions. I thought my life was over. If I hadn't had you kids relying on me..." He shook his head, not finishing the thought, but the words sent a chill through Dylan. "And now I know that some of the best parts of my life were still happening. Like you growing up."

Dylan's heart cracked open. *The best parts of my life.* To his horror, he felt dangerously close to tears.

He cleared his throat. "I don't remember Mom that much, but I know you really loved her."

"She was a wonderful woman. She could always look on the sunny side, you know? But she also kept me in line." *Sounds like someone I know.* The thought rocked him. "Maybe someday you'll fall in love. Then you'll know what I'm talking about."

"I think I might." He didn't even know if he was responding to the first statement or the second one.

Curiosity flitted across his father's features, but he only nodded. "Well, first things first. When do you move in?"

Dylan welcomed having a normal, factual question to answer. "It's not a done deal yet. The woman renting it had until this Friday to get the money to buy it, but it didn't work out. I think we'll close pretty soon, and it won't take me long to move." His clutter-free lifestyle, born more out of joyless workaholism than an actual style choice, would serve him well in this case at least. "You're right about the upkeep. Maybe after I move in, you can come over and give me advice about some of the repairs."

His father's face brightened. "I'd be happy to."

"It's going to take a lot to really get it in shape."

"Well, you've never been afraid of hard work."

The compliment hit home. His father did value him...and love him. He'd been a grieving widower, and he'd done the best he could.

Dylan said, "Maybe we could all have Christmas there again this year."

"Wow. That would be something."

"I know, right? You can help me put up Christmas lights."

"You want to do that?" It was no wonder his father sounded surprised. Last Christmas, Dylan had been talking about how he didn't decorate, because he'd just have to take it all down again.

"Yeah. Grandma and Grandpa always did." And Paige had gone all-out for Halloween. Christmas lights were the least he could do.

His father looked happier than Dylan had seen him in a very long time. "I'd like that."

A deep hurt inside Dylan was healing. It had been there for so long that he'd been used to it, but now he felt it lessening.

"We're going to have a lot more good times in that house."

His dad nodded. "I think we will."

Late that afternoon, people jammed the lobby of the big convention hotel in New York. Dylan had been in line for ten minutes waiting to check in. The couple at the front desk argued with the hotel employee. "I don't understand," the man was saying. "We made a reservation here."

Someone bumped into Dylan from behind and kept moving without an apology. Dylan felt his blood pressure rise. The woman said, "That's the other Dreighton Hotel, in the Theater District."

"The Theater District?" the woman wailed. "But we're here for the doll collector convention!"

Dylan did feel sorry for them. Still, as they got help from the woman at the front desk about how to get to the other Dreighton, and then advice on how to find a closer hotel room for the following night, Dylan felt sorry for himself, too.

He was trying to break that habit, thanks to Paige. But Paige was the reason this all seemed even more tedious than usual. He could've been spending time with her. Instead he was looking forward to nothing better than getting to his room, eating a mediocre thirty-some-dollar room service meal, and catching up on the hundred or so emails he'd gotten since Friday afternoon. Okay, so he would've had to deal with those emails if he'd been back in Denver, too, but he would've also had time to see Paige.

His phone vibrated, indicating a text message, and he looked down, expecting it to be her. Instead, it was Paul, telling him the guy they'd lined up to replace the windows at the cabin had abruptly decided to move out of state. Dylan texted back that it wasn't a big deal. He could find another contractor. And in the meantime, sure, the place was drafty, but he could build more fires.

Finally, he got his turn at the front desk and checked in. "Top floor," the woman mentioned, handing him his hotel key. He'd always like to be as high up as possible. The first time he'd been to this conference, in fact, had been his first time in New York, though he hadn't let on about that to Mark or anyone else. He'd been secretly excited to look out of his hotel window at the Manhattan skyline.

He tried to tell himself now that he was lucky, and should appreciate it. When he'd been in college, he would've done almost anything for this kind of job. That's what he should've explained to Paige before, when she'd questioned whether it was even worth it.

There was a line to get on the elevators. As it happened, the top floor was the worst choice.

"Dylan?"

He started at the familiar feminine voice. Who...? And then he saw his ex-girlfriend

Lauren, of all people, smiling and walking up to him.

She said, "Hey, stranger!" and went right in for the hug. Standard for an amicable breakup, he imagined, and theirs had been as amicable as could be. He returned her embrace, catching the familiar light scent of her expensive perfume—her signature fragrance, she'd always called it. It brought back a rush of memories. Late nights at the office. Binge-watching a particular television drama at her apartment. It almost disoriented him.

"How are you?" He hadn't even thought about running into her here, but he should've expected it. "You look great." The compliment, also, was standard. More than that, it was true. New York had apparently agreed with her, because she looked even more glamorous, like a movie version of herself: slimmer, in a gray sleeveless dress, her brown hair longer, shiny and smooth.

"So do *you*." The returned compliment sounded more than obligatory. "Are you still running?"

"Sometimes," he said. "How are things at Halcyon?"

Her eyes twinkled. "Oh, you mean the firm where I just made VP?"

"Congratulations," he said, meaning it. He of all people knew it couldn't have been easy. "You beat me."

She gave a fake-modest shrug. "Not by

much, I'm sure. Are you going to that cocktail thing tonight? It would be great to catch up."

"Oh, right." Dylan wavered. He'd been planning to attend, even if he hadn't exactly been looking forward to it. The whole affair would be a lot more comfortable with Lauren's familiar presence, too. Logically, he should go.

Instead, what came out of his mouth was, "I don't think so. I've got too much to catch up on."

"Oh, I get it. It never ends, right?" She gave a graceful wave to someone across the lobby and then touched Dylan lightly on the upper arm. "I'll see you around!"

"Yeah. Good to see you." The elevator doors opened and he squeezed on.

Why had he backed out of the cocktail hour? It wasn't only other firms attending the conference. There were also representatives from dozens, maybe hundreds of companies who were trying to learn more about investments, mergers, and acquisitions. The "social" gatherings were where business got done: conversations that led to follow-up emails the week after and then, sometimes, eventually, a deal.

But he suspected Paige wouldn't like it if she found out he'd run into his ex here. And it wasn't even an *if,* he realized. He was going to tell her, because the alternative was him hiding, or at least glossing over, the reality of his life. At work and elsewhere, he'd gotten good at doing that, but he didn't want to do it with her.

He'd told her things he'd never told Lauren, even after over a year of not only dating but also working long hours together at Hammersmith. And Lauren was a nice person, particularly by their profession's standards. But she'd never broken down his walls—maybe because she'd kept her own intact.

Paige had flitted into his life and demolished his walls, without even trying, it seemed, like some kind of superpowered butterfly.

He'd visited her the night before, right after kissing her that morning. There were rules about that kind of thing, he knew. After a date, you waited two days before calling or texting, or maybe three, depending on who you asked.

But he'd ignored the rules. They'd talked for hours the other night in front of a fire. Not watching TV. Not fiddling with their phones. Just talking. He couldn't explain why it was so easy with her, or so much fun.

Dylan reached the top floor, found room 4343, and locked the door behind him. With a huge sense of relief, he took off his jacket, tie, dress shirt, shoes, and socks, but he left his tee shirt and pants on because he was getting room service. Without looking at the menu, he called and ordered the grilled chicken sandwich and fries. Every hotel served some variation of that. Then he flopped on his back on the huge bed and picked up his phone to see if Paige had maybe texted him.

She had. *Let me know when you get there! I miss you already.*

He typed a quick text, a boring one, really—*I'm at the hotel. How are you?*—and hit *send.*

She didn't text back right away. Spending the evening alone struck him as a little depressing. His stomach growled. He couldn't remember the last time he'd been so hungry.

chapter twenty-three

In the second bedroom, her sewing room, Paige packed up fabric and craft supplies. She'd stored all kinds of things in there: books, old journals, photographs, and lesson plans. It was Wednesday night, and Friday was her last chance to make an offer on the cabin. Clearly, that wasn't going to happen.

She'd have to go to Walmart to get more big plastic tubs. How had she accumulated so much stuff in the time she'd rented this place? She couldn't take all of this with her. Some of it would wind up in the trash. Her filing cabinet held a horrifying number of half-written stories. It was a wonder she ever finished anything. She found the journal with the original drafts of the first Muffy and Kerfuffle stories, the ones she'd written so quickly and with so much joy. The ones that nobody liked. She'd written the date at the top of the first page: almost two years ago.

Then she came across fabric she'd bought

specifically for a tablecloth for the kitchen table. It wasn't hers any more, and now she knew it had never truly been. Jessica would no longer come over and sit at that table to prepare lesson plans or grade homework with her. In another box, she found squares of fabric she'd cut out to make a quilt.

So many incomplete projects. She needed to start looking for apartments. This had all been too good to last.

She had a lot to be grateful for. Her new relationship with Dylan, for one thing. Who knew where that would lead, though? She'd been happy about new boyfriends before, and they'd only disappointed her in the end. She pulled out a shopping bag filled with embroidery floss and canvas fitted on a hoop. When she flipped it over, she saw the cross-stitched words, almost complete: CABIN SWEET CABI

Her vision blurred with tears. *This was the best time of my life, and now it's over.* She'd somehow imagined that her life would get better and better. Why had she believed that?

Ugh. Sorrow tightened her throat. She couldn't go to Walmart in this state. She needed to get hold of herself.

Maybe her parents had extra bins. She walked to the bathroom, blew her nose, splashed water on her hot face, and blotted it with a towel. Then she found her phone and dialed. "Hi, Mom?"

In less than an hour, her parents came over, hugged her, and said all the right things.

"Changes are always hard," her mom said, and her dad added, "It's always darkest before the dawn." They'd brought more bins.

And more fabric. "Here, honey, before I forget. See if you like this heart print." Paige's mom pulled it out of her purse.

"It's cute," Paige admitted. "But I need help getting rid of fabric, not getting more."

"I told you. You don't have to get rid of it," her mom insisted. "We can store it at our house."

Paige's dad gave her a conspiratorial grin. "Sure, why not? I only have twelve bins of fabric in the basement right now."

"You're exaggerating!" her mom said.

Paige knew for a fact that he wasn't. Their banter cheered her up even more. "I think three will be enough."

"Let me help you pack it," her mom suggested. "If we fold it, we can fit more in there."

"All right. It's in the guest bedroom." Paige carried the storage bins in there, her parents following behind her. After she plunked down the bins, she opened the closet door. Grocery bags, both paper and plastic, lined the shelves and the floor, along with even less organized piles of brightly printed fabrics.

"Oh, my. You do have a pretty good stash," her mom murmured, clearly proud. She took out one of the grocery sacks and sat down on the floor next to an empty storage bin. Paige joined her, folding up wads and remnants of material.

"I still think it's terrible that you have to move out," her mom said. "Is it even legal? To not give you more notice?"

"It's legal," Paige said. She weighed her next words. She hadn't told her parents about Dylan yet. He felt far away, although they'd been together the night before, and the night before that. "The guy who's probably going to buy the place is really nice. He spent time here as a kid."

"Huh," her dad said thoughtfully.

Her mom was less charitable. "Well that doesn't mean that he can waltz back here and take over the place."

"Since he's got the money to buy it, it does mean that. Without literal waltzing."

As if on cue, classical music sounded from the other room. Paige looked to her father. "Is that your phone?"

"No, hon, I think it might be yours."

She trotted out to the living room to find it, picked up the phone—and took in a quick breath. *Alexis.*

She'd set up that ringtone several months ago, when she'd been filled with anticipation. Sadly, her agent had never called. Not even once. She seemed to believe that rejection was best communicated through email, and Paige couldn't really say she was wrong.

Why was she calling now? Paige picked up as she strode back to the room where her parents were, saying more loudly than necessary, "Hi, Alexis." Her parents both perked up, listening.

Ugh, was this a mistake, letting them know who she was talking to? Alexis might've called to tell Paige personally just how stupid *Log Cabin Princess* was, and how she'd better not bother her with any more of her worthless projects, ever again.

"Paige, how are you?" Alexis asked. "I have some news."

She was definitely not mad. *Oh my gosh, oh my gosh.* Paige's legs suddenly felt watery and she leaned against the wall. "News? About what?" Maybe this wasn't what she hoped. Maybe Alexis was giving up the agent life and moving to Bora Bora. Really, it could be anything.

"I sent your latest story right to the editor at Vandergast. The one who'd been a little interested in Mopsy and Kerfuffle." It was *Muffy* and Kerfuffle, but Paige saw no reason to correct her. "I caught her at the right time, and she's making you an offer on *Log Cabin Princess.*"

Making you an offer. Did that mean...?

Yes! They were going to publish the book!

Paige's heartbeat went crazy. She could hardly breathe. In a professional voice she barely recognized, she said, "Oh, that's wonderful to hear." Her parents stared at her, clearly desperate to know what was happening. Still in her super-professional voice, Paige asked, "Alexis, would you mind holding on a second?"

"That's fine," her agent said after the briefest of pauses. Paige set the phone face down on the nearby shelf. Then she ran over to her mom and grabbed her by the arms and made a high-pitched sound that wasn't completely human. "Yayyy!"

"What? What is it?" her mom demanded.

"I'm getting published," Paige hissed in a loud whisper, as if Alexis hadn't heard the piercing dolphin noise she'd just made.

Her mother's hand flew to her chest. "Oh, my goodness!" At the same time, her dad let out an uncharacteristically loud, "Yes!"

Paige scurried back to the phone and picked it up again. She cleared her throat and resumed her professional voice. "So they'll be sending...something for me to sign?"

"We'll have the official agreement in a week or so." Alexis didn't comment on the outburst. "I'm emailing you the terms we discussed right now. Since you're a debut author"— Paige could hardly believe how much she loved the sound of *debut author*—"it's not going to be a huge advance, but this is a big break."

"Right, right," Paige said inanely, breathless.

"I'll let you go so you can take a look, and we can talk in the morning about any questions you have."

"Okay."

STACEY DONOVAN

"Well, congratulations," Alexis said. "Have a good night."

"You too," Paige said. "Thank you." She hung up and bounced up and down. "Oh my gosh, oh my gosh, oh my gosh!"

Her father chuckled. "Cheer up, kid," he joked. It was one of his old jokes with her, because even as a kid, she'd been excitable.

This was a whole new level, though. "I'm freaking out," she said. "I'm so happy I feel like I'm going to throw up."

"Take a breath," her mom suggested, smiling.

"She sent me an email! Let me look at it." Paige pulled it up on her phone and gasped. "Okay. There's the advance."

"I take it it's good," her dad said.

"It's like she said. It's not huge." The fact that she was getting an advance, period, stunned her. "But. Along with what I've saved…it's enough for the down payment for the cabin."

Her mother hugged her. "Oh, this is amazing. And at the very last minute, too."

"It's funny how those things work out," her dad said meaningfully. She knew he didn't think it was funny, or a coincidence, at all. He thought it was God's plan; a bona fide miracle.

Paige's joy got cut short with a sudden dose of reality. "I don't really have the money yet, though. Let alone the loan. I don't know how long it's going to take for them to send the check." It could be weeks. Hopefully not months.

Her parents exchanged glances. Then her mom nodded and turned back to Paige. "Honey, I know you don't want to take money from us. But this is different, because you know it's on its way. We can give you a loan. You'd be able to pay us right back in no time."

Her spirits lifted, but she still hesitated. "I hate to ask."

"You didn't," her dad pointed out, amused. When she didn't say anything, he put his hand on her shoulder. "Hey. That's what families are for."

"Okay," she agreed with relief. "Thank you!" She gave him a big hug. "I'm going to go over to Harry's right now." She paused. "I need to call Dylan first, though."

Her mom squinted. "Dylan?"

"Yes. The other person who wants to buy it?"

Her dad was shaking his head. "I don't know why you'd need to do that."

"I uh, he and I have gotten to know each other." Understatement of the year. She could feel her face flush. "I'm going to call from my bedroom," she added, which immediately made her feel like a teenager. Again, her parents exchanged glances. Okay. She could check "tell Mom and Dad I'm seeing someone" off her to-do list. They were clearly up to speed.

She went in the other room and called. He

didn't pick up. Then she remembered that the conference was over, but he had dinner with a client. He hadn't expected to be back until late. When she came back into the other room again, her parents were murmuring to one another, which they abruptly stopped as they looked up to see her.

Her mom asked, "Did you get hold of him, honey?"

"No." Should she wait until she talked to Dylan before telling Harry? Maybe. But what if she needed some kind of document or form that she didn't know about yet in order to make an offer? She didn't want to miss out due to a last-minute technicality. Should she ask Jessica for her advice? No, she didn't need to. Jessica would tell her not to hesitate.

"You better go tell Harry now," her dad encouraged her. "You wouldn't want to miss out on a chance of a lifetime because of poor communication."

"Yeah, okay," she said. Her dad knew more about these things than she did. Dylan had already given her his blessing to buy it. And like her parents said, the timing was incredible. She was *meant* to buy the place. "Uh...do you want to wait here?"

"Sure," her mom said, standing up. "But I think we'll stop packing."

Paige went over to Harry's. As soon as she stepped outside, the night air hit her skin, much colder than she'd expected. She had a vague sense of foreboding as she walked to his house, and she didn't know why.

Once she'd told him the news, though, she felt better. He congratulated her, gave her a hug, and told her a silly joke about reading a soup cookbook. She started to walk back, but then she stopped in her tracks to gaze at the cabin. It was the coziest, most charming, perfect home she'd ever known in her life. And she would own it. As practiced as she was in gratitude, this overwhelmed her. *I'm the luckiest person alive.*

Maybe she could text Dylan. It seemed like such big news for a text, though. Or even for a phone call.

He was getting into town tomorrow. It would be much better to tell him in person. She felt another twinge of misgiving, but pushed it aside. He'd be happy for her. And like he'd said, he could come over all the time. It was going to be fine.

This was meant to be.

chapter twenty-four

On Thursday morning Dylan got to the airport several hours early, the way he'd done on his first-ever business trip, when he'd been an inexperienced traveler and fearful of missing his flight. This was much different. He just wanted to get home.

The dinner with the prospective client the night before had turned into more or less a prolonged session of them grilling him. When he'd finally gotten back to his hotel room, he'd seen that Paige had called, though she hadn't left him a message. He'd considered calling back—it was much earlier in Denver than in New York—but he'd felt so brain-dead, he'd decided against it. He needed to see her in person.

At the ticket counter, he told the guy, "I'm on the 1261 to Denver at two-ten today, but I was wondering if you could get me on the earlier flight."

"Let's see." The guy typed on this keyboard. "Ehh, flight 1682 leaves at eleven-forty-one, but I've only got business class."

"Can I put the upgrade on a separate card?" Hammersmith Capital wouldn't cover it.

"Absolutely." The man took Dylan's debit card. After a couple more questions and more typing, he handed the card back along with a boarding pass. "Gate C1. Enjoy your flight."

He still had a little time. Maybe he should get Paige a souvenir. She'd never visited New York, after all. Shopping held a lot more appeal to him than going to the gate and answering emails about bar graphs and sub-ordinated debt.

He found a good-sized gift shop and scruti-nized his choices. The Big Apple-themed gifts might remind her of their time at the orchard. But no, she was a teacher; she probably had enough apple-themed gifts to last her a life-time. Tee shirts? Guessing her size struck him as a potential minefield, especially as clueless as he was about such things...and did she even wear tee shirts, ever? They were a hard no. A snow globe with the Manhattan skyline? Sure, that seemed safe.

Then he laid eyes on a gift with no New York tie-in whatsoever: a kitchen timer, shaped like a turquoise cartoon owl. *Yes.* This was perfect. She liked woodland creatures, and she burned things. He asked the cashier about wrapping it, and she pointed him to the gift bags. While he was at it, he bought a greeting card to tuck inside.

His spirits light, he breezed through security and found a seat near the gate. He wrote a personal message on the card, making it clear that the gift wasn't a criticism by telling her that coming over for muffins she'd burned had turned out to be the best breakfast he could remember. After a moment of hesitation, he signed it, *Love, Dylan.*

It wasn't too much. Not the same thing at all as saying *I love you,* which of course, wouldn't be true. It was way too early for that. Wasn't it?

Everything he was doing with Paige lately—telling her all about his life, coming to see her twice in one day, avoiding his friendly and not even overly flirtatious ex-girlfriend, buying a gift, the *Love, Dylan*—felt like going out on a limb. A limb much slimmer than the one Paige had clambered out on, at the orchard. A twig, really, for someone like him, who'd given up on putting his feelings out there around the same time that he'd stopped climbing trees.

But as he boarded the plane, he told himself it was okay to be crazy about Paige and to have spent basically his whole trip actively yearning for her. He sank back into the relative luxury of the business class airplane seat and thought, with satisfaction: *She's crazy about me, too.*

At around four o'clock, Dylan pulled up to the cabin, ready to surprise Paige, only to see that her yellow VW bug wasn't parked in the driveway. She'd gone on some errand after work, he supposed. Just in case, he went up to the front door and knocked, but it hardly surprised him when no one answered.

He hung the gift bag on the doorknob, liking the idea of her coming home to a surprise. It made him wonder when her birthday was, and he made a mental note to find out. Maybe he didn't celebrate National Rainbow Day or National Kindness Day, but he could celebrate her birthday, which would be close enough.

While he was there, he supposed he might as well stop in to talk to Mr. Burke about the window guy. When Mr. Burke opened the door, he said, "Come on in. I thought you might drop by to talk." That struck Dylan as odd, but then again, he'd visited before, so maybe Mr. Burke considered them friends now.

"Yeah, I did need to tell you about something. The guy who was going to replace the windows is apparently relocating or something. I'll have to find another contractor."

Mr. Burke peered at him for a few moments. Then he said, "That reminds me of a joke."

Dylan wasn't surprised. "Let's hear it."

"Why did the man quit his job after he turned invisible?" He gave Dylan a moment to guess. Dylan could think of many career drawbacks to being invisible, but he just shrugged. Harry said, "He couldn't see himself doing it any more."

Dylan smiled and nodded. Sometime, when Connor and Noah were visiting, Mr. Burke was going to wind up telling them jokes. He suspected Connor would love them.

The older man asked, "Why don't you sit down?"

"Sure." He didn't mind staying for a short time. Maybe they *were* friends. Dylan could imagine sharing a cup of coffee or a beer with the guy once in a while, now that they'd be neighbors, like his grandparents had done. He sat down on the couch.

Mr. Burke settled in his easy chair. "It's very kind of you to worry about the windows for Paige."

"Um..." What was he talking about? Dylan gave an awkward laugh. "She probably will visit sometimes, but I'm mostly getting them fixed to keep the heating bill down."

Mr. Burke tapped a finger against his lips a few times, as though pondering the workings of furnaces and vents. Then he said, "Paige is buying the house."

"But she... What?"

"I'm sorry if I'm not the right one to tell you, but I didn't know how to *not* tell you, if you follow my meaning. She, ah…well, she got some very good news from her agent."

Dylan sat stunned. *Good news from her agent.* The rabbit and squirrel stories? Or was it the new one? How could she not have told him? After all they'd talked about with one another, all they'd shared? When she'd gotten the money, she'd gone straight to Harry.

No, he'd missed a call from her, he remembered. But she could've left a message. She could've texted, and she hadn't.

"I can't believe she didn't talk to me about it first."

Mr. Burke gave him a sympathetic look. "You know that place means a lot to her."

It means a lot to me, too. He'd thought Paige was out of the running for it. She'd told him as much.

And so he'd told his father about buying the cabin, and they'd bonded over it, talking about the good times they'd share. She'd ruined that.

That wasn't even the worst of it. He'd believed they were closer than this. On the trip, he'd thought about her constantly, but when it came to a decision that would have a big effect on him, she'd barely thought about him at all.

"I'm sorry it's a shock," Mr. Burke said, filling the silence. "I'm sure once you talk to her, you'll feel better about it."

"Right." It came out more sarcastic than sincere. "You know what, I'm going to go."

"Well, all right." Mr. Burke got up again. "Come by any time. Don't be a stranger."

Dylan headed back toward his car parked in Paige's driveway. Pausing, he glanced back at the bright pink gift bag he'd hung from her front doorknob, containing not only a present but what could only be described as a heart-felt love note. He went back up the front walk, took it off the doorknob, and turned around. What would he ever do with a kitchen timer shaped like an owl? He couldn't seem to think clearly about any of this, his mind frozen in disappointment too thick for words or logic.

He'd almost reached his car when Paige drove up and parked directly behind him. For some reason, the fact that she'd blocked him in stoked his mood to anger. He stared at her as she got out.

"Dylan!" At the sight of him, standing there grimly with a gift bag in his hand, her bright smile wavered. "I didn't think you'd be back already," she said, walking up to him. "How was your trip?"

"Fine." He pointed at the vehicle. "I can't get out. Your car's in my way."

"But you don't want to leave. I just got here." Worry creased her brow. In a softer voice, she asked, "What's going on?"

"I talked to Harry."

"Oh!" Her eyes went wide. "He told you what happened?" Dylan nodded.

"Well, shoot," she said in a forced light tone. "I wanted to tell you myself."

"Why didn't you talk to me first?" The only reason he could think of was that she hadn't wanted to deal with whatever he had to say about it.

"I was going to text you, but then...I thought it would be better to tell you in person. Why don't you come inside?" She searched his face as though looking for some sign of agreeableness. "I've really missed you."

This tugged at his sympathy, but he resisted it. She'd completely disregarded his feelings. "I can't stay long. Why didn't you talk to me first?" he asked again.

"You were at that client dinner."

"You could've called later. You could've waited to talk to Harry. You had until tomorrow."

"I..." She shook her head. "I wanted to make sure I could still get it."

"Okay, well." He shrugged and looked away. "Congratulations, I guess."

"You know, you told me that if I had the money, you'd want me to buy it." For the first time, her tone took a combative edge.

"I said that when I didn't think you *would* have the money."

"So you didn't mean it?"

Now she was making him look like a jerk, and that was completely unfair. She was the one who'd disregarded his complicated feelings about the place. He wasn't going to stand around and complain that she didn't care about him as much as he cared about her, and demand to know why. That would be pathetic.

"Fine, you're right," he said.

She didn't seem to know how to respond. That had been his intention: to leave her with nothing else to argue. She tried a different tack, pointing at the gift bag in his hand. "What's that?"

"It's nothing." Then he took the card out and handed the bag to her. "Actually, take it. I guess it's a housewarming gift." It wasn't like he had any other use for it.

She looked from the card in his hand to the gift. Her eyes reflected pain and worry. "Please come in. I want to tell you all about what happened."

He had no desire to talk. "I'm feeling too weird about things. I'm going to go."

She cringed. He'd seen her look like this once before. When? Oh, yes— when he'd found himself in her journal, depicted as the bad guy. Shouldn't that have been a warning sign for him? He was such an idiot. How had he thought this was going to work out? Maybe all the times she'd been nice had been about getting what she wanted. Maybe she'd never stopped seeing him as a rival.

She said, "Okay. Well, maybe come by later?"

"I don't think so."

chapter twenty-five

Paige went inside the cabin—*her* cabin, her real home now—and sat down at the kitchen table. *What just happened?*

He'd broken up with her. He hadn't exactly said those words, but clearly, he had. She couldn't believe it.

Even though he'd only been gone a few days, she'd been so looking forward to seeing him again. She'd gone over it in her head: showing him the email she'd sent to her publisher—his writing, almost word for word—and telling him about getting the call from her agent. No, The Call, capitalized, the one every writer hoped for. It was one of the most exciting things that had ever happened to her, and the fact that she couldn't share it with him stripped it of its joy.

He hadn't even told her about his trip. Had something happened in New York that had put him on edge? Probably not. He'd been cheerful enough to buy her a present, after all.

She dug into the gift bag, took out a small object wrapped in tissue paper, and unrolled it. A turquoise plastic owl? It was cute... *Oh.* It was a kitchen timer.

Her heart broke a little. She loved it.

He'd taken the card back. What had it said? Maybe something funny, or something sweet; likely both. Paige's mom had raised her to never give a wrapped gift without an accompanying card. She said the wrapping wasn't "finished" without it. But what would her mom say about removing a card from a gift? He hadn't even been subtle about doing that. It had been an all-too-tangible withdrawal of affection. She'd made him really mad.

No, worse. She'd disappointed him. Although she'd always lived alone in the cabin, at the moment, she felt very lonely.

She called Jessica, who picked up on the second ring. "Hey. What's up?"

Jessica had been through a rough time lately, but she still sounded positive. Her family's visit had done her a lot of good, and Jessica had told her that walking the dogs at the shelter was also cheering her up. Paige imagined that it cheered up the dogs even more.

"Hey. Do you want to come over and eat pizza and watch a movie?"

"Um, *always*. But you're not hanging out with Dylan? I thought he was back tonight."

"He is."

"And you're not going to have another long talk by the fire?" Jessica teased.

"No." Sadness filled her one-syllable answer.

"Oh, no. What happened?"

Soon after, when they sat on Paige's couch eating slices of pepperoni and jalapeño pizza, Paige told Jessica the whole story.

Jessica said, "But that makes no sense! He told you he wanted you to have the cabin!"

"That's exactly what I said." The defense now struck her as weak, even if it was logical. "I was so sad about packing up...I was crying. And then at the last minute, I got that call, and I got so excited. I felt like all of my dreams were coming true at once. So I ran right over to make sure with Harry that we had a deal."

"Of course you did! Anyone in your situation would've done the same thing." Maybe Jessica was right. Then again, the woman was loyal to a fault. If Paige had stolen someone's car, Jessica probably would've blamed the car manufacturers for designing such tempting sedans, all while researching auto shops that specialized in custom paint jobs.

"I was only thinking of myself, though." Paige got a hollow feeling inside. She always thought of herself as an empathetic person. She tried to be one. But this time, she'd ignored the small voice inside her telling her to slow down. She'd messed up. "I knew how many memories he had here, and his sister wanted him to buy it. I should've talked to him first."

"Okay, maybe," Jessica said grudgingly. "But give yourself a break. You didn't know he was going to run right over to Harry's and hear about it. That was some very bad luck."

This did make Paige feel a lot better. On the TV screen, the two people in the movie kissed. Jessica said, "Wait, those two are together?"

"I guess so." Paige hadn't been paying much attention.

"Do you think he'll try to outbid you?"

Paige set her pizza down. *Oh, no.* How had this not occurred to her yet? Her heart sank. "Probably."

"Text him right now," Jessica said. "Remind him he said he wouldn't."

"He knows what he said." She didn't feel like she had the high ground.

"Well, maybe he'll stick to it. And maybe he'll realize this wasn't a big deal. He'll probably get over it in no time."

Paige thought again of him taking the card back, and looking at her as though she were a stranger. "I don't think so."

"If he doesn't, he's not good enough for you, anyway," Jessica said. "If there's one thing I've learned, it's that you don't want to get serious with the wrong guy."

"I know." Paige couldn't help but add, "But Dylan really felt like the *right* guy."

"What do you mean? Like 'Mr. Right,' right?"

Paige shrugged. It was probably ludicrous.

"That's ludicrous," Jessica said, confirming it. "I'm sorry, but it is. You two barely dated. And you told me from the first that he wasn't your type."

Paige recalled this, but now... "What do you think my type is?"

"Oh, you know. Like, maybe he teaches at community college or works at a nonprofit. And he's very cute and wears hilarious tee shirts."

"You're getting very specific there."

Jessica shrugged. "Or maybe he's from another country and speaks in an accent that's to die for, and writes poetry about you."

"Where are you getting all this?"

"It could happen. The point is...there are a lot of guys out there. And it's easy to be wrong about Mr. Right."

"I guess."

"Who cares about guys, anyway? You're going to be a published author!"

"I know I'm super lucky." But it had been more than luck. She'd written a fun story... and, well, Dylan's expertise and encouragement had made a big difference.

"You and I need to have more fun together," Jessica declared. "I got so busy with the wedding stuff..." She shuddered. "This should be the best time of our lives! We're young and wild and free!"

"You're right," Paige said. Out of the corner of her eye, she caught a glimpse of the television. "Oh, now they're *shooting* at each other?"

Jessica squinted at the screen. "Maybe we should start over."

After the movie, Jessica left and Paige's spirits plummeted again. Her dreams had come true. Why didn't she feel better about it?

She set the little owl on the stove. "Well, buddy," she said to it, "it looks like it's you and me."

The owl stared back. She couldn't tell for sure, because he had a beak and couldn't really smile or frown, but he looked a little sad.

chapter twenty-six

It was Friday, November ninth. Dylan had been looking forward to it as the day he'd be talking to Mr. Burke's agent about buying the cabin. He sat in his office, his feet up on his desk, twirling a pen and staring blindly at the spreadsheet on the computer screen in front of him.

Should he make a higher offer?

The truth was, he could afford to pay twice the asking price. That might very well tempt Mr. Burke.

Unless Mr. Burke had decided to turn down any offer from him. Paige might've told the man how Dylan had said he wouldn't bid against her.

It didn't matter what she told Mr. Burke, really. Dylan couldn't stand going back on his word, no matter who else knew or didn't know about it. So Paige would get what she wanted, and he would get nothing. No cabin. No relationship with her. Just his old dreary life.

That's on you, something inside told him. Paige hadn't wanted to be finished with him. She was sorry she hadn't talked to him first. And...he had to be honest with himself. She hadn't expected that he'd hear about it first from Harry.

It had felt bad, hearing it secondhand like that, and he'd reacted accordingly. Maybe he'd been a jerk. Why had it set him off like it did?

Because he'd never let his defenses down the way he had with her, and he wasn't sure he liked it.

I should call her. But that would mean putting himself out there even more. Shouldn't she be the one calling him?

After the way he'd acted—taking that card back, wow—she probably wouldn't.

He needed more coffee. Last night, he'd barely been able to sleep, for whatever reason. Okay, for an obvious reason. He hadn't used the insomnia wisely, either, to get some work done. He seemed to be developing a lazy streak. It wasn't like him.

He got up from his desk and exited his office. Brian and Elaine stood talking near the water cooler, and Dylan raised a hand in greeting.

His boss intercepted him, seeming to materialize from nowhere. "Hey, Dylan. How was the conference?"

"Good, good. Made some new contacts." Maybe Dylan didn't break his promises, but it had been a long time since his virtue had extended to being truthful with Mark.

"Great! Hey, listen, we're going to need to start over on that pitchbook for Lionex. We need it ready to go first thing Monday."

Dylan's frustration flared. "It's going to take all weekend. Any way we can push that out?"

Ellen and Brian stopped talking and looked over. Dylan had never complained about a deadline before. Nobody complained about deadlines.

There was a first time for everything.

Mark laughed as if Dylan had made a joke. "I know, right? It is what it is. What are you going to do?"

Something inside Dylan snapped. "Well I'm not going to do *that*."

The moment of silence crackled.

It surprised Dylan as much as anybody else, but he had no desire to backtrack. He didn't even feel like he had a choice...or maybe, for the first time, he realized he did.

Mark's shoulders relaxed and he smiled. "Okay, I was going to tell you Monday. They always say share bad news on Friday, good news on Monday, right? But I know you've been grinding away lately. You're making VP." Behind him, Elaine's face fell, but Brian nodded slightly. "I still need to print out the stuff from HR. Including your new compensation!" He clapped Dylan on the shoulder—a completely unwelcome touch, as always—and said heartily, "Now get to work."

He'd been striving for this for so long. *I should be happy.*

Instead, he felt a heavy weight pressing him down, like somebody's boot in the middle of his back. With this promotion, he'd never be able to bring himself to leave—unless he moved to an equally soul-sucking position. The salary, the benefits, and the prestige would keep him stuck, giving years of his life to something he hated.

"I'm not working this weekend," he said.

Mark's impression of collegial good humor dissolved. His face reddened.

Elaine took brisk steps over to join them. "It's okay, Mark. I can take it." Dylan couldn't help but be impressed. She'd seen her opportunity and grabbed it, and by taking the latest assignment, she might also be taking the promotion away from him.

Mark said, "Thanks, Elaine. Dylan, see me first thing Monday." He walked away, leaving Elaine, Brian, and Dylan looking at one another.

Elaine asked quietly, "Are you drunk?"

"No. I'm very clear-headed." Probably the most he'd been in a while.

Brian said, "You just lost that VP job."

Dylan didn't care. "Elaine will do great. Heck, she's been here longer." She was the one they all went to with questions. Mark was always saying she didn't handle the clients

well enough, but it wasn't even true. Most
clients liked her fine. "I don't know why Mark
would promote me over you to begin with."
Why hadn't he considered it that way before?

Elaine continued to look at him as though
he'd lost his mind. "Thank you." She glanced
back at Mark's office. "Good luck on Monday."

"What do you mean, you're not making an offer?" Dee twisted around in her folding chair
to stare at Dylan. They both sat near the front
row at the grade school gym, where a temporary stage had been set up at one end. His
father, between Dylan and Dee, looked disappointed, but thankfully didn't say anything.

"Paige is going to have enough money for
the down payment," he explained. "I told her
I wouldn't bid against her." His dad nodded,
accepting this.

Dee raised her eyebrows. "So you two are
dating again?"

"No."

She half-rose in her chair to look around
them at the crowd. Most of the seats were
filled now with parents and grandparents,
talking among themselves, and a teacher
dashed out the side door where the child
performers waited in line. Another teacher in
the back of the gym fussed with sound equip-

ment. A speaker crackled. "Is she here?" Dee asked.

"No." He'd already looked.

"Oh. She was here last year."

Well, last year I hadn't made her feel like garbage.

If he did happen to run into her, he knew what he wanted to say: that he was sorry he'd overreacted. But Paige was avoiding him, and he couldn't really blame her. No one wanted to be in a relationship with someone who got upset too easily. He never thought he'd be that guy.

Dee got up and came to sit down in the empty chair on the other side of Dylan. In a lower voice, she asked, "Did you two have a fight?"

He loved his sister, but she was terrible at staying out of his business, especially where his love life was concerned. "I don't want to talk about it."

"You should call her! Or text her."

Dylan sighed. "Here's the thing. If I do that now, it might look like I just want her to not buy the cabin."

"Well, I don't want her to buy it."

He shook his head. "I'll call her in a couple of days."

He wouldn't be in the way of Paige getting the home she loved. And after she did that, there wouldn't be anything standing between them. They could start fresh...if she gave him another chance.

The lights dimmed and people clapped. A child emcee got on stage and welcomed everyone to the show.

"When's Connor on?" Dylan's dad asked in a whisper.

"He's up first," Paul said. "He still hasn't told us what he's going to do."

Dylan laughed. He hadn't realized Connor had still been keeping it a secret. "He's doing kung fu."

Dee's eyes widened. "He's doing what? He doesn't know kung fu!"

"That's what I thought."

"Oh, my gosh." She shook her head. "This is going to be bad."

Paul pressed his lips together. "At least he's going first. He can get it over with."

A popular song blared over the speakers. In response, some people in the crowd cheered and clapped their hands. The curtain opened to reveal a brick wall. Connor ran onstage in a white kung fu uniform. He danced around and did not-particularly-impressive kicks and karate chops as he lip-synched to the song, which had nothing to do with martial arts.

"Oh, geez," Paul muttered. "I don't know about this."

Dylan's dad had no secondhand embarrassment. He was chuckling more or less nonstop.

Connor dramatically kicked the wall with his bare foot and Dee let out a squeak. Dylan cringed—the kid was going to break a toe.

Bricks went flying everywhere, bouncing soundlessly on the stage. They were made out of foam. Dylan laughed and the crowd exploded into cheers and applause. Connor bowed and ran off the stage. The song wasn't over yet, so the guy in the back cut it off abruptly.

Dee spun to ask Paul, "Did you record that?"

He shook his head. "I was too scared."

She laughed and turned to Dylan and their dad. "That could've been a lot worse, right?"

"It was great," Dylan said. He wasn't completely sure about the propriety of doing fake kung fu, though. "You should get him real lessons."

Dee clicked her tongue. "You know? I bet he'd *love* that."

After the show, Dylan's dad asked Connor, "Whose idea was that? To make the wall with the foam bricks?"

"Brady's mom," Connor said. "I borrowed the uniform from Brady, and she had the bricks from a play. But the dance was all my idea," he concluded proudly. "Can we get ice cream?" Dylan and his dad shared an amused glance.

It was good to be here with them. Not everything was lost. Who knew what was going to happen with his job, or with Paige, but he could appreciate the good things he did have. Like his family. And his health. And the fact that, even if he did get let go from Hammersmith, he had enough savings to keep him from worrying for a while as he figured out what to do next.

He was thinking about what he was thankful for, like Paige did. All he needed was a sunrise.

Dylan walked into his office on Monday morning, booted up his computer for the first time since Friday, and scanned his inbox for any indication that he was being fired. The total of unread emails came in at a record-breaking high, but he didn't see anything out of the ordinary. Brian appeared in the doorway of his office. Clearly, the guy had been waiting for Dylan to come in. "Hey. Did you hear about Elaine?"

"No."

"She's the new VP. Mark's getting us together to announce it at nine."

Wow. It wasn't a surprise, but still. He and Elaine had been jockeying for the position for—how long now? Months. He didn't feel anything, and that was the strangest feeling of all.

"Sounds like a pretty unnecessary meeting," he commented. Then again, weren't a lot of them?

Brian stepped into his office and said in a lower tone, "I'm surprised. Even after what you pulled on Friday."

What he'd pulled? Brian made it sound like he'd insulted a client or taken an axe to the copy machine...not that he hadn't briefly imagined doing both of these things, on a couple of particularly stressful days. But he'd questioned Mark, and no one ever did that. "Why surprised?"

"Mark doesn't really *like* her."

"Mark doesn't like a lot of things."

Brian looked around wildly, "Dude, keep your voice down. He's going to hear you."

Dylan shrugged. He was fresh out of worries on that account.

Mark came up right behind Brian and said, "Hey, Dylan." Brian jumped about a foot, and Dylan swallowed a smile. "Come by my office when you get a chance, okay?"

"Sure thing."

Mark walked on, and Brian stared wide-eyed at Dylan. "What do you think's going to happen?"

Dylan shrugged again. "I'll tell you as soon as I know."

"Awesome," Brian said, clearly thrilled at being the first to get the scoop. Then he assumed a more sober expression. "I mean, I hope it's something good."

"It's not going to be good." Dylan got up and headed toward Mark's office.

When he got there, Mark said, "Come on in. Close the door."

Dylan obeyed. Mark didn't ask him to sit down, and he took a seat, anyway.

Mark said, "Listen, about what happened on Friday..." Dylan nodded. Things seemed to be going about the way he'd expected. "I know working here can be stressful. You haven't taken a vacation in a while. So I'm willing to let it slide."

Dylan blinked. This *wasn't* what he'd expected. "Okay."

"Personally? I think you need to blow off some steam more often. Like Josh and Kyle do. But hey. The point is, you missed out on the promotion, and I figure you've learned your lesson."

He *wasn't* getting fired. And he wasn't relieved. Instead his pulse kicked up higher, although he'd been so calm before. If he didn't get out now, he was never going to do it.

"I'm quitting," Dylan said.

"What?"

"Quitting my job," he clarified.

A look of horror crossed Mark's face. Then he licked his lips. "Now, let's not do anything rash. You're still getting a merit increase. In fact...let's look at a fifteen percent increase for you."

That was a great raise. He'd be a fool not to agree. "Yeah," he said. "Okay. Thanks."

He stood up. Mark did too, coming around his desk to clap him on the shoulder. "Think about what I said about blowing off steam."

Dylan nodded.

As he walked back toward his office, he felt numb. What had changed? A little more money? He still didn't like his boss. He didn't always like himself when he was at the office, either, and sometimes, he disapproved of the work. Out of habit, Dylan glanced up at the windowed partition of his office. It was dimmer than usual—a fluorescent light above had burned out, maybe—and he couldn't see his reflection.

Out of nowhere, he remembered the joke Harry had told him. *Why did the man quit his job after he turned invisible?*

He couldn't see himself doing it any more.

Brian poked his head out of his cubicle to whisper, "What happened?"

"Nothing." Dylan turned around and walked back to Mark's office. When Mark looked up, he said, "Yeah, no, I'm quitting."

Mark stared at him. "Are you serious?"

Dylan nodded.

Mark took a few brisk steps over to him. "Wait, wait. You can't leave me in a lurch like this with Lionex. Nobody else knows anything about them." Dylan recalled Kevin Jeffries, the guy who'd recently gotten fired. No doubt Mark had left Kevin in a lurch, what with his wife and new baby and all.

"You're going to want me as a reference," Mark said in a wheedling tone. "Stay another three weeks, and you can use me as one."

"Two weeks," Dylan said. His boss looked relieved. "And you write me a recommendation on LinkedIn today." He knew Mark well

enough to know that he'd only do it if there
were some immediate incentive.

"All right, all right," Mark muttered. "Where
did this even come from? Did you get another
offer at the conference?" Anger flashed in his
eyes. "Is it Halcyon?"

"I don't have another offer."

Dylan went back to his office. What was
he going to do next? Paige had mentioned
working for a charitable cause. At the time,
he'd dismissed the idea. One didn't make a lot
of money like that. That was why they were
called *nonprofits*, after all. But now, he might
consider it. He might consider anything. This
was such a surreal way to start a week.

Clean Slate Monday, he thought of Paige
saying. A fresh start. Anything could happen.

Brian appeared in his doorway. "What's
going on?"

"I quit," Dylan told him.

Brian's mouth fell open. "*Dude.*"

"You should get out of here soon, too. Do
another year, tops, so it looks good on your
resume."

"Why?"

Dylan had no reason now to refrain from
speaking his mind. "You were nicer when you
first started here, what was it, three months
ago?"

Brian gave him a disbelieving look. "You've
literally been telling me to be less nice."

"Yeah, I know. You shouldn't have listened."

chapter twenty-seven

On Wednesday afternoon, Paige filled the last few minutes before the school bell rang by reading a new story in her journal to the kids. "'Malarkey the Owl had the whole tree to herself. In the morning she watched the sun come up, and at night she watched the stars come out.'" Jaden already had his hand raised with a question. Chances were good that it would have nothing to do with the story, and that she'd have no idea how to answer it off the top of her head, but she always enjoyed learning where his thoughts had led him. "Yes, Jaden?"

"Umm, owls eat rabbits and squirrels."

Not a question at all, but a zoology lesson. "Well, yes, they do."

His small brow furrowed. "Is he going to eat Muffy and Kerfuffle?"

Suddenly, several children were staring at her as though she were a monster, although Tommy laughed.

"Oh, no! No, no, no," she assured them. "They're not going to be in the same story. Besides...only big owls do that. This is a little owl. Like this big." She held up a thumb and forefinger, a few inches apart, the size of the kitchen timer. "And...she only eats four-leaf clovers. That's why they call her Malarkey the Lucky Owl." Hmm, that was pretty good. Clara stuck her hand in the air. "Yes, Clara?"

"She's not lucky if she's lonely," Clara said.

"I didn't say she was lonely." Clara raised her hand again. "Yes, Clara."

"But she lives all alone!"

Paige said, "Just because you live alone doesn't mean you're lonely." Indignation warmed her ears and the back of her neck. Why, she'd lived alone for years, and she'd liked it. That was the truth.

The school bell rang and she instructed them to get their coats, hats, and mittens. It was truly cold out there now. Every time she looked out the window at the mostly-bare branches of trees, against a sky that had taken on the silvery gray color of the winter to come, she couldn't help but feel that the season had slipped through her fingers too quickly.

A couple of hours later, Paige sat at Harry's kitchen table with Harry, a pile of forms, and Trent Jackson of Paragon Realty. "This is one of the easiest deals I've done in a while," he said. "No contingencies, complications."

He talked about the boring, minute details of the contract, such as PMI and taxes. She did her best to pay attention. Dylan probably knew about all of that stuff. Finally, Trent said, "Let's go ahead and get your signature on this first page."

Looking down at the blank line, she clicked on her ballpoint pen. She should be overjoyed, but everything felt wrong. She clicked it again and then, embarrassed and stalling for time, looked up at Harry with a forced laugh. "I'm a little nervous."

"It's normal. I see it happen all the time," Trent said. "It's a big commitment."

"Oh, I don't know about that," Harry said. "A *marriage* is a commitment. Having a child is. A house?" He shrugged. "A house is nothing."

He was right. Commitment to a person meant a lot more than a commitment to a little cabin. And what was a house, anyway, without the people you loved? Paige's chest ached.

Trent nodded. "True, true. And Paige, you may have to budget a little more, but you should be fine. That place is only going to appreciate in value."

She nodded. Buying the cabin was not only what she'd hoped for, but also the sensible thing to do.

She began to sign. The pen was out of ink.

She tried scribbling in the margin of the document, but nothing came out.

"Hang on, I've got another one," Trent said, digging in his bag.

She felt sick. This was a sign. She knew it.

"Actually, you know what?" she asked. "I want to talk to someone else about this."

Trent's face fell. "A lawyer? This contract is standard, I promise you. There's nothing in here that's going to raise a flag."

Harry spoke up. "Well, now, if Paige doesn't feel comfortable signing without talking to someone about it, that's perfectly fair."

Reluctantly, Trent nodded. "Of course." Paige didn't even blame him for trying to talk her out of it. He'd wanted to finish the deal, get his commission, and be done with it. But as she gathered the papers and stood up from the table, for the first time that day, she knew she was doing the right thing. She went back into the cabin, sat down on the couch, and took out her phone.

Then she paused. What if Dylan didn't pick up because he didn't like her anymore? Now that she'd annoyed him by not telling him first about the cabin, he might've realized a lot of other things about her bothered him, too. Maybe he'd come to his senses and realized he should be dating another high-powered executive, not a first-grade teacher who wrote stories about squirrels.

She pressed his number and the phone

rang four times. *Ugh*. Then he answered. "Hey Paige, what's up?"

He sounded casual, as though it were no big deal that he'd gotten mad at her and then stopped talking to her. Maybe he was so over her, he didn't have any feelings either way.

"Hi. I was wondering if you could come over?" She should clarify that. "Just for a few minutes. To talk."

Silence on the other end of the line. She felt like putting her head down on the coffee table.

"Yeah, absolutely," he finally said. "Be there in, uh...forty minutes, I guess?"

Which meant he was leaving right now. Her nerves settled. He wasn't mad at her. But if he wasn't, why hadn't he called her? "Great."

It was chilly. She should build a fire before he got here. In fact...she recalled the idea she'd suggested to Jessica, about ritually burning everything to do with Steve. Paige could do some ritual burning of her own. Then Dylan would understand.

She tried to build the fire in the same way he had, but her version turned out quite a bit less symmetrical. It didn't matter, of course. He wasn't coming over to judge her fire-building skills. As an afterthought, she lit a couple of jar candles. *This isn't romantic*, she assured herself. They smelled like pumpkin pie, after all. Would he want something to drink? He didn't like tea. She never had coffee at night, but maybe he'd want some, so she started a pot, just in case.

When she heard him knock, she glanced up at the cuckoo clock. He'd gotten there as quickly as he'd said he would. She opened the door. He stood there, dressed in jeans, a plaid shirt, and a leather jacket she'd never seen him wear before. He gave her a slight smile. "Hey."

"Hi! Come on in. Thanks for coming. Do you want anything? Coffee? I made some coffee." She was talking too fast.

He looked surprised but shook his head. "No thanks."

"Have a seat," she said brightly, sitting down herself. He went toward the couch—not in the other armchair next to her by the fire, where they'd sat together before and talked for hours. It felt weird, their being polite to one another and keeping their distance. No, not weird. Bad. Every muscle in her body felt tense. He looked at the fire and then the glowing candles on the mantel. Was he getting the wrong idea about why she'd invited him over here? He might think she was trying to get back together with him again. *Was* that the wrong idea?

"I won't keep you for long," she said. "I know you probably have a lot of work to do. You always do." That came out sounding like a criticism, and she gave a nervous giggle to make it clear she hadn't meant it that way.

He got an expression on his face. "Uh actually, I'm going to be working a lot less."

"That's good." Strange, though. "How come?"

"Well…" He gave a rueful laugh. "You're actually the first person I've told about this. I quit."

"What?" Her voice must've gone up an octave, she was so shocked, as well as many decibels of volume. "You didn't!"

"I did."

"This is so exciting! What are you going to do next?"

"Not sure," he said.

After centering his whole life around his work, the change had to unsettle him. "How does it feel?" Maybe she had no business asking such a personal question anymore.

"Uh…uncomfortable, and right." He gave her a crooked smile. "You told me I should quit. I guess I listened to you after all."

She squirmed. "I hope you're glad you did."

He held her in his gaze. "But that's not what you invited me over to talk about."

"No." She twisted the strap of her purse, which she'd plunked down next to her on the couch. Since he'd quit his job, and didn't know where he'd get another one, he was probably in no position to buy the cabin, after all. "But it doesn't matter now."

"What is it?"

He might as well know she'd had second thoughts, for what that was worth…which was probably not a lot. "I brought something." She unzipped her purse, pulled out the folder with the closing papers, and handed it to him.

He opened the folder to the contract on top. "It's yours," he said. "Congratulations."

He hadn't really looked at the papers. "I'm not—"

"Let me say something first." He held up a hand. "I'm sorry I got mad. You were right. It was stupid."

Paige's mouth dropped open. "I—I never said that," she faltered.

"I just..." He took in a deep breath and let it out. "You know, one of my first bosses told me, 'Don't mess up an apology with an excuse.' And I guess that's what I'm going to do. But I want you to understand."

He didn't even need to apologize. She opened her mouth to say that she was just glad he'd forgiven her, but he continued. "When I was in New York, I couldn't stop thinking about you." It touched her heart, but then he said, "And I ran into my ex-girlfriend Lauren."

Her stomach dropped. "Lauren," she repeated numbly. He hadn't mentioned her name before. What had happened? Well, what did she *think* happened at conferences when single people ran into their old flames?

"Yeah, and I—I avoided her the whole conference." Paige felt a surge of happiness. She was only human. "All I could think about was you. Wanting to get back to you. And I, uh..."

He scrubbed his mouth with his hand. He wasn't looking at her at all, and Paige could barely breathe.

"When I heard you'd gotten a book deal, and you'd already told Harry you were buying the cabin, I felt like...you hadn't been thinking as much about me."

Paige knew it wasn't easy for him to open up, but he was letting down his guard completely—for her. It touched her to the core. He grimaced at his own words. "It was immature. I'm sorry."

She didn't deserve this. "I wanted to tell you *I* was sorry. I wouldn't have even gotten a book deal if it weren't for you. You're the one who told me to send the cabin story. And I used your email word for word."

He smiled with obvious self-satisfaction, surprising her. "I wondered about that."

It only added to her guilt. She felt shaky. "You were right. I should've talked to you first."

He shook his head. "I'd just talked to my dad about buying it, and it seemed like it made things good between us...I don't know."

Ohhh. If talking about the purchase had brought them closer together, for the first time in...well, almost forever, then it must've been all the more of a shock. "That's great that you're talking to your dad. I mean really talking." She'd encouraged him to give his dad a chance, and as soon as he had, she'd undercut it with her own thoughtlessness. She hesitated, and then said, "My dad told me I should go talk to Harry right away." Now who was messing up an apology with an excuse? "It's still my fault, though. I'm an adult. I got so caught up in thinking it was meant for me, and..." Thoroughly ashamed now, she hazarded a glance up at him. "I should've known better."

"It's okay. I hope you love it here, Paige. I know you will."

"I—I didn't buy it."

Confusion clouded his expression, and he glanced back down at the document. "What?"

"I didn't sign them. I want you to buy it. Except now, I guess maybe you can't, because you quit your job." She swallowed. "I was thinking about you when you were gone, too. And then after I made you mad, I felt so terrible, and..."

She reached over, took the papers back from him, and tossed them into the fire. One of them didn't land in the flames, and she made a frustrated noise and reached into the grate to move it.

Dylan grabbed her arm. "Careful," he said sharply. Dazed, he looked toward the fire, where the rest of the papers were already a small pile of black ash on one of the logs. Sometimes, she thought, her talent for burning things did come in handy.

He stared back at her, his mouth parted, still holding onto her arm. "You didn't have to do that."

"Yes, I did." A tear leaked from her eye and she swiped at it. When had she become such a crier?

He got up. "Come here." He urged her to sit next to him on the couch. "Don't—please don't cry, okay?" With unbelievable gentleness, he brushed away the tear that had fallen, and the pad of his thumb felt cool on her hot cheek. She realized, with a shock, that his own eyes were glistening, and he gave an unsteady laugh. "I can't stand to see you cry. So stop right now."

She nodded in agreement, also with a laugh that was mostly a release of tension. He took both of her hands in his. It felt so good to have him touching her again that she closed her eyes for a moment, in gratitude and relief.

He said, "As far as this place goes...I could still buy it. I've got at least a year to get another job before I even start to worry. The mortgage would be less than my rent."

She brightened. "Oh, I'm so glad. And I mean...you have very marketable skills, right?" Everyone needed people who were good at money and numbers.

"Extremely," he agreed. "I just want to find a job that won't take up my whole life...and that I feel a little better about, I guess."

"Exactly. You deserve that."

"You are so sweet, you know that?" he murmured. "But I'm not buying the place. You are." She shook her head. "No, I meant what I said before," he said firmly.

"Dylan, I—"

"I'm falling in love with you."

Her heart skittered at his words. She'd never seen his face look more serious or more filled with joy. She remembered when she'd told him, *I could see you as a knight.* He looked like one now, and it awed her.

"You're the most amazing woman I've ever met," he continued. "You're kind, and you have this unique way of looking at things. Everywhere you go, you brighten things up... and you call me on things, and sometimes I need that. I want to be with you. That's all I want."

"That's all I want, too. I'm falling in love with you, too," she managed to say, though her voice shook. "Except—maybe not just falling."

Dylan laughed. "Yeah, same here."

"It's your fault I'm crying now."

He kissed her. She felt his sincerity and passion all through her body and soul. It was impossible to cry while being kissed like that.

When he'd released her and she was able to catch a breath, she said, "I'm only buying it if you come over a lot."

"Obviously," he said.

"I mean it. Like every day."

Amusement glinted in his eyes. "I'm positive we can work something out."

Was he thinking what she was thinking? Maybe the cabin was destined to belong to both of them…because maybe they were destined to belong to one another.

"Will you come over in the morning? Before work?" she whispered. "I promise not to bake."

"You should bake. I didn't buy you that timer for nothing," he teased.

She dared to ask, "Can I see that card now?"

He paused and then shook his head. "I'm getting you a new one."

"Okay." She smiled. "Come over and see the sun rise with me."

"Hmm, I don't know. Do I have to do the gratitude thing with you?"

"Obviously," she said, although of course he didn't.

"Okay, you're on. But you already know what I'm going to say." He kissed her again.

She wrapped her arms around him. For all her optimism, she'd never dared to wish or pray for someone as wonderful as he was, and she'd been blessed with him, anyway. She'd never in her life had more to be thankful for, and her joy felt like every color imaginable, purples and pinks and oranges and the brightest, truest gold…a sunrise in her heart.

epilogue

Paige faced Dylan, holding both of his hands. Could he feel her shaking? One would've thought they were getting married in the dead of winter instead of early June. The weather was perfectly comfortable for her sleeveless maxi dress of white lace. It wasn't fussy or fancy, or even strictly a wedding gown—she could've almost sewn it herself—but a small backyard ceremony next to a little cabin didn't call for too much formality. Dylan simply wore his best suit. He hadn't worn it in months, because his new job as the financial manager of the Colorado Wilderness Foundation was decidedly casual.

They'd set up chairs near the pond, leaving an aisle in the center, with a string quartet to provide the music. They didn't even have a wedding party, although Jessica had stepped up a few moments ago, as planned, to take Paige's bouquet for this part of the ceremony. Paige loved the arrangement of pink and purple tulips mixed with white roses and baby's breath. The tulips she'd planted the previous autumn had bloomed weeks before.

Dylan visited her at the cabin a few nights a week, and they spent most of their weekends together. On most Sundays, they went to Paige's parents' church, which was maybe their church now, too. After the service, they'd sometimes come back to the cabin for Sunday Muffins. Paige couldn't imagine getting married anywhere but here, and the pastor hadn't minded.

He spoke now of the symbolism of the rings—precious, with no beginning or end. A movement in the corner of Paige's vision distracted her. In the front row, Connor had donned a pair of sunglasses, and he wildly gestured for his little brother to do the same. Noah complied, and Connor folded his arms across his chest in satisfaction. In their suits and shades, the boys looked like pint-sized Secret Service agents. Paige and Dylan exchanged a look and his mouth quirked up.

The pastor said, "Dylan, will you take this ring, and place it on Paige's finger?"

As Dylan took it, his expression became serious and focused. He slid the band of gold on her finger and spoke his part of the vows, which they had both memorized.

"I give you this ring as a symbol of my promise to love, honor, and cherish you..." He held her gaze, conviction in his steady voice.

"With all that I am, and all that I have, in all times, and in all ways, forever."

Paige ducked her head and blinked. When the minister prompted her, she took the ring and put it on Dylan's finger. He gave her a slight smile of encouragement. She spoke her promises to him, meaning them with all of her heart.

Dylan took both of her hands in his again. They bowed their heads as the pastor said the Lord's Prayer. Then Jessica gave Paige her bouquet as the pastor delivered a final benediction. He concluded by saying, "Dylan, you may kiss your bride."

"Yay," Paige said quietly, and immediately realized this was not traditional. It had just slipped out. Dylan laughed, amusement and pure joy in his warm brown eyes, and then pulled her close and kissed her, long enough that someone yelled, "Wooo!" As he stepped back, people stood up, cheering and applauding.

Paige's parents came up to hug them both, and then a teary-eyed Dee did the same. Paige told her, "Thank you so much again for the veil." Their grandmother's bridal veil had been her "something old." When she'd first seen it two years ago, at the bottom of a cedar chest, it had sparked her curiosity and sense of romance, but she'd never dreamed she'd wear it at her own wedding someday. "And the sixpence, too," she added. The coin lay under her toes in her left shoe, for luck.

"Of course!" Dee said. "I'm so happy for you both. You were just what he needed."

"He was just what I needed, too," Paige said, earning a look of gratitude from her handsome new husband. If this talk kept up, she'd have to use her "something blue" again—the delicate blue handkerchief, already damp by now. Thank goodness for dresses with pockets. The dress, of course, was "something new," and for "something borrowed," she wore her aunt's pearl earrings.

"Congratulations, son," Dylan's father said, holding out his hand. Instead of shaking it, Dylan hugged him. Paige's throat tightened. She'd never seen them hug before. But they'd grown much closer in the past months. Dylan had watched Broncos games at his father's townhouse during the late fall and winter, and they'd taken him out to dinner a few times lately at the Italian chain restaurant he liked.

His father cleared his throat. "It looks like those trees are holding up. I was a little worried about the storm the other day." The abrupt change of subject surprised Paige, and then she saw that his eyes were misting. He was trying not to be too emotional.

He'd bought Dylan and Paige several Scotch pine saplings and, since his back hadn't been acting up lately, had helped Dylan plant them in a row along the west side of the property. Most of their wedding gifts had been more for Paige than for Dylan, which had troubled Paige, even though he insisted he didn't mind at all. The trees, though, had really been for him. Right now, they were small, only a couple of feet tall, and Dylan had said they weren't particularly fast growers. Still, she liked imagining what they'd look like ten and even twenty years from now.

"They're looking good," Dylan said. Paige knew that both men were extremely proud of the results—justifiably so, she thought, since neither of them had planted trees before—and they'd been glad to have it done before the big event.

Several long tables had been set up closer to the cabin, with ribbons tied to the backs of the chairs, and the caterers had set out a buffet. Paige and Dylan headed that way. They hadn't really considered a reception line, and people simply mobbed them.

"Yay," Jessica said to Paige, teasing her, before smooshing her in an embrace. One of Dylan's new friends from work, Aaron, came up to shake his hand and clap him on the back. Paige was so grateful that Dylan not only liked his new job, but also the people there.

Paige said, "Jessica, this is Aaron. I don't think you two have met yet." It occurred to her that they might actually have something to talk about. "Aaron's interested in adopting a dog. Aaron, Jessica volunteers at Furever Friends. She can probably give you some good advice."

Jessica stood up a little straighter. "I adopted an older dog, right before Christmas. It was a present to myself."

Aaron said, "And I bet it was the best gift the dog could ever get."

Jessica's eyes sparkled.

Paige smiled to herself. Her friend hadn't really dated since she and Steve had broken up. It would be nice if she hit it off with Dylan's coworker.

Aaron pointed to the end of the buffet table where beverages were being served. He asked Jessica, "Can I get you something to drink?"

"I'll walk with you." As they moved away, she said, "So we're looking for more volunteers for the charity ball…"

Harry came up to greet them. Although he lived in Albuquerque now, Dylan and Paige had sent him an invitation, along with gift cards for an airline and a hotel chain. It had been Dylan's idea. They'd included a note to make it clear that he still wasn't obligated to attend, but the older man had RSVP'd immediately, with his daughter as his plus one.

"What a beautiful day," Harry said. "And what a beautiful bride."

"Definitely," Dylan agreed.

"Paige, when does your next book come out? Your mother said it's about an owl?"

"Malarkey the Lucky Owl," Paige confirmed. "January of next year."

"Oh, isn't that wonderful." He looked to Dylan. "And you're moving into the cabin with Paige."

Dylan flashed a grin. "That's right."

"I have to admit, I thought of that as a possibility," Harry said. "It's snug for a family, but I'm sure you can make it work."

"We're going to build on," Dylan explained. "It'll have a second level." They wouldn't change the history and the memories, but they'd add to them. Paige hoped they'd have children soon, and she often imagined them growing up with Connor and Noah as their cool older cousins.

Harry looked thoughtful. "You both deserve it."

Paige looked back at the cabin. It had always felt like such a special place to her, and now she knew why. In the past, it had held so much love...and it would again, as she and Dylan made a life there together.

The End

sunday muffins
(maple pecan streusel
muffins with cider glaze)

A Hallmark Original Recipe

In *Sunrise Cabin*, Paige comes across an old muffin recipe tucked away in a kitchen drawer...the very same recipe that Dylan's grandmother used every Sunday during his childhood. You can make your own sweet memories with these autumn-inspired maple pecan muffins, finished with a buttery-rich streusel crumb topping and a simple cider glaze.

Yield: 12 servings
Prep Time: 20 minutes
Cook Time: 17 minutes

INGREDIENTS

Streusel Topping
- ¼ cup all-purpose flour
- ¼ cup rolled oats
- ¼ cup brown sugar, packed
- ¼ teaspoon ground cinnamon
- ¼ teaspoon real maple extract
- ¼ cup cold butter, cut into pieces
- ½ cup chopped pecan pieces

Muffins
- 1¾ cups all-purpose flour
- 1 cup rolled oats
- 1 tablespoon baking powder
- ½ teaspoon ground cinnamon
- ¼ teaspoon kosher salt
- 1 large egg, lightly beaten
- ¾ cup brown sugar, packed
- ¾ cup milk
- 1/3 cup canola oil
- ¼ cup real maple syrup
- 1 tablespoon real maple extract
- 1 cup chopped pecan pieces

Cider Glaze
- 1 cup apple cider
- 1 cup powdered sugar

DIRECTIONS
1. Preheat oven to 400°F. Line 12 muffin tins with muffin baking cups.

2. To prepare streusel topping: combine flour, oats, brown sugar, cinnamon and maple extract in bowl of food processor fitted with a steel blade. Add cold butter pieces and pulse until mixture is coarse and crumbly. Add pecan pieces and stir to blend. Reserve.

3. To prepare muffins: in a large mixing bowl, combine flour, oats, baking powder, cinnamon and salt. Whisk to blend; reserve.

4. In another bowl, combine egg, brown sugar, milk, canola oil, maple syrup and maple extract; whisk until blended. Add to flour mixture and stir to blend. Fold in pecans. Spoon batter into muffin cups, filling two-thirds full. Top muffin batter evenly with streusel topping.

5. Bake for 15 to 17 minutes or until a toothpick inserted in center comes out clean. Let cool in pan for 15 minutes before removing.

6. While muffins are baking, simmer apple cider in a small saucepan over medium heat for 5 minutes, or until liquid has reduced to ¼ cup. Cool. In a small bowl, combine 3 tablespoons cider syrup and powdered sugar; whisk until smooth (add additional cider syrup, as needed, to adjust glaze). Drizzle cider glaze evenly over muffins.

Thanks so much for reading *Sunrise Cabin*. We hope you enjoyed it!

You might like these other books from Hallmark Publishing:

Love on Location
In Other Words, Love
Country Hearts
A Simple Wedding
A Cottage Wedding
Love at the Shore
Dater's Handbook
Beach Wedding Weekend

For information about our new releases and exclusive offers, sign up for our free newsletter at hallmarkchannel.com/hallmark-publishing-newsletter

You can also connect with us here:

Facebook.com/HallmarkPublishing

Twitter.com/HallmarkPublish

about the author

Stacey Donovan grew up in central Illinois, earned her MFA in Creative Writing at the University of Arizona in Tucson, and was a Master Writer at Hallmark in Kansas City, where she wrote several gift books and children's books. She now lives in Los Angeles with her husband and their three rescue dogs. A true optimist, she loves stories with happy endings, random acts of kindness, and adventures big and small.

You might also enjoy

JOURNEY
Back to Christmas

Based on the Hallmark Channel Original Movie
Written By Marie Nation

Leigh Duncan

Chapter One

December, 1945

Her purse meticulously balanced in her lap, Hanna Morse crossed her ankles and pushed down a quiver of anticipation as the heavy curtains pulled away from the movie screen. She aimed a brave smile at the tall brunette sitting beside her, glad she'd let Dottie talk her into coming to the theater tonight. Moping around the house certainly wasn't doing her any good.

It had been six months since that terrible day when the telegram arrived. Six months, and she still couldn't make it through the day—or the night—without tears.

But tonight, she'd let Dottie convince her to take in a picture show. While she'd never get over the pain of losing Chet, she needed to escape her grief just for a little while. To laugh, to enjoy life. At least, long enough to watch a movie.

Lights flickered on the screen. Hanna

straightened. Dottie had promised the movie was a good one—a comedy starring Frank Sinatra and Gene Kelly. It had been so long since she'd laughed out loud that she'd nearly forgotten what her own laughter sounded like. Looking forward to it, she let herself relax.

But instead of the opening credits, the screen filled with images of soldiers marching through New York City. Unprepared, Hanna tensed as the voice of the newscaster filled the theater.

"New York pays tribute to the American foot soldier. These men were chosen to represent all the ten million soldiers of the United States Army. Gliders fly overhead as the city roars its welcome home to the thirteen thousand veterans who fought from Sicily and Italy through Normandy, Holland and Germany. Four million New Yorkers line the four-and-a-half-mile parade route to greet the men..."

She pressed shaky fingers beneath her eyes, straightened her shoulders, and took a breath. She could do this. She could sit here while the boys—everyone else's boys—marched beneath the ticker tape thrown from tall buildings while crowds cheered. She could keep a smile on her face while wives and mothers welcomed husbands and sons home from the war. Chet would expect her to do that much. He'd be the first to remind her that others had sacrificed far more than she had. He'd tell her to think about the Sullivan family and all they'd lost. He'd...

But Chet wasn't here. He wasn't among those who were coming home.

And she wasn't that strong.

Abruptly, she stood. Thankful she and Dottie had chosen seats on the aisle, she grabbed her coat and hat and headed for the lobby. As she rushed up the aisle, plush carpet silenced the sound of the black pumps she'd bought especially for this night, her first night out in half a year. The swinging doors opened into a lobby filled with twinkling Christmas lights and bright red ribbons. The decorations announced the happiness of the season. She blinked, struggling against her tears. She thought she had a pretty good chance of winning the battle over her emotions until a whiff of pine from the boughs that hung over the doors and around the window sills reminded her of Chet. The mask of cheery goodwill she did her best to maintain threatened to collapse completely.

Why, oh why, had she agreed to go out with Dottie tonight? She had no business being here. She needed to go home, to lose herself in memories of better times, of better days. Lately, it was the only way she ever got through the long, lonely nights. Even then, she slept in fits and starts. When she did manage to drift off, she dreamed of Chet dying on a field in a foreign country with no one there to comfort him.

Tears stung her eyes in earnest now. Fighting them, she slipped her arms into her coat. She had to leave.

Dottie caught up to her before she made it halfway across the lobby.

She turned to the woman who'd been the best friend a girl could ever ask for during those first, awful days after she'd received the news. "Oh, Dottie," she said, tugging on her gloves. "I don't want you to miss out because of me. Go back inside and watch the movie. I'll be all right. I just…" She sniffled.

"I wouldn't dream of staying without you." Sympathy glinted in Dottie's dark eyes. She overrode Hanna's protest while she put on her own coat. Together, they hurried toward the exit. "Oh, Hanna, I didn't know there'd be a newsreel." Dottie's breath spiraled into a cloud the instant she stepped from the warmth of the theater onto the sidewalk. Behind her, colorful Christmas lights outlined posters of the coming attractions.

"It's not your fault." Hanna stabbed at her tears with gloved fingers that did little more than smear the dampness onto her cheeks, where they froze faster. "Silly me, I... I just, ah..."

"Here." Always prepared, Dottie handed her an embroidered handkerchief she'd pulled from her purse.

Hanna swallowed a sob. Dottie was so kind. Far kinder than a weak-willed woman like her deserved. What was wrong with her? Why couldn't she be stronger? Why couldn't she bury her sorrow and pain? Chet had willingly fought for their country. He was the one who, like so many others, had given his life protecting their freedom while she'd stayed home to watch and wait and support the war effort by buying bonds and saving tin foil. Yet, here she was, in tears again.

Standing in the cold in front of the theater wasn't going to help her get past this, but a walk might clear her head. Mindful of the beautiful but treacherous ice and snow, she started down the sidewalk toward her car with Dottie—bless her—at her side.

She whispered, "I just miss him."

"Of course you do," Dottie agreed.

"Seeing all those soldiers coming home. It just, ah, it breaks me up." She twisted the handkerchief in her hands.

"Of course it does." Dottie leaned down, her voice growing fainter when two women passed them headed in the opposite direction on the sidewalk. "He's your husband."

"Was," Hanna corrected. She had to remember that Chet was gone. Otherwise, a fresh wave of grief would wash over her whenever she thought of him.

"Oh, Hanna, honey. He's still your husband. Nothing changes that."

If only that were true.

More tears hovered near the surface. Any second now, they'd burst through the protective barriers she'd erected around her heart. She tore her gaze from the rooster tail of slush and snow that trailed the tires of a passing car and cast a pleading glance at the friend who was trying so hard to make her feel better.

"Well, you know what I mean." Dottie struggled to offer the right words. "He's still in your heart. You're always going to be Mrs.—" Hanna's expression must have finally registered. "Oh, I'm just making it worse, now, aren't I?"

A muffled sob escaped. The dam broke, and the hot tears ran in rivulets down her cold cheeks.

"Go on and blow." Offering the same kind of advice she'd give one of their patients, Dottie motioned to the handkerchief. She patted the side of a well-stocked purse. "I've got another one in here."

Though her eyes swam, Hanna smiled. No matter how bad things got, she could always count on Dottie to make her laugh. She'd discovered that the day they'd both begun nursing school. They'd been best friends ever since.

"Oh, look at me blubbering." Hanna struggled to pull herself together. "And when all our boys are over there doing something heroic."

"Aw, have a good cry." Dottie patted her shoulder. "Not all of us are born to change the world."

"Yes, but nothing ever got solved by blubbering on a sidewalk, either." That was it, wasn't it? Now, with Chet gone, what use was she? "I'm lost, Dottie," she admitted. "I used to know who I was. I was Mrs. Chet Morse, wife." She sighed. The yellow telegram hadn't just announced Chet's death. In a way, it had marked the end of her life, too. "I wasn't out to change the world. I just wanted to make a happy home for my husband. And now..." She shook her head.

Now, what?

"I don't have any purpose at all." There, she'd said it. Without Chet, without a husband to make a home for, without children to raise, what was she supposed to do with the rest of her life?

"Well," Dottie tilted her head, "you could walk me to the square."

The suggestion was so surprising that she *tsked*. "That's not exactly a purpose."

"You never know." Dottie smiled slyly. "Even the smallest stone makes a ripple in the water."

Hanna glanced at her friend. She didn't understand what Dottie meant and let her eyebrows bunch. "What stone?"

"It's a saying," Dottie answered with a laugh. "C'mon. They're decorating the gazebo."

Well, she'd wanted to take a walk, she conceded while Dottie threaded their arms together. Maybe her friend was right. A walk past Henderson's Hardware and down Main Street to the gazebo might perk her right up. It couldn't hurt to wander past the Christmas trees the shop owners had erected with such care along the sidewalks. Or to take in all the decorations. Everywhere she looked, greenery tied with bright red ribbons gave windows and storefronts a festive look. The colorful lights against the backdrop of a night sky added such a merry touch that they warmed even her heart. Throughout Central Falls, people were trying so hard to make this a cheerful Christmas homecoming for the soldiers and sailors who'd been away at war.

How could she do any less?

By the time she and Dottie reached the center of town, she'd dried her eyes and banished her tears. She even hummed along when Dottie, hearing the carolers on the square, burst into song. As they approached the gazebo, she squared her shoulders and hid her pain. She refused to dampen the mood of her neighbors who were pitching in to decorate the gathering place at the heart of Central Falls. To prove she'd caught the Christmas spirit, she pulled her camera from her bag and snapped a photo of the women in winter coats and heels who busied themselves untangling strings of lights, while men in suits and hats threaded the strands through hooks attached to the gazebo's eaves. Spotting a former patient, she stopped to say hello.

"How are you doing, Mr. McGregor?" She watched closely, ready to spring into action, as the older gentleman wearing a bowler hat leaned from a tall ladder to place an ornament on the Christmas tree. Mr. McGregor had taken a bad fall last year and broken his collarbone. She knew it still gave him fits. "How's your shoulder these days?"

"Ah, you know. The old rheumatism acts

up when there's a storm coming." Carefully, Mr. McGregor worked his way down the rungs of the ladder. Once he had both feet on the floor of the gazebo again, he rubbed his arm. "And I can tell there's a doozy coming in tomorrow."

Hanna nodded. At the hospital this afternoon, she'd overheard sweet old Doc Smithy talking with her favorite patient about a blizzard. "That's what everyone's saying."

Mr. McGregor glanced up as if he could see through the gazebo's pitched roof. "It's a shame, too. Cloud cover is going to hide the comet."

"Oh, darn," Hanna exclaimed with an unexpected pang of disappointment. "I didn't think of that. I was looking forward to seeing it." She shrugged. There were worse things than not seeing a bright light arc across the sky. "But, a big snow storm. It'll be a good night to nestle in, I guess."

Or it would be if she had someone to nestle in with.

She shook the thought aside. Maintaining a brave face, she drew in a steadying breath and issued herself a stern reminder to stay cheerful and upbeat.

But Mr. McGregor only pinned her with a concern that saw through her false bravado. "And how are you holding up?"

Heat flooded her cheeks. Her act wasn't fooling anyone, not if Mr. McGregor's rheumy eyes could see through it. Determined to try harder to do her part, she mustered a smile. "Oh, now, don't you go worrying about me."

"Someone's got to, Nurse Hanna," the old man protested. "You're always taking care of the rest of us."

Genuine warmth deepened her smile. Though she and Chet had talked about moving to the city, people like Mr. McGregor made her glad they'd decided to settle down in Central Falls.

"You'll come to the lighting tomorrow evening, right?" he asked.

The tradition had always been one of the season's highlights. Dressed in their winter finest, practically everyone in town would gather at the square. In the past, she'd enjoyed watching the children, so eager with anticipation that their eyes sparkled while their little feet danced in the snow. There would be caroling and hot chocolate. Some of the younger boys might even have a snowball fight. How could she miss that? Suddenly her plan to spend another evening all alone didn't seem like such a good one. "Oh, I suppose so," she agreed. "I always like seeing the whole town come out for it."

Mr. McGregor studied the gray skies overhead. "Let's just hope the snow holds off."

The words "yes, let's" were on the tip of her tongue. Before she had a chance to say them, though, Dottie rushed over, holding the enormous silver star that would soon grace the top of the gazebo. Holding it up to her face, the brunette struck a silly pose. Hanna had just enough time to snap a picture before they both laughed.

Coming here was a good thing, she decided as she watched her friend act the clown. After all, they said laughter was the best medicine, and Dottie had given them all a healthy dose of it.

Get the book!
Journey Back to Christmas
is available now!